THE END OF INNOCENCE

ALEX J. FISCHER

For my Family and Friends

1

Jim looked under his television to the bright red numbers denoting ten twenty-seven. He glanced over at the darkened window and cleared his throat. His right hand dug into his pants pocket and fished out his smart phone. He clicked the button on the side and unlocked it by inputting the code. His thumb swiped to the side as the screen glowed bright white causing his blue eyes to squint in the dimly lit room. He sighed. "Nothing yet, huh? It'll be soon." He picked up the remote control from the arm of the sofa and turned the television off. He tossed it aside as he stood up and walked over to the nearby light switch to flip it on, illuminating his small but cozy living room. "They always do. They can't help themselves. I'm too damned good at what I do."

Crossing into his kitchen he retrieved a cup from the nearby cupboard and filled it with water before he took a swig. A loud tone interrupted him mid-drink coming from his pants pocket. He pulled out the tool and brought it up to eye level. A small smirk appeared. "Always." His thumbs danced across the screen. "Now let's go in for the kill, shall we?" An almost feral grin appeared on his features, his teeth bared as he stared at the screen. He read the words on the screen. "How about tonight, sweetie? You said your parents wouldn't be home."

"That's right. Mom's out of town, and it's the first time I'm home alone." He spoke aloud as he replied. He hit the send button and shut off the nearby faucet before placing the now discarded glass into the sink. He flipped the kitchen light off and moved back into the lit living room. He leaned into the side of the door frame and glanced about the room. The sofa facing the television, the chair adjacent to him, and the stairs leading upward in the corner of the room caught his eye along with the front door. "Probably shouldn't have taken mom's decorating tip of 'Be frugal' quite so literally. Two pieces of furniture is pretty spartan if I do say so myself." A tone shook his attention off his décor choices and back to the luminescent screen. "Excellent. He will be here soon. I should prepare for his arrival. It's only fitting as a good host, and I pride myself on being just that." He moved to the door, unlocked it, and leaned back against it while typing his last message. "Door's open. Come on in." Wasting no more time he hurried upstairs, his hand sliding along the railing.

He moved into the door on the right and into his sparse bedroom. His unkept bed clashed with the cleanliness of the nigh empty room. He moved to the only other door in the room and flung open the door before leaning forward and digging past the shirts and assorted jackets hanging there. He got onto his hands and knees and pulled out the trunk at the bottom of the cramped space. He input the numerical code on the padlock and opened the container. Inside were numerous weapons ranging from pocketknives, hunting knives, his 9mm pistol, and enough boxes of rounds to fill the remaining spots in the enclosed space. He picked up the hunting knife and the firearm. He ejected the slide and looked inside, nodding to himself. He inserted it back into the weapon and cocked the hammer back with a smile. He closed the box and placed it on his double sized bed, leaving the lock beside it.

He exited his room and concealed his newfound insurance into his belt line, under his shirt. He hitched the knife's sheath onto his belt line afterword and did his best to hide the bulge it created at his side. He pulled it out in a hurry a few times. "Have to be sure and all," he muttered to himself. He glided down the stairs and moved to the sofa. He turned the television back on and turned the channel to a children's channel. Animated images of talking animals danced across the screen before he vacated the front room, leaving the lights on. He moved into the kitchen and into the adjoining bathroom. He closed the double wooden doors and turned the shower on. His phone chirped to life after he closed the shower door. "Be there in five minutes." He slid the phone into his back pocket after sending the text "In shower. Be out in a few minutes."

He exited the now quickly steaming bathroom, moved into the adjacent room, and grabbed a tripod and a mask sitting in the nearby corner. He moved a brown lock of hair aside, donned the mask, and pushed a button near the top of the camera. The red light turned green, and he leaned down. "Good thing I sprung for the advanced version with streaming capabilities." He clicked an option and looked over his shoulder before turning back and talking to the camera. "Hey, everyone. Sorry for the late stream, but we got one coming over right now. He'll be here in a few minutes, so I need to get moving. Enjoy the show." He moved it into a dark corner facing the living room and the couch, then draped a nearby cloth over the bright light. He leaned down and glanced at the screen, making sure the feed was unobstructed. Nodding to himself he moved back to the bathroom and shut the door.

As soon as he entered the now fully steamed room, he heard a loud chiming come from the front room. "About time," he muttered to himself. He whipped out the phone and sent a message. "Come in. I'm just getting out of the shower now."

He heard the front door open and an undoubtedly male voice could be heard. "I'm here. I brought pizza!"

Jim brought his phone up and played a prerecorded message at a loud volume. The voice was that of a young girl. "Out in a minute. Make yourself comfortable."

"Such a nice young girl," Jim heard the voice say quieter. "I'll leave the pizza on the kitchen table for us and settle in front of the tv then. Shall I?"

Jim scrambled to find another prerecorded message to play. "That's fine. Thank you." He waited until he heard a quiet thud and footsteps leading away before a soft grunt. He let out a deep breath and whispered to himself. "Showtime, Jimmy boy. Don't fuck this up." He pushed open the door and crept out of the room and into the kitchen. He made it to the living room before straightening his posture and clearing his throat. "Well, what do we have here?"

"Oh shit," his guest said. "Are you Amanda's father?"

"Her father? No. You're quite mistaken. I'm someone else entirely. That's not the point though." He moved to the front door and leaned his back against it. "Now sit there, and let's have a nice chat."

"I don't want any trouble. I'll just leave."

"No, you won't. Now be quiet." Jim glared at the overweight, balding, middle-aged man sitting on his couch. "Amanda does not exist."

"This can't be happening."

Jim continued unabated. "You really shouldn't be messaging little girls with unsolicited dick pics, man. See, I'm here to put a stop to that."

"What? Are you an undercover cop or something?" The man's face became saturated with sweat as he wiped it away with the back of his arm.

"Not quite."

"A vigilante then?"

"Heavens no. What, you think I want to go to prison myself? Now don't mistake my denial as being a pussy. I am armed, so don't try anything stupid. Well, more stupid than you already have. Now if you'd be so kind, Mr. Dick pic, let me finish." He kicked off the door and pointed to the darkened room, near the camera. "Look over there please, and tell me what you see."

The man turned and looked where Jim pointed. "It's a dark room. What about it?"

"You really don't see it? Lean forward and look harder."

The man leaned over the side of the sofa and squinted his eyes. "You got a point? I'm getting impatient and will be leaving one way or the other. I don't have to stay here you know."

"Of course not, but thank you for complying. See, I know where you work. I know your family, and you just showed your face to the camera for all the world to see. What do you suppose would happen if that footage got out? Do you think your employer would keep you on the payroll? Now, it's not official, but no self-respecting company is going to keep a suspected pedophile on their payroll. Now your wife, that's another story."

"You are getting into dangerous territory here, pal." The bulbous man stood up and pointed a finger in Jim's direction.

"Aw," Jim smirked. "Did I upset the guy who sends dick pics to little girls? Tough titties. I don't really care what pedos think. Now calm down, big guy. I'll let you leave as soon as I'm done. Just let me say my piece. You're quite lucky you messaged me and not some of the other guys in this hobby of mine. They'd have not been quite so tame as me."

"What will you do exactly? Scare me with that little Halloween mask?"

"No. I'll leave that part as a surprise later. What I will say is that you have a lovely wife. Maybe spend some of that energy toward her."

"Don't try and give me marital advice."

"Fine. Be that way." Jim grabbed the door handle and twisted, pushing the front door open. He backed up and signaled outside. "Now leave, and don't get any bright ideas, Kevin."

"Don't call me by my name, asshole." Kevin stormed off the couch and stopped beside Jim. He leaned forward, his face red, "You will regret tonight, you moron. You have no idea who you're fucking with." He stomped outside and hurried to his car before getting in and speeding away.

"Sure, sure big guy. I'm sure you believe every word you're saying." He closed the door shut and locked it with both locks before moving over to the camera and kneeling. "You all saw that? Well, I'm going to report that to the local police along with all the other evidence. I'll be offline for a while and no doubt will have to go give my statement at the local department. Also, did you see how greasy that slime-ball was? Guess I should be used to the type, but good Lord. Hope everyone has a good sleep tonight, God bless. See you all later." He turned the stream off and saved the clip to the local memory card. He dismounted the camera and took off the mask. "Guess I've got a long night ahead of me. So worth it to keep that scumbag away from more kids though. What's one night of discomfort to save a kid a lifetime of trauma, right?" He chuckled to himself.

2

"I saw what you did last night," Cynthia said to Jim from across the diner booth's table." She blew a strand of red hair out of her face. "Nice work, vigilante. You invited a dangerous child predator into your house while you were all alone and antagonized him. What was your grand plan? Piss him off until he charged you, and you could claim self-defense? Because it sure looked like it. You realize he might get off free with your little stunt. He's going to claim entrapment at best."

"Thanks, Cyn." Jim rubbed the bridge of his nose with a yawn.

"Oh, sorry," Cynthia mock apologized in a sarcastic tone. "Did you want me to pat you on the back for the job you did last night? Well, the best thing I can say about it is you got a hell of a lot of followers on social media from it. You probably made the guy's life a living hell. Some of the more trolly types are saying they're going on a crusade against the guy's personal life."

"Good."

"No, not good." She rolled her green eyes. "You need to

publicly denounce that kind of shit, or it's liable to blow back on you legally. You ever heard of defamation, or how about accessory to harassment? You don't want to be anywhere near the loonies on your side. They'll take your so-called victory and turn it into a pyrrhic one."

"Noted. I'll do that now." He whipped out his phone with a grumble. His digits danced across the screen before placing it on the table and pushing it toward her. "How's that?"

Cynthia angled her view down and frowned. "Let me fix this. God, you are tone deaf sometimes." She set upon the still forming post and edited. "What would you do without me?"

"Go to prison probably."

"That's not something to brag about. Besides, I'm just an aspiring law student, I'm not actually a lawyer yet. Don't take everything I say as gospel. I can be wrong. Regardless," she placed the phone down and slid it back over, "how's that? At least that doesn't feel manufactured, and it keeps you looking human to the masses."

"Fine by me."

"And how did your little visit to the station go last night? I assume they gave you a speech about doing their job for them?"

"Something like that. Said the evidence would probably be inadmissible in a court of law even if they did want to use it."

"Exactly as I said." Cynthia sighed and wrapped her pink lips around the straw in her strawberry shake before pursing her lips and gulping down the sweet mix. "All you really accomplish with this kind of crap is ruining the guy's life socially speaking. Yeah, you may get him divorced, fired, and socially cast out, but what will that really accomplish?

He can still go after kids if he so desires; in fact, easier since now he'd have nothing to lose. Or even worse."

"Not sure there's anything worse if I'm honest." Jim took a sip of coffee from the mug and shoveled a piece of apple pie into his mouth.

"I meant someone who's lost it all might just come after you if he ever finds out who you are - which would be easy by the way, you idiot."

"Would it now? I had my mask on."

"You did indeed have your mask on," she said in a calm voice; however, it quickly changed to a more biting tone. "But you invited the man to your own address. Did you ever stop and think that someone could easily find out your real identity from that? Because it sure wouldn't be hard. You can find someone's address in the blink of an eye nowadays. He could simply run it through a service online, and he'll get your real name. Hell, if he's too lazy to do that, he could just swing on by and be waiting with a gun when you get home. He wouldn't even need your identity for that." Her tone calmed. "My point is, be careful for God's sake. Don't get yourself killed playing hero."

"If I didn't know any better, I'd think you're worrying about me." Jim gave a shit eating grin.

Cynthia looked out the nearby window. "Maybe I am. Would that be so wrong?"

"No, just a change of pace. Usually, you're all piss and vinegar."

Cynthia gave a wry smile. "That's because your dumb ass responds better to it. Someone has to try and keep you alive and out of the big house, don't they? Who better than your best friend?"

"Truer words have never been spoken. Now then," Jim

finished the remnants of dessert on his plate and drank the last of his coffee, "was there anything else?"

"There's always something else when you do one of these jobs." She leaned forward, bringing a hand to her mouth, her tone changing to a hushed whisper. "You are armed, yes?"

"Always. You know I got my concealed carry last year." He flicked his head causing a lock of brown hair to fall behind his ear. "You really think the guy will come looking for trouble?"

"Do I think a mentally ill man you recently screwed over might come looking for revenge amidst a social media shit-storm? Gee, what could give you that idea? Human nature maybe?"

"Smartass."

Cynthia smirked. "Seriously though, watch yourself out there. That wasn't your first mark."

"No, but most of the others are behind bars now. I don't live in the same place as I did when I got them, so I'm good on that front."

Cynthia slurped up the last of her drink. "Yeah, but this was the first job in the new place. Tell me something. Are you planning on keeping this up?"

"Yes, and don't try to talk me out of it again. You know I'm stubborn."

"Stubborn as a horse's ass. Anyway, if you absolutely must do it again, might I suggest you meet in a public place next time? Minimizes the sketchiness and, you know, maxi-mizes the chances that you will come out without a new stab wound or lead poisoning. Besides, if you want my honest opinion, it's more believable. A small girl would want witnesses when meeting with an older man. You've just been getting the ignorant morons who think with their dick."

"I'll take it under advisement. Where would a girl even want to meet?"

"You're asking me?"

"You're the one without a y chromosome, and I'm pretty sure you're female, based on that one time I accidentally walked into your room after you'd just finished changing."

Cynthia's arms rushed forward pushing the palms of her hands over top of Jim's mouth, her face turning crimson red. "Shut up, you insensitive jerk. I told you to forget that memory. You promised me you would."

Jim nodded and waited until her hands fell back to the table. "And you believed a teenage boy that he'd forget. What does that say about you?"

"I'm an idiot. Anyway, to answer your question, it depends on the time of day."

"I was thinking the food court at the mall."

"Sometimes I wonder if you get all your ideas from media. Jesus! No, just no. If you're talking teenage girl, try a restaurant. You could even try this diner. I will warn you though, if management finds out about any of your little stings, they could ban you from their establishment. So, I wouldn't use anyplace you like. Owners tend to not like that kind of bad publicity and possible violence if the guy snaps. At least that way you'd have witnesses too - so you could prevent a murder one charge."

Jim shook his head. "You always did think of the cheeriest outcomes for everything."

"Because you always do stupid crap."

"Guilty as charged. But you love it."

"No." Cynthia caught his gaze lowering to her modest

chest. She moved a hand to his sightline and pointed up. "And my eyes are up here."

"I know." Jim laughed. "I moved them down purposely. That old memory came flooding back in perfect detail."

"You are an insufferable prick. You know that?"

"Is that what they call that when it lasts for more than six hours, because maybe you can help me with that if you got some free time later."

"I hate you sometimes."

"Dinner later then?"

"Sure. At six."

Later that day

Jim heard a honk from out in front of his house, moved to the windows, and peeked out. He sighed in relief. "Just Charlie. Must have gotten out of class earlier than usual today." He threw the door open. "What's up, dude?"

A bearded man wearing a psychedelic styled shirt got out of the beat-up car and made his way toward the door. His messy hair was held in place with a tie dye hairband. "Man, I had to come over after the response I got earlier."

"Surely you're not referring to last night."

"What else, man?" Charlie slapped Jim's shoulder. "You cornered that chomo and broadcast it for the world to see. Every time you do, my street cred goes up."

"Oh, you know why I do this I see."

"Seriously though, I was surprised a bit considering…" Charlie pushed his way inside the house and paled a bit. "Wait a second. This looks familiar." He moved to the angle the camera portrayed. "Oh shit. You did it. The rumors were true. You actually recorded in your own place."

"That's right," Jim said. "You've not been here since the move. What do you think of the new place?"

"Spacious compared to the crappy apartment you used to live in. Just let me suggest something."

"I'm not going to invite anymore here. Cynthia gave me the whole speech at lunch earlier today."

"She always was the smarter of the two of you. Now can you explain something to me?"

Jim motioned to the sofa and took a seat on the far side as he watched Charlie sit on the other. "Go ahead."

"How many diddlers have you got locked up now? Ten? Twenty maybe?"

"Eight if you must know, with two with pending court cases. Why? Does that matter?"

"The ones locked up getting out anytime soon?"

"One's getting out in a year I think." Jim pulled out his phone. "Let me look. Here," he poked the screen, "it says June 18th on one."

"That's today."

"Huh. What a coincidence. What about it?"

Charlie stretched his hairy legs out in front of him and rested a hand on his shorts clad leg. "All I know is if you'd screwed me over and got me years in the slammer, I'd be none too happy, my man. You really screwed the pooch last night, man."

"Fine, it may have been a little rushed."

"A little?"

"Okay, maybe very rushed. I thought I had to reel him in quick, or I would lose him. I improvised the quickest place I could control the environment."

"Fine." Charlie exhaled. "I'm sure Cyn gave you the

hullabaloo about how dumb it was already, so I'll spare you that speech. Excluding that, there was another reason I reached out today, and it didn't have to do with your hobby."

"Shoot."

"I don't suppose you want to go to a party tonight?"

"I'm not really a party kind of guy. You know that. Why are you asking me when you already know the answer?" Jim picked up the nearby remote and changed the channel. "You must have an alternate reason. What do you need me for?"

"You're so cynical. Fine. For your information I could use a little help tonight."

"You need a designated driver is what you need. Just come right out and say it, man. I'm not going to judge."

"I can't help that the ladies love me more after a few drinks, can I? They always love my jokes, and I need to loosen up before I can perform."

"Insert joke here about they're not laughing with you, they're laughing at you. Sorry though, I got my own stuff to deal with tonight. You might notice," Jim gestured around the sparse room, "that I haven't even fully unpacked yet. I prioritize that over partying."

"Are you sure? Cynthia will probably be there."

"Are you trying to imply something?"

"I'm saying I know you like her deep down. You don't want her getting picked up by some random guy, do you? I can only do so much before I'm labeled a clam jam. You need to put some work in if you want her."

"She's a big girl. She can make her own decisions. Besides, I'm meeting her at six for dinner." Jim whipped out his phone and his thumbs danced across the screen.

"What are you doing?"

"Asking Cyn to help me unpack after dinner."

"You're a conniving one, aren't you?" Charlie reached

over and gave a mock punch to Jim's shoulder. "Trying to get her away from potential suitors while spending more time with you. I doubt she'll come though - back breaking labor, or a fun party?"

A chime lit up Jim's phone. "She's coming here. What was that you were saying?"

"Never mind. Didn't figure her for the type to pass up a good time."

"Always have to have the last word, don't you?"

"Yes."

3

Cynthia's lithe frame hefted a box from the floor and followed Jim out into the upstairs hallway. "If I'd known I'd be doing heavy lifting too, I'd have reconsidered my offer."

"Aw, come on. It isn't that bad. Besides, who else would I get to help? That lazy stoner Charlie? I'm lucky if I can get him to set the table whenever he's over for dinner. This?" He nodded to the boxes lining the thin hallway, "There's not a chance."

"Surely you have more than us. Call your parents, cousins, uncles. Anything would have worked and sped up the process."

"Complaining doesn't befit a woman of your stature." Jim led them into his bedroom. "Just put them on the bed."

"Next to this box?" Cynthia dumped the cardboard box onto the bundle of messy blankets on top. "What is this?" She reached down and flipped the lid up. "Whoa." She backed up. "Explain. Now! Why do you have numerous knives and ammunition boxes holed away up here but have basic amenities still packed?"

"Protection," Jim said before dropping his box beside hers. "Seemed smart at the time."

"Smart, but creepy. Jesus! But why do you have ammo and no gun?"

Jim reached behind him and removed the weapon. He brought it in front of him facing to the side. "Here."

"Is that thing loaded?"

"Not much good otherwise. Yes, it's loaded."

"You were ready to kill the guy?"

"If he wanted to kill me, sure. I was hoping it wouldn't come to that though." He plucked one of the knives out of the box, flicked the blade out, and flipped the blade around in his hand. He jammed the blade into the tape sealing the box and drug it across the line of adhesive.

"Next time don't insult them. Just get them on camera and then ask them to leave. Humans are like animals - back them into a corner, and they can get aggressive."

"I didn't put him in a corner," Jim said while placing a digital clock on the newly added nightstand beside his bed.

"No," Cynthia said pulling out a stack of clothes, "you just stood in front of the door and told him that his life was over. Not letting him leave and trying to piss him off was stupid."

"Well, when you say it like that, you might be right." Jim got onto his hands and knees, grabbed the hanging cord from under the table, and plugged it into the nearby outlet.

Cynthia looked at the flashing red digits. "I'm always right. I'd thought you'd have learned that by now."

A chime interrupted their conversation.

"Oh, that's me." Cynthia reached into her jacket pocket. She bit the inside of her mouth. "Jim, take a look at this." She beckoned him over and showed him the screen once they were side by side.

Jim's brows furrowed as he leaned closer until they were shoulder to shoulder.

"I didn't say molest me." Cynthia frowned and took a deep breath.

"Sorry." Jim focused on the text on the screen. "Get out of there. Now!"

"Scary and creepy." Cynthia exhaled a deep breath. "What do you think it means? The obvious connotation being leave this house, but who would even have this number? You think Charlie is fucking with us?"

"That's not Charlie's number." Jim placed his hand on the side of the phone near Cynthia's and angled it toward him. "Unless he got some random persons phone just to mess with us, I doubt it."

"Doesn't sound like him." Cynthia bit her lip.

"Don't be scared." Jim placed a reassuring hand on her shoulder. "It's not like I'd let anything happen to my besty."

Cynthia gave a long look at the hand on her shoulder before shooing it away with a sly smirk. "I don't need a knucklehead like you looking for me. I can do it myself."

"Yadda, yadda, empowered woman. My bad." Jim let go of the screen. "It's a little odd how such a strong woman is still scared of storms though."

She tucked the phone away where it came from, stomped up to him, and pointed a finger up to his chest. "I told you that in confidence, Mr. Benning."

"My apologies. I just try and have the last word and go back to what I know."

"Jerk." She backed up a few paces and moved over to the lone window in the room. "You really need blinds for these," she remarked, tracing the outline of the window. Turning her attention to the road, her eyes widened. "Who is that?" She refrained from pointing but stared at a lone, overweight man standing on the sidewalk outside the house. He stood under the nearby streetlight illuminating him against the dark backdrop of the suburban neighborhood.

"Who?" Jim came over. "Oh shit. Get down, and on the other side of the bed. Don't come downstairs."

"What?" Cynthia's tone changed to one more hysterical. "You're not serious. Don't be stupid."

Jim's tone gained a steel edge. "Do not move. Let me handle this." He quickly left the room leaving Cynthia alone.

"Don't get yourself killed," she said in a dejected tone as she sat down on the floor beside the bed. She felt the wall on her back as she slid down to a sitting position. "This is my life now. Hunkering in a room with a creepy guy outside while he goes and plays hero again." She blew a strand of crimson hair out of her face. "Why do I do this to myself?"

Downstairs

Jim rushed over to his mask sitting in the next room and donned it before flipping on the nearby camera still pointing at the front door. He moved over to the front door, got on his tip toes, and leaned in close to the peephole. A familiar silhouette greeted him, now closer to the door. He raised his voice. "No visitors tonight. Go away."

The darkened figure wore an oversized coat and ambled its way closer before banging on the door. "You bastard. Get out here." His words were slurred, and his balance teetered as he came closer. "You cost me everything, you insufferable bag of cunts."

"Colorful fellow, isn't he?" Jim muttered to himself. He

raised his voice. "I'm not interested in getting yelled at by a drunk guy. Go home and sleep it off. You're disturbing the peace. Do I need to call the police for your loitering and trespassing? I may even be able to up it to stalking if you keep this up."

"It doesn't matter." The drunk man's voice rose. "Even if they send me off to the clink, I can't lose anymore. Because of you," the man took a swig of the brown paper covered bottle in his left hand before continuing, "I lost my wife and access to my kids. Not to mention I've been laid off work now. I need to pay you back. Open this door," the obese man fell against the door with a thud, "or I'll bust it down. I'll do it. I don't give a shit anymore."

"Son of a bitch," Jim swore under his breath. "I can't just let him in though. Who knows what he'll do in a drunken rage?" He cleared his throat and raised his voice. "If you keep causing such a racket, the neighbors will call the cops for me. You want extra charges on top of your other impending ones? Because I can add to my testimony about your harassment if you like."

"You shithead!" A loud thump erupted as Jim felt the door shake. He saw his mark slamming against the door causing creaks and slams to emanate in his ear. "Where do you get off talking to me like that. You're just a nobody vigilante that falsely accuses and entraps people to ruin their whole life."

"You sent what you thought was a young girl unsolicited groin pictures. Get down off your high horse, you sicko."

The creaking grew louder as the force escalated with each tackle. Jim heard Cynthia's voice from upstairs. "Calling the police."

"Police have been called. This is your last chance to back down. They'll be here inside of three minutes. You know they're only a few streets over, and given our history they'll make it a priority to come over here."

"Bullshit." Another ram caused a more audible creaking and groaning to the new door. "I'll have my way come hell or high water."

Jim saw the man take more than a few feet further than normal. "Here we go." He moved a few feet to the side of the door and brought his hand to his side, grasping the knife in the holster.

The front door opened with a deafening crack along with a howl of rage from the intoxicated belligerent. He crashed forward into the staircase in a crumple and fell into a ball at the foot of the stairs.

"Guess I'm buying a new door tonight. I'm going to have to install it myself too. You're a right royal pain in the ass, aren't you?"

"You think you're so suave, don't you?" The drunkard stumbled to his feet and leaned against the wall. He stared down at his feet as he spoke, barely keeping vertical. "Think you can just say whatever and do what you want to whoever. You think you're so virtuous." He stumbled toward Jim and fell to a knee before pushing himself up to his feet.

"Sir, this is a castle doctrine state I'll have you know. I really don't want to harm you."

"Too bad for you then," he said with a lunge toward Jim.

He deftly dodged to the left away from the man and reached behind him and retrieved his firearm. "Sir, please just leave. Don't do this. For both our sakes just go home and sleep this off." Jim's voice cracked. "I don't want to use this."

"I don't care if you kill me or not. My life's over anyway. So do it already, because I'm not stopping," he said with another roar and sprinted forward faster this time.

"Fuck!" Jim raised the weapon to face the intruder and aimed center mass before squeezing his index finger three times in quick succession.

His target tumbled forward into a crumpled heap in front of him. Moans of pain and incoherent noises met Jim's ears as he writhed on the floor.

"What the fuck was that?" Cynthia's voice was now closer until Jim could see her at the top of the stairs. "Oh my God. Oh shit. Oh fuck. What did you do? Is he dead? You know what this will do to my education if my school finds out I was here? Oh no." She brought her hands up to the sides of her head and sat down on the top stair. "They'll kick me out, and I'll be ostracized from all legal professions. I can't be a part of this."

"You weren't. You were upstairs when he broke in." Jim took a wide berth around the quickly slowing man on the floor. "Look at his hand there, one has a bottle, the other a knife. He was trying to kill me. What would you have had me do? Get shanked? Now calm down, and don't have a panic attack."

"Calm down? You killed a man."

"In self-defense."

"Yes, but I mean..." She stopped mid-sentence and let out a shaky breath. "Fine."

The distant sound of sirens interrupted their exchange.

"Ah no. This will take all night, and I have a test in the morning."

"Sorry."

The man on the floor stopped moving, and his back stopped rising.

"He won't make it four minutes," Jim said, "You think they'll make it in time?"

"I doubt it, but I don't have medical training to make an

accurate guess." She stood up and, with shaky legs and one hand on the railing, made her way down the stairs. "Don't get anywhere near the body. They'll construe that as manipulating evidence. That thing is registered, right?" She pointed at the weapon hanging at Jim's side in his grasp.

"Of course it is."

"Good. That's one less headache in a hellish night to come. Just tell the officers exactly what happened, and try not to leave anything out. Don't get smarmy, and don't be a smartass. Just answer what they ask and do what they say. Got it?"

"Yes," Jim said before moving beside her on the bottom step and sliding down into a sitting position and leaning forward, cradling his head into his elevated knees.

"Starting to hit you what just happened?" Cynthia asked. "Yeah, I bet." Her voice lowered. "Thanks for protecting us," her voice raised a tiny bit, "though we wouldn't have been in the situation if you hadn't had your little hobby." She was met with silence from Jim. "Sorry, not the right time. Though if you are crying, that will probably work in our favor with the cops. Still not talking huh?" She looked toward the open door and saw flashing red and blue lights on the pavement outside. "They're nearly here. Just remember what I said. We'll be done by morning, and uh, I guess you can stay at my place until this mess is figured out since this is a crime scene with no door now."

"Thanks," Jim replied before the sounds of car doors slamming and rapid footsteps approached.

4

"So that's why we're at Cyn's place instead of yours," Charlie said. "I'm happy you're alright," he said from the beanbag chair in the corner of the room. He leaned his head back against the orange fabric. "Was it the same guy?"

"The very same," Cynthia said from across the room, sitting at her dining table with a laptop in front of her. Her hands danced across the lit up keys as she spoke. "Bastard rammed the door so hard it broke the hinges. His whole house is a crime scene now.

"You've been quiet, buddy. What's wrong?" Charlie asked the man sitting on the lone recliner in the room, staring blankly at the widescreen television mounted on the wall.

"He's been like that since last night. Probably in shock from having to put that pedo down like the animal he was. He charged him with a knife, but you can't stop the human emotions from doing what they do," Cynthia said. "I figure give him a day. He hasn't slept in two days now, so that probably doesn't help."

"No doubt," Charlie nodded. "Why don't you take a nap, man? Get the cobwebs out."

"Yeah." Jim's right arm reached down and pulled the lever, causing the footrest to snap out, and reclined back into a laying position.

"Oh no." Cynthia stopped typing and groaned. "I just looked up who that creep was."

"So?" Charlie asked. "What about him? Who cares who some scumbag was?"

"The guy kept asking if we knew who he was, right? Both last night and the night before. He wasn't just some nobody living in his mama's basement." Cynthia turned the laptop toward Charlie's direction and beckoned him over with her index finger. "Look."

Charlie hefted himself out of the beanbag chair and plodded over to the table. He planted a hand on the table and leaned into it. His head lowered as he read. "So what? He was some bigwig at a law firm?"

"Yes, the premier one in the city. Aka the one I had my eye on. The police now know I am involved with his uh," she looked over toward the recliner, "adversary."

"Killer." Jim's voice said in a dejected tone. "You can use the word. It's what I am now. Don't treat me like a five-year-old."

"Right," Cynthia said. "Well, the point is, I guess I'll be looking toward a different firm to intern with now. And no, I don't blame you for this."

A grunt from Jim and a rustle indicating he'd switched positions in the chair was his only response.

Charlie's voice fell to a whisper. "I've never seen him like this before. He's always been so self-assured and, honestly, a little reckless."

"Everyone goes through their own trials and tribulations," Cynthia answered in a quiet voice. "His just happened to be after a self-defense shooting. Anyway, he wasn't just a 'big wig' as you put it. He was their top lawyer. He had more sway and clout in the place than anyone else. The only reason they're not coming after him is because of the mass amount of damning evidence, or Jim would be in the legal battle of his life."

"Geez." Charlie stood up and arched his back. "So what?"

"So," Cynthia huffed, "these aren't the type of people who just give up because of a technicality. Odds are they knew their guy's proclivities and wanted to keep it quiet. This event is a stain on their firm's name now. We're now radioactive to them. If they wanted, they could make it difficult for me to get a job with any firm now. Thankfully there are always other options."

"There are?"

"Yeah. I could start my own legal firm and make my own business. They can't do bunk about that."

"Now before when you said these were powerful people, are they vindictive too?" Charlie asked. "Because they could still try something."

"What?" Cynthia asked. "Like sending assassins or something? Come on. You watch too many movies. That'd be a legal disaster if it ever got traced back to them. Not to mention the fact it wouldn't even make a difference at this point. The information's already out and open to the public now. There is no winning in that stratagem. Now the real problem could be if any others there are of the same persuasion. They could hold a grudge and target him."

A soft snore met their ears from the other side of the room.

"He is damned good at what he does. You may have a point. If any more of them are kiddie diddlers, they could want him out of the way. But that goes back to my last question."

"I doubt they'd hire a hitman."

"Doubt does not mean certainty," Charlie said. "So, you're saying it could happen."

"So long as he doesn't keep his hobby, they'll likely leave him be. Judging from how he's reacted, I'm hopeful he'll quit."

"Or it'll go the other way. He could toss himself into his 'work'. Then we'd be in a potential mountain of shit."

"What ifs are not a productive area of discussion. We'll cross that bridge if we come to it."

"Getting off that subject then..." Charlie's voice raised a little, not loud enough to wake Jim. "Are your niece and nephew still coming into town today?"

"Sure are. They should be getting dropped off in a little bit according to this email from sis. They should be here in a little under an hour. Why?"

"Of all the places, they should be safest here with you two. It'll almost be like your own little family play. You know the game kids play? House, I think it is. Now you two will be the mommy and daddy. Did you two ever play that as kids? You two seem like the type. Now you're playing the adult version."

"Here I thought he was the biggest joker of them all and yet you prove me wrong."

"Who said I was joking?" Charlie asked, back stepping away from the table toward the front door with a cheshire cat smile. "You two need to open your eyes and seize what's in front of you. It's painful to watch." He threw open the door and stepped outside before shutting it, leaving the two alone.

"What does he know?" Cynthia pouted, pursing her

luscious pink lips together. "Fricking stoner hippy hipster. Always thinks he knows everything with that annoying smile of his." She glanced over at the back of the recliner and fixated on it for a few minutes before turning away. "I should get back to work instead of trying to make sense of his drugged-out brain. That's what I should do."

5

"Finally got them in bed." Cynthia shut the door behind her with a quiet squeak. "Wait." She saw Jim standing at the front door with a bag in hand, "Where the hell are you going at this hour? It's ten at night."

"I'm going for a walk."

"A walk where? You can't just leave in the middle of the night. Not in the state you're in."

"Worried about the kids? Because I am. I wasn't asleep earlier you know. If I am a target, I'll be damned if I put them in danger like I did to you."

She planted her hands on her hips. "Trying to get a superhero complex now? It doesn't suit you. What's in the bag? Why do you need that on your little walk?"

"I'm not answering any more questions. You do keep a firearm here, yes? I know you do. Make sure you're ready for anything. I'm going now." Without waiting he exited through the door leaving her speechless on the other side."

He quickly made his way to his vehicle and slung the back door open, tossing the bag inside. He entered the driver's seat and saw Cynthia's modest one floor house's front door open revealing an irate woman stomping toward his car. She stopped beside his car and started slapping the window. "Get inside and we can talk about this. You're scaring me. Don't do this."

Jim pushed down a button on his left causing the window to lower a few inches and allowing him to talk in a calm voice. "Head inside. You might scare the children. I'll be back before you know it." He mustered his best smile. "Where else would I sleep for the night. I really am just going for a walk. Now take a step back. I wouldn't want to hurt your feet."

She did just that and watched the car back away a few feet. "You better be back here by midnight, or I swear to God I'll slap some sense into you."

Jim rolled the window up and gave a wry chuckle. "I believe that." He backed out of the driveway and pulled out onto the two-lane road. As the vehicle lurched forward onto the empty, dark road, Jim leaned his head back. "Need to get gear first before I kick this off. I need a new mask, gloves, a hair net, and a pair of binoculars. That should keep my DNA and prints off anything, and give me something to scout with if I'm going to pull this off." He turned the wheel after pumping the brake and came onto a brighter road, with the occasional car. "Ah, main street - got to love how empty it is at this time of night." He slowed as he approached the local all-night mall and chose a parking spot near the entrance.

He twisted the key and pulled it out before leaning his head back and adjusting the rear-view mirror. He gave his reflection a long hard look. "I'm already a killer, may as well be one for good. Right?" A lingering doubt inched its way into the back of his mind, but he shook his head. "No, I can't think like that. I'm not planning a murder. I'm just assessing the situation. That's all. Or is that just what I'm telling myself? Maybe I'm not in the mental head space to make these kinds of decisions like Cyn said. It's not like I'm going to come to a conclusion out here. I may as well get my stuff ready just in case."

He flung open the door and shut it behind him. He pressed a button on the handheld remote on his keychain to hear his car give a chirp, then ambled toward the store.

He stopped in front of the glass double doors and stomped on the mat causing them to slide open. When he looked up he saw a familiar face.

"Son?" A graying haired man asked while standing next to a nearby aisle. He rubbed his mustache and turned back to the cereal in front of him. "Come on over here and talk with your old man. It's been too long."

Jim sauntered over and stood side by side with his father. "How's it going, Dad?"

"Late night shopping. You know how your mother gets if I forget something on the way home from work. 'Dennis, why didn't you get the groceries? I told you before you left work. It's like you don't even pay attention when I speak.'" Dennis scoffed. "When she gets like that, I will admit I do tend to zone out and not pay attention, but nobody likes getting harped at. Right, Son?"

"Right, Dad."

"Of course I'm right." Dennis glanced over at his son. "What's wrong? Don't say nothing either. I can tell. I haven't seen that face on you since you were dumped on prom night in your senior year."

"You didn't hear the news? Someone broke into my new house, Dad."

Dennis's attention snapped off the boxed food and over

to his son. He placed both his hands on his son's shoulders. "You're alright though, yes?"

"I'm fine, Dad. I just had to defend myself is all."

"Did you kill him?"

"Yes. He charged me with a knife after busting open my front door, so I aimed center mass and put him down."

"Good."

"Good? I killed a man," Jim said in a hushed tone and looked over his shoulder.

"So what? I don't give a damn if you put down someone trying to kill you. If I learned anything in my time on the force it's that you defend yourself, and that's that." He patted his son's shoulders with a gentle smile. "I care if my boy is still alive or not. That's what you have to do if someone is trying to harm you or yours. I know you probably feel like crap and the like, but don't. All that matters is that's you're okay."

"Cynthia was in the house too at the time."

"Did he get near her?"

"No, but I am staying at her place tonight, seeing as my house is a crime scene and all."

"She sent you out for groceries this late too? Women, right?" Dennis chuckled. "It's the same no matter what generation. Let me give you a little bit of advice, Son. Just do what they say, and you'll be happier; but don't be afraid to stand up for yourself. They'll never respect you otherwise. Know when to pick and choose your battles. This though, just do it."

"Something like that."

"I'll accompany you then." Dennis tossed a nearby box into his shopping cart and turned to Jim.

"Thanks, Dad."

In the car

Jim waved at his father and let him back his car out first. "Sorry, Dad. I couldn't tell you everything about tonight. I have my own plans." He looked in the back seat at the food. "Guess I'm buying Cyn's groceries, but he'd have been suspicious otherwise. Hope she likes what I bought. Anyway," he backed the car out and pulled onto the road, "now to get on with it."

His eyes danced to the clock near the radio. "Ten forty already? Guess I may be late. Hopefully she doesn't wait up. Thankfully the place isn't that far away. In fact," he slowed the vehicle down, "there it is, right at the end of main street." He pulled the car over and parked on the side of the street.

He turned the car off and dug around the plastic bags in the back to retrieve the binoculars. He brought them up to his face and grunted. "Still hard at work I see." He peered into the glass windows lit up with people still in them. "Probably trying to distance themselves from their little kid hunter. Ah, I can't see shit from here. What am I even doing? The only way I'm going to get answers is to get personal with one of them. I think I'll do just that."

He hefted one of the plastic bags to the front passenger seat and dug through its contents until he found the new mask and hair net. He pocketed the hair net and hid the mask beneath his shirt. He put on the new gloves after tearing off the tags and exited his car. He walked down the nearly abandoned street until he was in the alley between the law firm and the neighboring one. He found the back door and donned all his new apparel.

He bent down and made sure his jeans were tucked into his shoes and placed his back to the wall near the back door. His right hand extracted the blade from his side and held it at the ready.

The door opened and a lanky man in glasses exited.

Jim sprang into action. He wrapped his left arm around the man's neck and jammed the knife into the guys back. "Now be quiet and pay attention."

"Don't kill me, man. I'll give you my wallet and anything else. Just don't kill me."

"Quiet." Jim tightened his grip around his neck as he spoke through his teeth. "All I want is information. Don't try to turn your head, and answer my questions. Do what I say, and you'll go home tonight and sleep with your wife."

"I'm not married."

"Not the point, chuckles." Jim moved the knife from his back and brought it in front of his target. "See this? Six inches of cold steel is standing between you and home. Now only speak when I ask a question."

His quarry nodded.

"Good, you're learning. Now then, you're aware of the recent incident with one of your co-workers?"

"Yes, sir."

"Are you familiar with his charges?"

"He lured young girls and did God knows what to them, I think. All I know is I'm the new guy, and my job was to help the higher ups gain deniability."

Jim moved the knife out of the man's line of sight and placed it on his shoulder. "Very good. Now do you know of anyone else in your little workplace who shares his interests? Surely you've heard a few rumors around the water cooler."

"The only thing I've heard is Susan likes the little boys,

but that was just a rumor, man. I don't know if it's true or not."

"Susan? Susan who? Give me her full name."

"Susan York. She works as the receptionist. She's on duty right now as a matter of fact."

Jim loosened his grip but shoved the tip of the knife into the man's shoulder instead. "Give me the full story you heard."

"Christ! Alright already. I'll tell you." He pawed at the arms choking him. "This was before the whole incident. Susan and Kevin were chatting in his office, but the door was cracked open. I was running an errand for my boss when-"

"Skip the crap."

"I overheard them talking about their little hobbies. Kevin was going on about how he'd been angling for another meeting with another one. He said it'd be his twelfth. I had no idea who he was talking about but it's obvious now. Susan said something about how her next boy toy was set to graduate in a few years. They were real chummy. One thing I remember her saying was that she was going to get him to come over to her house real soon and stay the night. That he should tell his parents he's staying with a friend for the night."

 ` "Birds of a feather flock together," Jim growled. "You said graduate, she didn't mean college, right?"

"I thought so at first, given the words used but her next comment solidified it. She said that her boy's third grade teacher was a real hard ass. Started going on about how he was complaining to her about him being mean or some such. Apparently, the teacher was asking questions about who the kid was hanging out with after school. Kid had a big mouth it seems. Turns out they went after him because he was getting too close to finding out about his extracurricular activities if you catch my drift."

"I do remember seeing a teacher get fired and disgraced in the papers recently. Okay, here's what's going to happen," Jim said. "I'm going to let you go. You're going home and never telling anyone else what happened here. You get me? You really don't want to test me."

"No, sir. I don't. I just want to keep my job. Talking to vigilantes about office gossip isn't conductive to that."

"God bless human selfishness. Oh, and one more thing. Why didn't you ever say anything if you knew Susan was a piece of human garbage touching a young schoolboy? Did you not care? Were you only worried about your little job enough to cover for them?"

"I had just got the job, dude. Did you want me to jeopardize that by blabbing to the police over a theory?"

"For a child's innocence? Yes. Yes, I did. So sorry. I lied to you earlier. You won't be going home tonight. Not with you covering for child molesters for a little money."

"What?"

Jim didn't answer verbally but instead jammed the knife into the neck of the man and slit from left to right. He pulled the blade out with a sickening squelch, pushing him forward and taking off into a sprint back the way he came. He wiped the blade clean with his gloved hand and holstered the weapon. He checked his clothes to see no crimson on them. Before reaching the street, he took off the identity hiding apparel and concealed them on his person before calmly walking back to his car. "Susan, huh? You're next on the list."

He climbed into his car and investigated his rear-view mirror before pulling out into the nigh empty road. "Should be back in time for Cyn to not be suspicious too. All I did was take a nice little walk after all." A devious grin overtook his features. "Still, need to get rid of this shit before I get home. Just need to find a metal bin to burn these gloves, mask, and such. A quick wash should cleanse the knife when I'm sure she's asleep. Then finally get some sleep myself." He rubbed his eye with his left hand, keeping his right on the wheel. "No one will miss that little weasel, right? Who doesn't report possible activity like that when a kids involved? People these days - what's wrong with them? Maybe I have gone crazy, talking to myself this much. Shit, I wouldn't put it out of the realm of possibility. Not to mention I need to keep working if I want to keep this façade up. At least I work from home and have access to my phone. Should be easy enough during the day." He exhaled a large breath. "I hope I know what the devil I'm doing."

6

"It's about time you got home." Cynthia sat at the recliner and angled her neck back to see the door. She got out of the chair and approached Jim when her nose crinkled. "What is that smell?" She sniffed around him. "Is that smoke? Why do you smell like smoke?"

"Teenagers were having a bonfire in the park as I walked by. Oh, and I bought us some groceries." He lifted his hand holding the white plastic bags. "Figured I should do something useful if I was going to stay here."

"Huh," Cynthia took one of the bags, "thanks. I thought you were..." she trailed off, "Never mind that. I did get an interesting call from your mother a few minutes ago."

"Is that right?" Jim carried another couple bags over to the kitchen counter and started unpacking them. "What did she say?"

"That she just heard about your little event yesterday. You didn't tell your own mother you were nearly killed?"

"I feel like this is a loaded question no matter what I answer, but no. No, I did not. Precisely because I knew how she'd react."

"You decided having her find out this way and worrying herself sick was better?"

"Can we not talk about this? You know how she found out? Because I do. I ran into my father at the store, told him what happened, and he informed her. So, in a roundabout way, I did tell her. So kindly get off my back."

"Not the same thing, but fine. It's not my business how you talk to your own family. She was just distraught, and I hated listening to her so frantic about her baby. I barely managed to get off the phone with her by the time you got home."

"Home?" Jim asked. "I appreciate the hospitality, but I don't consider this my home." He closed a cupboard. "Not yet anyway."

"Yet? Oh, don't you do this. Don't try and embarrass me like that. It was a slip."

"A Freudian slip maybe." Jim chuckled and came up behind her. He slipped his hands around her waist and leaned his chin onto her shoulder. "Should I call you honey and take you to bed then?"

"Get off of me." She shook him off and looked away. "You're mentally well enough to joke again, that's a good sign at least." A slight crimson blush colored her cheeks. "How did your father take the news?"

"As good as can be. Told me not to blame myself and that all he cared about was that I was safe. Typical parenting things I assume. Made me feel better if nothing else."

"Always a good thing. Can you answer me one more question though?"

"Go ahead."

She backed up a step and crossed her arms, looking at him "Why did you go to the law firm?"

"Excuse me?"

"You think I'm dumb or something? You leave in the middle of the night, go to the grocery store, and then park near the same law firm Charlie and I were talking about? Why? I used the gps locater on your phone by the way. Don't try and deny it."

"If you tracked that, then you know I just sat there watching the building. I just wanted to see where the man I killed worked. That's all. To see if they were planning anything on me."

"To protect me I'm assuming. How did you even plan to find out anything from a half mile away inside your car? By looking for people in masks and guns visible?"

"I realized the flaw of my plan a few minutes in. I never said I was a flawless planner, did I?"

"You're an idiot. A compassionate man, but an idiot you know. Next time get a directional microphone. You'll look like a creeper, but you might actually get results."

"Ever consider becoming a private detective? Sounds like you have a knack for it."

She slapped his shoulder. "No. Stop trying to change the subject. I appreciate your trying to look out for me, but you're not a superhero. You can't stop everything. You're still a human being. You need rest the same as the rest of us. Probably more so now that I think about it."

Jim led the pair further in toward the kitchen as he spoke. "Appreciate the concern, but the nap earlier charged my batteries a bit. I just had to get out and get some fresh air."

"Right. Did it help?"

He started unloading another bag's contents on the table "Certainly did. How are the nephew and niece doing?"

"They're still in bed. One did get up and ask for water,

but uneventful since. They're so well behaved - not like us when we were kids."

"Remember when we'd sneak out and go on adventures outside?"

Cynthia sighed, setting her bag down beside Jim's. "I'll tell what I remember. I remember us nearly getting jumped by hooligans after hours and managing to sneak away back to my mom's house only to get yelled at for an hour before getting forced into bed. She was up all night watching that door afterward you know. I still feel bad making her do that."

"We wouldn't have been caught if you hadn't slammed the door so hard. We'd have been in and out without anyone noticing."

She pulled out the various boxes and bags of food in the remaining space as she spoke. "And we'd never have learned our lessons if we had. Sometimes failure is a part of learning."

Jim crumpled up the white bag and tossed it into the nearby trash bin. "Got me there."

She smiled. "You should learn by now not to argue with me. I always best you."

"Sure, sweetie. If that helps you sleep at night."

"Get to bed already, you bum." She pointed toward the living room. "Just use the couch. I'll get you a pillow and a blanket. Feel free to use the television, just keep it real low. I have classes in the morning." She exited the walk-in kitchen and moved to her bedroom door before stopping. "Did you ever get your laptop from your house?"

"I think it's been seized as evidence in the ongoing investigation. I know the camera has been."

"I doubt it'll take long to get it back. Feel free to use mine to work when I'm at class tomorrow. Professors don't let us take them into class, so someone may as well get some use out of it," she said before disappearing behind her door. Muffled sounds of fabric moving rustled behind the wooden blockade until she emerged and dumped them on the sofa. "There you go. Don't say I never did anything for you as my guest."

"Perish the thought." Jim came over and sat beside the presented gifts. "For real though," he said in a somber tone, "thank you for having me over and being worried. I know you deny it, and it's adorable, but I can tell. I don't know what I'd do if you weren't here."

"Don't get all sappy on me now." She turned around and hurried to her door before stopping without turning around. "Good night."

"Night."

7

Jim watched the loaded car pull out of the driveway from in front of the door and gave a wave along with a smile. "She's a saint getting them all up and ready to move at this hour," he mumbled to himself. He watched the car speed down the road and turned back to the home. "Guess it's time to get to work." He entered and wandered over to the laptop. "Left it logged in, huh? Appreciate it. It would have been awkward if she hadn't, considering I don't know her password. Question is, do I actually do work, or a little research?"

He navigated to a new browser's webpage. The banner above read "Privacy from prying eyes. Your history is so private, even you won't know where you went afterward."

Jim chuckled and clicked the install button. "Research it is. Can't have her knowing though. I'll just uninstall it before she gets back." He clicked the prompts and watched the progress bars fill up until finally a new window popped up.

"Here we go." He typed in the name of the law firm he'd visited the night prior to see the place's official website show up first in the search results. "Susan York, where are you? There." He clicked on the name. "Receptionist. Yes, I know that. Hard working, personable - legalese for she's nice. Blah, don't know what I expected to find on their official site. Guess it's time for something unofficial. "Let's try another avenue. Need to see where she lives and get a handle for my next plan."

He navigated to a different website entirely. "This will do nicely. It may cost a small fee, but modern-day cryptocurrency will keep me anonymous. It's a good thing I memorized my virtual wallet's credentials. Just need to wait for the confirmations, and I will have all the information about Susan York in the Oklahoma nearby area. There should only be one or two, and I can cross reference the photo on the official page to make sure I get the right one."

He got up from the bar stool, moved to the sofa near his black bag, and opened it. "This is useless." He picked up the firearm he'd defended himself with recently. "It's registered and would lead right back to me. Another hurdle in the life of a vigilante. Guess I can find ways around it. I'd rather not rely on my knife for all the dirty work. That tends to be too messy. The last thing I need is their blood on my clothes."

"Cyn will get suspicious if I end up burning all my clothes. I'll have to get an unregistered one or come up with something different. I'm not sure what that'd be though. I don't have the local underworld connections I'd need to pull that off. Not unless I want to go to the seedier part of town and ask around. I don't savor that option though." He carefully placed the handgun back into the bag and pulled out a notepad and pencil before moving back to the kitchen bar. "Three confirmations, and we're good."

Photos of two different women turned up on the screen.

Only one he recognized from the law firm's website. "Here she is." He clicked on the profile and data replaced the previous screen. "Address, date of birth, maiden name, parents, even where she went to high school. Damn, this is a thorough site." He wrote down the address, and other pertinent bits of information before closing the web browser and uninstalling it.

"Address, job location, and everything's in order. Now to just observe and plan an attack. I need a location for the deed, an exit plan, somewhere to leave the body, a new firearm, and a change of clothes. That and everything else to conceal my DNA, but that's easy to get. I suppose I could take a day off work and do a little scouting today. Right? It wouldn't hurt. I'll leave my phone here this time. No sense giving Cyn a heart attack and reason to suspect anything." He reached into his back pocket and left the cell phone on the bar.

He jogged over to the front door and threw it open. Shutting it behind him, he power-walked over to his car and got inside. He pulled out into the road and reached into his back pocket to retrieve the newest burner phone he'd bought. He kept his eyes on the road and placed the device into his lap. "Bad form to use while driving, but during red lights it isn't so bad. Right?" He pumped the brakes at the intersection and dialed Charlie's number.

He answered in two rings. "What's up? Who is this?"

Jim switched it to speaker phone and redirected his attention back to the still red light above. "Hey, man. It's me - Jim. Can you direct me to your bud plug?"

"That guy's in the seedy part of town, man. You sure you want his addy?"

"Dude, with the past few days I've had, yes. Yes, I'm sure."

"I get it. He's at 1208 Charred Avenue."

"Charred?"

"Scared?" Charlie's playful voice asked. "I am too every time I make a pickup. Just tell him I sent you. He doesn't do walk-ins, but referrals are fine. Here, I'll text you his number. He should be cool if you give him advance notice. Just keep your hands steady, and don't go near your belt line."

"Why? Is he the paranoid type?"

"Obviously, but he also deals in uh," Charlie paused, "hardware."

"Got it. Thanks, man. How's class going?"

"Teach is gone from the room now. She's late to class. How long was it before students can leave?"

"I'd give it half an hour."

"Damn," Charlie said. "Got it. You have a fun day. Sounds like you will alright. He's got that sticky icky good stuff."

"Thanks, man. Talk to you later."

"Later."

Jim reached down, still staring at the traffic in front of him and touched the screen, ending the call without looking. He gave a quick glance down to confirm the call was in fact ended before raising his attention back to traffic. "Now I know where to get an unregistered piece. That solves one problem. I should have enough cash on me."

He took a turn onto an unfamiliar road. "New objective - don't get shot," he mumbled to himself. He saw numerous people on either side of the road sitting on their porch watching the cars go by. "Such a welcoming lot, aren't they?" Most turned their head as his car passed by. "He's a few minutes out, so I should give him a call and drop Charlie's name. Don't want to surprise him." He stopped at a nearby stop sign ahead and quickly dialed the number Charlie had texted him, making sure it was on speaker again.

"Who the fuck is this?" a rough voice asked.

"Hey, Charlie referred me. He said to call you before I stopped by. Is that alright?" Jim accelerated and kept going toward his destination as he spoke.

"Yeah, if he sent you my way it's cool. Park down the road a bit and meet me in my backyard. The gate's open. What's your name anyway? I like to know who I do business with."

"It's Jim."

"Oh yeah. Charlie's talked about you before. Great. Come on over."

"Be there in a few." Jim hung up and stuffed the device into his front right jeans pocket. "Awfully accepting fellow. Maybe Charlie and him have a rapport. That, or I'm walking into a trap. Not like I can do much in this neighborhood if I am. He has all the friends and home field advantage. Then again, who said gearing up for doing the right thing was easy or safe?"

He glanced to his right. "Judging by that house's number, it should be up here in a few more places so I'll park right here." He slowed down and parked by the side of the road. "Now don't stand out, and we'll be good." He checked his side mirror before opening the door and stepping outside into the sun saturated asphalt below.

He shut the door and locked it. He walked around his car and hopped up onto the cracked sidewalk before continuing to the dealer's house.

"You lost? Don't look like you belong in this neighborhood," a man to his right heckled.

"Just on my way to an acquaintance's place."

"Oh, I know why you're here. Just try to stand out a little

less." A wild laugh met his ears and grew quieter as he passed further ahead.

He faced numerous other hecklers both sides of the street as he walked, with one notable one in his ear as he approached the house. "Whatever you do, don't go into that backyard. It's only trouble back there, rich boy."

"Right."

"Don't listen to them." The man he was there to meet met him at the gate. "Come on back to my office." He led him between houses and into the small fenced off back yard. "You know," he said, "normally I don't take new clients, but you did drop Charlie's name. Since he's vouched for you in the past, I'm making an exception. What those idiots were referring to was that I've had a few walk-ins come back here without notice."

"Don't take surprises well I take it?"

"Oh, I take them well. I treated them as an intruder on my property because they were."

"Understood."

"Good, my name's Emmanuel." The tanned gentleman offered a hand toward Jim.

Jim took it and grasped it firmly before shaking it. "It's Jim Benning."

"Mr. Benning, what did you come to my humble shop for? Same as Charlie? Need a little relaxation in your life. I heard you had your own little intruder problem recently."

"Not quite," Jim said. "I'm looking for a little protection."

"Ahh, you're here for my other business side. A man can't have too many guns, right? This is God damned America after all. How much you got to spend?"

"I can spend two hundred."

"Two hundred can buy you a simple handgun with ammunition. Now it is modified before you get in a huff. I added the laser sight and calibrated it myself. Come inside and I can show you. Wouldn't want you buying blind, would we?" He motioned toward him and slowly walked inside the already open door. "I know the place ain't much, but come on in."

"It's a fine house. Don't short change yourself. It's cozy."

"Quite polite, aren't you? That's a rare thing around these parts. I like you already." He led the pair through a small kitchen littered with assorted unwashed dishes on the counter and inside the sink. "Don't mind the mess. I haven't got around to doing the dishes yet today." They continued through into a smaller room off the main hallway into a door. "Here we are. Just hold on a second."

Jim leaned against the door frame and reached into his back jeans pocket. Fondling his wallet he spoke. "Don't suppose that price gets me any ammunition?"

"Sure does. You'll get two boxes. That should be enough, right?" Emmanuel opened the nearby closet door and leaned forward, pushing clothes out of the way.

"Sure, I have nine-millimeter ammunition, but I wasn't sure of the caliber this thing is."

"This little daisy's a forty-five. Still plenty of stopping power for any self-defense needed. Trust me on that one." He dug out a small shoe box and plopped it on the nearby bed. "Here we are." He took off the lid revealing an assortment of small arms packed inside. "This here's the one I'm speaking of." He fished one out and ejected the magazine, confirming it was empty before reinserting it. He checked the chamber and handed it over. "What do you think?"

Jim took it with great care and turned to the side away from Emmanuel before raising it to a shooting position.

"You turn on the sights like this." Emmanuel leaned over

and flicked a tiny switch, causing a low hum to emit along with a red line to appear on the opposite wall.

"I like that."

"I thought you would."

"I have one quick question and it may be a stupid one."

"Shoot."

Jim relaxed his stance and angled the firearm, inspecting it. "No serial numbers?"

"None. Totally untraceable. Be aware though, that if you're caught with that thing, it's a mandatory five years in the slammer. Now, you don't know me if you're caught. If you squeal on me, I will be..." he paused, "angry."

"I get it. Good. I was looking for this precisely."

"You're an odd guy. Most would-be shooters always shit their pants when I say that. Can't tell you the number who go pale and give some excuse and leave. You just say, "good". I'm not going to ask why you want that, but now you know the risk. Don't let a cop find that thing, and you're good."

"Simple enough to remember. Keep the registered piece if there's a chance cops are around, this thing if not."

"I said I won't ask, but I'd be lying if I said I wasn't curious why you want an untraceable piece."

"I won't answer that, just like how I won't ask how you got this."

"Smart man. You know the value of privacy. I respect that. So with the modification and two boxes of ammunition, that will be one hundred and eighty dollars."

Jim retrieved his wallet and cracked it open. He rifled through the crinkled bills inside and pulled out the required amount. "Done deal." He handed over the green paper and took his new purchase.

"Let me get you your ammo, and you can be on your way." Emmanuel moved to the foot of his bed and opened the chest before extracting two small rectangular boxes and handing them over. "I'm assuming you know how to load the magazine yourself then?"

"Safe to assume as much."

"Just have to be sure. Some folks are green and wouldn't know how to use it If I didn't ask."

"I appreciate your time. I'll get out of your hair then." Jim tucked his new purchase behind him in his belt line and covered it with his shirt. "Don't want to take up too much time."

"Appreciated, friend. Now I'll escort you out." He led Jim back through his place. "Try to ignore the peanut gallery. They know not to fuck with my clients."

Jim followed, "You're the big boss man here, huh? Good to know."

"Something like that. There's always a few young bucks who want to challenge the status quo, but most of the time they have sense enough to not try me. If someone does, you let me know. I'll sort it out."

"Thanks." Jim reached the gate and nodded at Emmanuel. "I'll be going then. Have a good one."

"You too Mr. Benning. Try not to use that thing, eh?"

"No promises."

"No, there never is in this business."

Jim left the man without further words and headed back in the direction of his car. "Next, to pay a special little visit to Susan tonight." He passed the assorted hecklers and got back to his car and climbed inside. "I should go there tonight. She may be trying to get the kid over there tonight. I can't let that happen. I'll have to take her out before the kid gets there. I can't let him in. If he does…" He lightly punched the steering wheel with a growl, "I can't let that happen. Either he watches me take her out, or he gets violated. Neither is acceptable." He jammed the key inside the ignition and twisted.

The engine roared to life, and the car pulled out into the road to its next destination.

"To the shopping center again. I should probably buy the hair nets, masks, and such in bulk, huh? Or would that be too suspicious? Maybe. Guess we'll see."

8

"There she is." Jim watched Susan's house as a car entered the driveway and a lone blonde, slightly overweight, middle-aged woman climbed out. "That's her alright." Jim put down the binoculars and surveyed the street. "I've been waiting long enough." He glanced down at the clock by the radio. "At least she got home earlier today. It's only six. Should give me time before the kid gets here. Best case scenario, the kid knocks on the door and heads home when she doesn't answer. Worst case, he has a key to her place and finds her." He bit his lip. "Shit. Can't let that happen either. Mental scarring of that nature isn't much better."

"A better question is how do I get inside?" He scanned the surrounding buildings amid the rapidly darkening sky. He spotted a ladder leaning against her neighbor's home. "Someone was cleaning their gutter and got lazy. I can work with that. Judging by the no lights thing, they're probably not home. Now for a point of entry." He turned his attention back to the two-story home. "There are certainly enough windows, but I can't break in from the front - too many potential witnesses. I'll have to wing it and check the sides when I grab the ladder. It's more dangerous, but I can't let some honest Joe see me breaking a window and climbing in from the street. He'd call the cops in a heartbeat. Plus, she'd be alerted by the noise and be waiting with heat pointed in my direction." Jim brought a finger up to his mouth and bit down softly.

"No sense waiting here playing the what if game. I can't let the kid get here, so I need to take action soon." He climbed out of his car, closed the door gently to avoid unnecessary noise, and walked toward her house. "Nice day for a walk." He directed his attention upward toward the sky and shielded his eyes from the setting sun before looking over his shoulder to see no moving cars and no pedestrians behind him. He glanced side to side to see nothing but houses on either side with parked cars in front of them. When he got near enough, he ducked between the houses. He checked again to make sure no one noticed his entrance. Satisfied no one saw him, he turned to his target's domicile. He reached into his pants pocket and retrieved the black leather gloves before putting them on

Two windows overlooked the alley he was in, one on the first floor, and one on the second. He hopped the waist high fence splitting the properties and fell to a knee. He crept along the side of the house toward the back yard. After he made the turn into the backyard, he surveyed that side to find another window, this time only on the second floor. Making another turn, he found a nearly identical two windows on this side as well. "Dealer's choice then. May as well try the first floor first." He tried the nearby window to find it locked tight.

He stalked around to the ladder side of the house and tried the first floor window there only to be disappointed when it too was firmly locked shut with no way in other than to break it and climb through. "Guess we're climbing and trying that," he whispered. "Who locks their second story window, right?" He peeked into the window he was just trying to get in and saw her in her kitchen with her back to him holding a phone to her ear. He got out of her potential line of sight and sighed in relief. He hopped back over the fence and seized the ladder. He gingerly lifted the ladder over the mini blockade and leaned the ladder on the fence before vaulting over it again.

He positioned the ladder below the window and, with great precision, leaned it against the two story house.. He lifted his shirt and donned the hair net and new mask he'd recently bought. He climbed the first step and took a deep breath. His hand snaked around to his back to the newly acquired weapon before extracting it. He ejected the magazine, making sure he'd done his job well loading it in the car. Satisfied, he nodded and whispered to himself, "Moment of no return. Let's do this. Just remember to leave the way you came and return everything to the state it was in before you got here."

Using only his left hand he scaled the rickety old ladder up to the second floor and used his left hand to try the window. Success! The window inched upward a few inches until it opened easily. He climbed into the bedroom and readied his weapon as soon as his feet touched the floor. "Go time," he said under his breath. He brought the weapon up to a ready stance. Aiming down the sights, he moved forward toward the only door in the room.

He placed his ear to the door to hear a faint female voice. He placed his free hand on the doorknob and twisted. Pulling with great care the door opened without a squeak. The words from downstairs became a little clearer now.

"Yeah, I'm home, sweetie. Feel free to come on over whenever. I'll leave the door unlocked, so you feel free to come right on in. I'm going to get a bath really quick. Alright? Aren't you sweet? I'm just a little tired from working so hard today."

Jim grimaced and readied his weapon again when he heard footsteps approach. He ducked back into the room and got out of the doorway. He placed his back to the wall near the door. The footsteps grew louder. "You did tell your mom you're staying at a friend's house tonight, yes? Good boy. It'll be our little secret." The footsteps and voice were just on the other side of the open doorway now. "I'll be expecting you in the next fifteen minutes then. Be careful on your walk over. Oh yes, don't worry. I'll help with your homework as well, dear. Okay now. Bye, sweetie." A low click was heard before another door further down the hall could be heard slamming shut.

Water could be heard running, along with the muffled sounds of shuffling clothes. Jim emerged from his makeshift hiding place and moved down the hallway at a deliberate pace toward where the sounds were coming from. He took a position outside the bathroom by the side of the door and waited.

"Finally," the feminine voice from inside said. "It took this damned water long enough to warm up, just like the kid. It just requires patience." The sound of running water ended and was replaced by the low sound of water shifting along with a feminine sigh and eventual silence.

"Now or never," Jim said under his breath. He checked the chamber, confirming that there was in fact a round loaded, and took a step away from the wall. He reached out with his left hand and grasped the knob. His eyes closed for a few seconds and opened before throwing the door open and a piercing yell meeting his ears.

"Who the fuck are you and how did you get in my home?" The naked woman's shame was covered in bubbles and water.

"Sit down, and don't get any wise ideas." Jim's voice was filled with steel.

Susan's eyes wandered to the firearm and back to Jim's steely blue eyes behind the mask. "Are you robbing my house? Take it all. I don't care." She slid back into the opaque liquid, her tone taking a defeated tone.

"You have a guest coming over soon. Does he have a cell phone?"

"What? Why do you know that?"

"Think I'm deaf?" Jim pulled the hammer back. "Bad answer."

"Okay, fine." Susan raised her sudsy hands in front of her. "Yes, yes he does. Don't hurt him, please! He's just a little boy."

"Quite the proverbial balls on you. You abuse the child and then tell me not to hurt him. Not everyone is like you. Now quiet, and do what I tell you." His eyes darted to the nearby cell phone sitting on the sink. He kept his weapon pointed at her and ambled over to said phone. He picked it up. "Catch." He tossed it underhanded with his left hand and watched her catch it. "Now call him, and tell him to go home. Make up an excuse, I don't care what. Just do it now."

"Why should I?" Susan asked.

"Because if you don't, I kill you now."

Susan stared down the barrel for a few terse moments before flinging her right hand relatively dry and complying. "Fine. So long as you don't kill me." She pressed a number, and the sound of automated dialing could faintly be heard by Jim. "Yes, honey, I'm so sorry. I've been called into work for overtime tonight." She paused. "Now don't you worry. I'll help you with your homework later, but it'll just be a little later. Just go to the arcade, alright? I'll call you when I'm home. You're such an understanding young man."

Jim's eyes narrowed into a glare at the woman, his index finger wrapping around the trigger.

"I'll see you later." She hung up and looked up at Jim. "Happy now?"

"Ecstatic." His dry voice remarked. "You have any firearms in this place?"

"Robbery huh? Yeah, in my room. Not like I can get to them right now anyway. What caliber is that thing anyway?"

"It's a forty five."

"Same as mine."

"Perfect." Jim moved toward her within a few feet and squeezed the trigger. A crack, a flash of light, and momentary look of terror crossed Susan's features. A circle appeared on her forehead and her body slumped back. The once pristine water now being tainted with red and tinges of gray matter. "Now to get said firearm and make it look like a suicide before someone calls that shot in."

Jim ran out of the room and barged into the remaining rooms he'd missed. In the first room he tried, he saw a gun cabinet already cracked open. He grabbed the forty-five-caliber weapon and ejected the magazine. Taking one round out, he jammed it in his pants pocket and reinserted the magazine before returning to his latest work. He carefully placed it inside her hand dangling outside of the tub and without delay returned to his entrance point. He hopped up onto the windowsill and down onto the top rung of the ladder. He closed the window and slid down the climbing tool. He moved it to the other side of the fence and removed his gloves, mask, and hairnet before calmly walking back to his car.

Along the long walk back he saw only one other soul. Three quarters of the way back, he saw a lone man exit his front door and look behind him toward the house he'd just exited with a cell phone to his ear. "Just in the nick of time." Jim made it back to his car and hopped inside before taking off without pause.

9

———

"He seems to be doing better recently," Cynthia said. "He's actually going out and doing things. I don't think he's blaming himself as much as that first day after."

"Could be a momentary thing."

"If you don't mind my saying, Mr. Benning," Cynthia said, leaning back against the sink's counter.

"Call me Dennis."

"Very well, if you don't mind my saying, Dennis, I think he might be swinging too far the other way now. He's not working too much, and he's out all hours of the day relaxing. I'd rather he do this, but too far in either direction isn't exactly healthy. I guess him not having his own laptop doesn't help that."

"What happened to it?" Dennis asked, crossing his arms.

"Taken into evidence from the recent incident. I doubt he'll get it back anytime soon. Maybe in a month or two if he's lucky. I've been lending him my laptop when I'm in class, but he hasn't been using it much."

"Pardon this old fuddy duddy for asking, but how do you know how often he uses it if you're not home?"

"System logs. Like today it said it was in use for twenty minutes while I was gone. Then when I got back, he was gone. He's yet to get back."

"He's always been a free spirit." A larger framed woman said from across the bar. "He'll come back when he's ready. I'll just have to give him a little push in the right direction."

"You're right, Jill," Dennis said to his wife. "He's definitely headstrong - just like our host when she was younger."

"The difference is I matured as I grew up a bit more." Cynthia brought a hand to her face to hide her chuckle.

"We do appreciate you taking care of our boy in this rough patch though." Dennis gave a small bow. "He's too prideful to ask us. If you hadn't offered, he'd probably be living in his car, knowing him."

"Not like I'd let that happen," Cynthia said with a wave of her hand.

"We know, darling." Jill held her quivering hands in front of her. "We just worry is all. It doesn't matter how old they get, we worry. Our boy would be lucky if you two got together."

"I, what?" Cynthia stuttered as a red hue enveloped her cheeks.

"Don't embarrass the poor girl, dear," Dennis smirked. "Besides, they're already living together. They're only a step or two away now."

"I see where he gets his sense of humor from now," Cynthia said. "Sorry for you coming all the way over and him not being here though. I'm sure he'll be back any minute now. Frankly, I'm surprised he's not here already."

As if on cue an engine could be heard outside, along with a door slamming shut.

"Speak of the devil, and he appears," Dennis said with a mirthful chuckle.

"I'm home," Jim said, flinging the door open.

"Did you hear him? He said home. He must be quite comfortable here." Dennis glanced over at Cynthia.

"Yeah. I figured I'd give the lot of you something to chat about." Jim closed the door behind him. "I saw your car outside."

"Where were you, son? You had your little missus all worried to hear her tell it."

"Is that what she said?" Jim's eyes darted over toward a heavily blushing Cynthia. "I was out taking a drive, clearing my head."

"Get much work done today?" Jill asked.

"I hate tying up Cyn's work laptop for long. That, and I'd have to download a few programs - and that's disk space."

"You know I wouldn't mind. There's a reason I offered. You sure you're not just getting lazy?" Cynthia said, facing away from the group now. Her hands washed the leftover dishes as she spoke.

"It won't become a habit." Jim walked past the group, sat on the empty sofa, and looked back at the group. "I promise."

"Just like the time you promised to stop skipping spelling class, and then we got a call from the principal the next day?" Jill asked. "Sorry, honey. I'm just concerned. I don't want you forming bad habits and troubling this sweet young lady."

"I appreciate the confidence, Mom."

"We should trust our son." Dennis left the bar and moved over to the sofa, close to his son. He stood behind him and placed his hands on his shoulders. "We raised him right, and we didn't raise a freeloader. Possibly a trouble-maker, but not a leech."

"Thanks, Pop," Jim said. "Look, I'll get back to a normal working schedule tomorrow. I promise. I'll be on her laptop all day tomorrow when she's at class working my life away. Then when she gets home and it's fully charged, she can thank me. I'm nothing if not a perfect house guest."

"We will see about that, but that's good. We were just concerned." Cynthia turned the faucet off and faced the group now that her face was back to its normal shade. "See anything neat out there today? News has been lighting up the past few days. I was worried."

"News? What happened?" Jim asked from the nearby sofa.

"In the past two days two people have been murdered," Dennis said. "One by a knife to the throat, one by a supposed self-inflicted gunshot wound to the head. If you ask me though, it doesn't fit. Based on the details released, it sounds like a homicide to me."

"You're retired, dear. No sense getting up in arms about it." Jill soothed her husband.

"I might have just been a detective, but I know a setup when I hear one. 'Investigators suspect it to be a suicide'. They used that same line when we had our suspicions, but no evidence. My only thing is who would want some random woman dead? I'd need access to the database to see though."

"Who knows?" Jim kicked back with an exhale. "Maybe she pissed someone off. You never know what the rich and powerful will do to keep people quiet."

"Could be," Cynthia said. "She was with the most powerful law firm in town. Quite a string of bad luck happening with them lately. I wouldn't want to work there now. Karma is after them like a bloodhound."

"I did not know that." Dennis rubbed his chin. "That's interesting to say the least. Those kinds of places are always getting mixed up with the worst kinds of scumbags, by nature of the business."

"Don't encourage him, Son," Jill said. "You know how he gets when he starts up. His blood pressure spikes."

"Sorry, Ma. Just tossing my two cents into the discussion. It is weird though."

"They'd have the resources for it too." Dennis's eyes lit up. "Maybe I should call some of the old boys on the force and see if they've thought of her work connections. On the other hand, it might just clutter up their investigation chasing down false leads. Ah hell, what should I do?"

"Just calm down and forget about it. If they need your help, they'll call. They know more than you do about this," Jill cooed. "Leave it to the younger men. They know what they're doing. You trained them before you retired after all. Have more self-confidence."

"You're right, sugar." Dennis moved back to his wife and gave her an embrace. "It was just fun to think about. Imagining myself helping the boys solve crimes and put low lives away again."

"I get that," Cynthia said, cracking open her laptop. "Fulfillment from a job is a strong motivator, and hearing about a killer on the loose would pique that interest whole hog."

"They'll catch him," Jill said. "They always catch them."

"Well," Dennis said, "not always, but most of the time. This guy seems smart though. The one guy I did call earlier said there was no foreign DNA at the crime scene. Making suicide seem more likely. Still, the last two dead both worked at that law firm. That coincidence is concerning."

"Getting off of the dead people chat," Jill attempted to change the subject, "we should be heading back home soon." She winked at Cynthia. "Let the lovebirds settle in for the night."

"You both are incorrigible," Cynthia said with a sigh. "Do we really look like that?"

"Yes," both parents answered without hesitation. "But we're biased," Dennis said with a wicked grin. "We just want our boy to find happiness. Is that so wrong?"

"We think you'd do a great job with that," Jill said, guiding her husband closer to the door. "Are we wrong?"

"No," Jim said looking away.

"Don't you start too." Cynthia pointed at Jim. "Don't encourage them."

"The lady doth protest too damned much methinks."

"Why do you remember Shakespeare quotes now, but you flunked that test back in high school?"

"Selective memory. You know how it goes when it comes to you."

"I think you just like pissing me off."

"It is indeed fun."

"Good night you two. Have fun." Jill opened the door and waved to the remaining two occupants.

"Have fun." Dennis winked at his son and shut the door.

"Your dad was really into his job, huh?" Cynthia took a seat on the opposite end of the couch. "Never seen him get so worked up like that."

"He was always the go getter. Him and Ma used to argue about him coming home late when I was a kid. It's why I had the habit of sneaking out my window. I hated listening to them argue."

"It's all coming together now. Wait, your room was on the second floor. How did you get out?"

"I got good at tying my bedsheets together. I simply made a rope, opened the window, tied it to my bed, and climbed down. Well, I say climbed, but it was more of a sliding motion."

"Getting back in the house?"

Jim smiled at the memory. "Not quite as elegant a method I assure you. I kept a spare key on me. I'd come back and wait until the lights went out, then go in the front door; or resigned myself to face the music if they noticed, since they didn't go to bed if they saw I wasn't in my room."

"My parents were mortified the time we snuck out during our sleepover. I was grounded for a month and got a lecture every single day of it about how they were mortified by my behavior, and how you were a bad influence."

"Nice to know your parents didn't like me." Jim looked over at her. "What kept you coming back?"

"You ever told a child they can't do something? It makes them want to do it more."

"So, our friendship was based on childish stubbornness?"

"The base of it was indeed cemented around it." Cynthia clicked a button on the remote control, changing the channel. "It was the beginning of the fun part of my childhood. I was sheltered growing up."

"Glad I could be of assistance as a young troublemaker. Happy to spice your life up."

"Too bad you're still a bit of a bad influence." She laughed and looked over at Jim's dour expression. "Aw, don't take it so seriously. It was a joke, you dolt."

"Yeah." Jim's smile didn't reach his eyes. "I know."

"You've made a lot of progress recently, but just know you don't have to act a certain way. If you're still bummed, say it. You can be honest."

"I wouldn't call it depressed, more like drained. You always have these daydreams in high school about what it'd be like to actually end someone's life, but to actually do it - it's a different beast altogether. What you thought would be cathartic really makes you feel a bit hollow. It's difficult to explain. Like I shouldn't be as okay with it as I am, and I know it. Everyone tells me I did the right thing, and they're right, but it doesn't feel like it." He clenched a fist as he spoke. "It feels like I did an abhorrent thing for the right reason."

"And what reason was that?"

"You want to know what I was thinking when it happened?" Jim paused, leaned his head back on the sofa, and paused. "Fear mixed with keeping you safe. Self-defense was in there, but my first thought was you upstairs hiding behind my bed. I couldn't let him get near you - not that kind of man. I wouldn't allow it. After it was done, I realized the only reason you were there was my own selfish-ness and impatience."

"You really are getting a hero complex I see. It's not your fault I was there. Good God, melodramatic much? I do have a brain of my own you know?" Her spare hand's index finger raised up and tapped the side of her head. "It is nice to hear that, however. You may be impulsive, sometimes arrogant, and more than a little idealistic, but you're indeed a good person as I see it."

"Let's hope you're correct."

"Haven't you learned yet that I always am? Or do I have to prove it again?" Cynthia brought a leg up onto the sofa and extended it to kick Jim in the thigh. "Just shut up and listen. You just might learn something." She took a deep breath. "I give you a lot of shit, and we both know I'm not often serious, but this is one of those rare times. You always do what you believe is right, for better or worse. You know what that requires - willpower, ability, and yes, even stubbornness. You're kind generally speaking, stern when needed as you've shown, and have good people skills. Even if you do have a dangerous hobby, I'm not afraid to spend my time with you because you make life more enjoyable. Enriching people's lives isn't all sunshine and rainbows. Without darkness there is no light and all that first-year philosophy stuff. Point is, I choose who I hang out with, and I chose you. Now don't make me say this mushy shit very often, alright? It'll make me lose my image. I'm just doing this to cheer you up, that's all. You're too slow to realize the obvious, and I have to fix that."

"Aren't you chatty tonight? My parents must have really riled you up. I will think about what you said though, since it's so rare you pour your heart out and all." He gave a sly grin and looked over at her without turning his head.

"Always need to be difficult, don't you? Some things never change." Cynthia arched her back, showing off her modest figure with a massive yawn. "Now, since the kids aren't here tonight, you can use the guest room instead of this sofa. It's comfier than this thing." She patted the cushion below. "Follow me. I got the sheets washed while you were out today." She grunted as she got up from the furniture. "Come on, lazy bones. No time to feel sorry for yourself."

"Such a slave driver tonight." Jim followed the order and walked behind her.

"At least you're getting back to normal now." She pushed open the door he'd not entered yet to see a small, but cozy room. "Glad to see I did a good job as always."

"Your classes going well?"

She picked up a folded blanket and tossed it on the foot

of the bed. "I got my homework and project done before you get home - well, at least for the past couple of days. Lectures are the same as always. Legalese can't be boiled down. That's why it's called such - incredibly wordy and boring."

"Enthralling." Jim pulled down the sheets and sat down.

"Now don't go sneaking out of here, mister." She walked back to the doorway and grasped the doorknob. "I have class tomorrow and can't be up all night like your mom."

"I wouldn't dream of it."

10

J im closed the laptop and pushed it away. "I'm done for the day." He glanced at the bottom right of the screen. "Been working for six hours apparently, that means Cyn should be back soon. At least I have income coming in again, but it's just not the same as my laptop." He hopped off the stool until a chirp on his phone stole his attention.

He reached into his back jeans pocket and brought the device to his face. "A message from an unknown number. I have a bad track record with those. Let's see what this one says." He poked the screen. "I know what you've been doing. Come to the address I text you tonight at one a.m. if you want me to keep your precious secret. You're not the only one affected by this. Don't be stupid."

The sound of a car engine decelerating and eventually stopping outside caught his attention. He quickly stuffed the phone in his pants pocket and moved to the door. He peeked through the peep hole to see Cynthia climbing out of her car in the driveway. He opened the door with a smile. "Hello there. Welcome home."

"Aren't you cheerful today. I didn't think work worked

that way." She brushed past him, and he closed the door behind her. "I don't suppose that has much of a charge left?" she asked, leaving a lingering gaze in the laptop's direction.

"I just stopped. It showed it's at twenty percent left. You do have your charging cable, right?"

"Sure." She exhaled and plopped down on a nearby stool in the kitchen.

"Tell me where it is. I'll go get it for you."

"You'd do that?"

"Sure. What else is a house-husband for? Now where is it?"

"I'll ignore the smartass remark. It's in my room on my night table. Don't go rifling through my dressers. I don't want a repeat of when we were teenagers."

"A teenage boy goes through your panty drawer one time, and he never hears the end of it." Jim headed toward her room and stopped just outside. "I still hold to my story. I was just looking for my cd I lent you."

"In my clothes dresser? It's still not believable."

"Whatever you say." He headed inside her room and immediately saw the cable beside her bed. He walked over and grabbed it. He surveyed the room momentarily. "Nice room she's got here." He shook his head. "Get those thoughts out of your head," he whispered to himself.

He emerged from her room and trotted over, tossing the cable on the bar. "Here you are."

"That was quick," she grumbled.

"Rough day?"

"Professor had a royal hard on for calling on people today - chief among them was me. If he had a question, he called on me whether I raised my hand or not."

"You tick him off recently?"

"Not to my knowledge."

"Maybe he likes you. Seriously, some teachers call on students they like, not knowing how bad it can be from their perspective. Anyway, getting off school stuff, you want me to cook dinner tonight? Charlie called earlier and wanted to come over. I know you probably have homework to do, and I'm more than happy to alleviate however I can."

"It'd be a huge help." Cynthia plugged one end of the cable into the laptop and the other end into the nearby electrical outlet. "Just make whatever. I'm not picky. What's Charlie want anyway?" She started typing.

"There are no parties going on tonight, so he's probably wanting to party here. You know him - always chasing the highs, wherever they lead him."

"They just so happen to lead his ass here when he's not out candy flipping. I see how it is." Despite Cynthia's serious tone, the smirk on her face betrayed her true emotion. "Thankfully since the teach was so gung-ho on lecturing, I only have an hour's worth of homework tonight. I should be done by the time he gets here. If he gets here early, be a dear and entertain him, won't you?"

"Obviously. I doubt he'd want to get an earful from you anyway." Jim retrieved a cup from the nearby cupboard and pressed it against the lever on the front of the refrigerator. Water fell into the container. "Now you focus on your work." He took the cup away when it was three- quarters full and placed it well to the side of the laptop. "Enjoy this water when you get thirsty. I'll get the place ready for our guest for the night."

"What would I do without you?"

Later that night

Jim glanced down at the car's clock and read that it was currently twelve forty-five. "This is where they wanted me. The question is who are they, why do they want me here, and what do they plan on doing?" He looked over to his left at the designated empty lot. "This is a sketchy as fuck location they chose here, isn't it? I don't see anybody; then again, I am fifteen minutes early. At least I'm relatively sure they're not here already. I drove around it four different times. Another question is how they managed to get my phone number, and how that slimeball got Cynthia's number on that night. All questions I need answered, and this person may well be my only source."

His phone lit up again with a new message while he was muttering to himself. "I know you're here. Get out of the car and head into the property. I'm waiting nearby. Do not keep me waiting."

"Impatient buggers, aren't they? Fine, if that's what you want." He put on his mask, stepped out of his vehicle, and checked both ways before crossing the street. His neck swiveled as he entered between the buildings.

"You're early." A digitally disguised voice said from his right. A figure with a mask emerged from the alley.

"Why did you call me here, and who even are you?" Jim asked.

"I'm not here to answer your questions, rather the opposite. So be quiet. You've caused the wrong people quite the amount of anguish recently."

"I didn't know they'd miss one guy all that much. Especially one with such despicable interests. What? Was he their ringleader on capturing small children or something?"

"I know nothing of their plans yet, nor do I wish to know. It's above my pay grade."

Jim crossed his arms with a frown. "So, you're just a grunt they sent out here then?"

"Who I am doesn't matter to you. What you do need to know is you've made powerful enemies in this town. The type of people who have connections to the worst kinds of people. Now you might think it's cute being on their shit list, but I assure you it's not."

"Are you here to threaten me or warn me? I'm getting mixed signals here."

"I am not here to take direct action against you, rest assured. I will not reveal my orders. Now shut up and let me finish monologuing before interrupting. Have you never heard of manners?"

"Getting lectured by a creepy stalker now. Take a look at my life." Jim rolled his eyes. "So, what's your message, Mr. mask donning Mysterion? Besides what you already said."

"You are insufferable. Anyway, I am not affiliated with your enemies. In fact, my organization has been keeping an eye on your progress."

"I don't know what you mean by that. All I've been doing is laying low."

"There are no media here, Mr. Benning. You need not deny who you've become with me. Very well, you keep denying it. It matters not. We know you were contacted on the night of your recent incident. Have you never wondered how that unsavory individual got your girlfriend's number? It seems quite suspicious, no?"

"How could you possibly know that? We've never told anyone that."

"Modern technology is a marvel. The question remains, don't you wish to know how they knew she was there and her number?"

"More than anything, but something tells me such information isn't easy to come by."

The masked figure's modulated voice chuckled. "You are beginning to realize how this works. We are not altruistic; everyone has a price for their aid. My people are no different. Our goals just so happen to coincide with your recent world view change."

"Awfully verbose tonight. Get to it already."

"Do not rush me." An annoyed tone tinged the digitally enhanced voice. "We are in need of your newfound skill set."

"Don't know what you're talking about."

"You have a mask on, and you're still feigning ignorance after I used your real name? Either you don't believe we have evidence on you, or you're quite stupid. I caution you to not underestimate us. We can ruin you if we so desire."

"Blackmail then is it?"

"That's such a dirty word. Think of it as merely choosing your next target."

"You still never told me who or how they got my friend's number. Do that before getting ahead of yourself here."

"If I reveal that information, will you agree to help us? I assure you, it's right in your wheelhouse."

"We will see. If they are indeed scum, then I'll do it. But I will be researching them to verify their character. I am not an assassin for hire. Understand that right now."

"Oh, perish the thought." The electronically garbled voice said. "You're an avenger for the downtrodden and innocent, yes? That's what you picture yourself anyway. Since you agreed, fine, I'll tell you. I've been authorized to anyway. Your friend - Cynthia was it? You're wondering how the fellow you put down the other night got her number. Yes?"

"Yes. She's never had any contact with their law firm."

"Are you sure about that? Because my sources say she did in fact visit them not too long ago and inquired about their interning program. She willingly gave her cell phone number over to them to call back. It would be a simple matter for a disgruntled employee to back trace her number and find her connection with you. He did know your address after all, and he found her connection with you. Even the worst kind of man has a line he draws somewhere. Judging by the text he sent her, his was innocent women. Ironic, isn't it? He had no problem ruining the innocence of children, but grown women were his bane. Human nature is a mysterious thing sometimes."

"Your sources? You have an in with the law firm?"

The masked figure held up a lone index finger and wagged it back and forth. "Now, I don't reveal sources to unvetted wildcards. That's bad form. All you need to know is their information is good. Your friend wanted a lucrative future with them, but she didn't know who she was trying to crawl into bed with. She should be more careful in the future. Now that her connection with you is known, I have it on good authority they are incensed with her."

"She's in danger?" Jim asked, taking a step forward. "You tell me who's after her, right now."

"Quite the sore spot, eh? That's part of the job I was talking about earlier. Well, half if we're speaking literally. First you take care of the other half, and then I tell you who's targeting your friend."

"And if I wanted the other info first?"

"What you want is immaterial. Her threat is not imminent, yet. If that changes I will inform you, provided you accept the other half of the job. What do you think I am, a monster?"

"I don't know what you are. That's the problem." Jim kept a wary watch on the figure's arms. "And keep those hands where I can see them."

"So paranoid. That's the life of a vigilante though I suppose," he sighed. "Will you undertake our task for us? I promise it would be mutually beneficial."

"Your promises mean squat to me, but I don't have much choice here. Yes, I will do it provided I see a reason for such an undertaking."

"Scout them out to your heart's content. You will come to the same conclusion as us. I'm going to approach and hand you something. Is that alright?"

"If you wanted to try and kill me, you'd have done it already. Go for it, nice and slow."

The figure took strides toward Jim and stopped a few feet away. "Here, look over these in private." He handed him a folder. "I trust you'll see what I mean when you do."

"How do you even know of me?"

"I can't give away all of the secrets, now can I? What's the fun in that? Just know that we'll be watching. Don't go to the cops with this. Let's say the method in which this was gathered wouldn't hold up in court, and you do not want this guy getting off on a technicality. Right? Do what's right. Now without further ado, I bid you farewell."

"Wait a second." Jim reached out to no avail as his contact bolted in the opposite direction and dashed behind a nearby building. "Guess that's all I've been deigned to get from his group." Jim looked down at the manilla folder in his grasp. "I don't like this. I'll have to vet this carefully, or possibly not if Cyn's in danger. I need to know who's coming after her."

He shook his head. "No time to think like that now. I have to get home before she gets suspicious." He turned and made his way back to his car. He climbed inside and checked his surroundings before turning on the above light and opening the folder to inspect its contents. The first page had a picture paperclipped to the top of the paper. "This must be their intended target. Walter Evans. He's younger than the typical kid toucher I've encountered. Can't be more than thirty. Blonde hair and blue eyes. He could have any woman he wants. What's so bad about this guy?"

His eyes perused further down the dossier and read his past charges. "Drunk and disorderly conduct, public indecency, and it says here he was tried in a case about sexually assaulting a twelve-year-old but got off due to the boy being too scared to testify. The extra note says the child committed suicide shortly afterward. Good God." He flipped the page and continued reading. "It says the lawyer that got him off scot free was none other than Kevin Reiner. I know that name." His eyes widened in realization. Images flashed through his mind's eye of a man crashing through his front door and attempting to tackle him only to be brought down once and for all.

"That's quite the coincidence. Or, as Dad always said, when they start piling up like this they cease to be coincidence and turn into evidence." His gloved index finger trailed down. "It even gives his address, employment location, and a list of vices. He works at a local arcade. Okay, major red flag there. He likes his drugs I see - meth, grass, nose candy, ecstasy, and LSD. Jesus, how did they even get this much information. I thought Charlie was bad with his habits, but this guy went hard in the paint. It probably clouded his mind and brought this about if I had to guess." He shut the folder. Doesn't matter right now. I need to focus on a strategy of keeping Cynthia safe now. Either I do this job," he jammed the key in the ignition and twisted, "or gamble that they're taking their time on the revenge against her."

He took off down the road and the informant's words played again in his head. "Her connection with you is known. I have it on good authority they are incensed with her. Her threat is not imminent yet, but if that changes I'll inform you."

He growled and tossed off his mask at a red light. "Can I trust them to actually tell me though? Not really. I don't know these guys from a hole in the ground. Hell, this could all be false intel, trying to goad me into doing their dirty work for them. They seem to know what pushes my buttons and it makes it all seem too good to be true." He watched the light turn green and stepped on the gas. "Shit."

11

———

"Worried about something? I should be the nervous Nellie here." Cynthia shoveled the nearby stack of books into her backpack and jogged to the door. "I'm the one running late for class. Now be a good boy," she said, throwing open the door, "and work hard."

"Yes, sweetie. I'll be a good house-husband," Jim smirked, "for my sugar-mama. Good luck getting there in time."

You're always so weird." She turned away, hiding a spreading crimson on her cheeks. "Bye." She disappeared behind the door and slammed it behind her.

"She's too easy to embarrass. I'll have to change it up to keep it from getting boring." He got up from the recliner and ambled to the window to watch her car pull out of the drive-way. "No time to focus on work today. It's all this new project." He waved as she pulled out onto the road with a smile and turned away once she was out of sight. He made his way into the spare bedroom and over to the bag hidden underneath the bed. He pulled it out and rifled through its contents. "Here." He fished out the manilla envelope and brought it into the main room. "First to identify if this guy is really who they say he is. If after a little background check the info checks out, I'll do a little more personal scouting. Methodical is the only way to do this safely." He plopped the notes next to the still open laptop and opened it to the first page.

He reinstalled the browser from previously and headed back to the same website as before. "Now to see if their info is good." He made the necessary digital arrangements and sent the requisite cryptocurrency before hitting enter. He turned his attention back to the notes and kept reading from where he left off the previous night. "Likes brown haired, pre-teen boys. He has no second job, and lives in a shitty motel. Nothing sketchy about that at all," he grumbled. "Has been known to invite children back under the premise of getting them more quarters."

"Well, they're believable if nothing else. I'll need to check this place out and keep an eye on his behavior to confirm. Following him back home would probably be prudent too. If I decide he is a worthy target, I'll need to find a place to do the deed. A motel wouldn't do. The walls are too thin, and tons of people are around. It'd have to be outside his house. Unless I used the knife and surprised him - then I guess it could work. It'd be a lot messier. On second thought, there's no way I could get into his place and surprise him. Bad idea. What was I thinking?"

He looked back to the laptop's screen and saw it was done. "Looks like the preliminary information was good. The name matches," his eyes danced between the folder and the screen, "the address matches, and the photo looks similar. Shit." He exhaled. "Guess I'll have to check him out." He removed the browser and stood up again.

He plucked the house key hanging near the door and swung it open. He exited and locked the door behind him before pocketing the key. "Guess I'm going back to my roots." He walked to his car and entered it. "Haven't played video games in years." He started the engine and got out onto the road. "I know where this place is." Memories came to the forefront of his mind. "Only too well."

"You need to focus more on your goals for the future." The memory of Cynthia tapped on Jim's shoulder as he hunched over a nearby game cabinet. "Or else you'll never get a decent job."

"You always act like his wife. If you keep doing that, people will start talking." Charlie leaned against the side of the cabinet with a stoned grin plastered on his face. "Well, more than they already are."

"Let them misunderstand. If they wish to be ignorant, then so be it."

"The haughty attitude is sexy and all, but most guys are sick of it. I'd be careful if you have any prospects at a future boyfriend," Charlie laughed.

"I don't need such things."

"No more than him. I see how it is."

"I'm ignoring you now." Cynthia turned back to Jim.

"I'm done for the day." Jim straightened his posture and rolled his neck around, eliciting a crack.

"Goodness." Cynthia covered her mouth, stifling a laugh. "You think it was loud enough?"

"Feels better now." Jim rubbed the back of his neck.

Jim came back to reality and noticed he was already at his destination. "Probably shouldn't daydream and drive again. Luckily, I know the route like the back of my hand." He parked around the corner. "Never thought I'd be here again or that they were still open after all these years." He climbed out of the car, jamming his hands into his jeans' pocket. He kicked the door shut and began the familiar walk back to his childhood hangout.

He pushed the door of the familiar building open. It no longer smelled of smoke; instead, the lingering scent of plastic and cheap cleaner hung in the air. He glanced over to the clerk at the counter, mentally confirming it as the same guy in the folder. He made his way to the change maker machine and inserted a five-dollar bill before pocketing the torrent of quarters it dropped.

He maneuvered himself to a nearby cabinet that gave a sight line to the prize counter without looking suspicious and inserted his first quarter. Looking around him, he was surprised to see he was not the only adult there indulging. They were outnumbered three to one by the teenage clientele though.

He saw nothing out of the ordinary, so he simply inserted the required coins into the machine in front of him and waited.

Five minutes later he noticed a child walk up to the counter and start talking to his mark. He made sure not to stare but kept an eye on the pair. The child was not carrying a line of tickets or any paper in his hands, so it wasn't to collect a prize is all that echoed in Jim's head.

The two were talking for a few minutes until the boy turned and left, a smile on his face, a new rubber ball in his possession. *He's buttering him up.* Jim thought. *Kid didn't even have any voucher or tickets. That was a gift. Now why would a grown man give a child a gift? To make his day? Possible, but not likely.*

He kept playing at the cabinet for a few more minutes until he saw the pair talking again out of the corner of his eye. This time the man slipped the boy a piece of paper after writing on it. A kind smile painted on the man's face all the while.

Surely, he's not about to do what I think he is, Jim thought. *Then again, that was smooth. No one noticed except me.*

The screen in front of him flashed with game over text. He sighed and moved for the exit. He gave the guy at the counter one more once over before exiting the building.

He walked back to his car and entered it. "That was all I needed to see." He put it into drive and relocated to the front of the establishment. "The kid matched his preferences too. Can't let it happen - not on my watch. The only question is - when is his shift over? I think the folder said at three. So, I know he won't do it before then. I need a plan before that. First of all, where am I doing this? It's broad daylight, so I'd rather not do it on the street. Not with all the traffic cams around. I'd be asking for my license plate to be seen or worse. I'll check out his place then." He put the car back into drive and headed toward the motel in question.

"Gun or knife?" he asked himself. "Gun's quicker, knife is quieter. Which one will matter more? Guess it depends on how cruddy the place is. If there's no cameras or traffic cameras nearby, the gun will work fine. It's only a few more blocks, and I can already tell I'm heading into a seedy part of town. The boarded-up window motif is especially welcoming." There were small crowds of youth on every street corner that stared at his car as he passed by. "That's not creepy at all. At least I can see the place now."

A small run-down motel was off in the distance and steadily coming closer with every passing second. "Can't see much yet. We'll park there and inspect it from closer. I doubt they have a camera." His eyes drifted right toward another group of youths. "Or maybe they do with the natives being how they are. Who knows?" He pulled into the parking lot and into the parking space below the beat-up sign above signaling they had vacancies. "I don't see any cameras on a cursory glance."

He overlooked the dirty, stained parking lot and saw few cars besides his own. "Not a very popular spot and for good reason. Probably just used to bang hookers and shady drug deals, along with other unsavory acts - or if you're down on your luck." He got out of the vehicle and walked along the neighboring sidewalk surrounding the establishment.

He made mental notes as he walked in the circle. *North side has windows the rooms look out of, no cameras on this side.* He looked the other way to see a citizen sitting on his front porch staring in his direction. *Not a good place to enter from though. Nosy person lives on this side. Mark that off.* He turned the corner. *East side looks like the back. Service entrance or fire exit's right there. Would make a quick getaway or entrance point, and there's no residential onlookers on this side. Good find right there.* He finished his circle, finding nothing else of interest. He leaned against his car and looked up toward the roof. *Would just need to find a way into the proper room. Oh, this could be easier than I thought - a little riskier, but easier. I'll just tell the kid to bugger off, slip him a twenty, and knock in his stead. He opens the door and bam, it's done. Not flashy, but it'd get the job done.*

His inner musings were interrupted by a scraggly man pushing a shopping cart marching by on the sidewalk clearing his throat. He approached Jim and spoke in a brittle voice. "Say, sonny, you wouldn't happen to have a little something for an old man down on his luck?" The clearly aging man stopped the cart with a squeak and tilted his head.

Jim turned his attention to him and shrugged before reaching into his jeans pocket. "Here you go." He extended a hand holding a ten-dollar bill. "Don't do anything I wouldn't do with it."

"That's it?"

"Excuse me?"

"I don't mean that in an ungrateful way." The old man pocketed the bill and held his hands up in front of his person in a non-threatening manner. "I mean, you don't want me to do something? Most here make me earn it."

"You're an honest one, aren't you?" Jim asked with a grin. "Most would take it and be on their way. What do people around these parts make you do to earn it?"

"Depends who's asking, sir. It ranges from dancing for their amusement, making me eat things I'd rather not, all the way to..." he trailed off. "I'd rather not speak of such actions."

"I don't want to imagine what I think you're alluding to. Say, instead of making you do physical labor, I bet you know a fair bit about this place, yeah? Could you give me some information? If it's good, there might be more in it for you."

"I live around the corner." The man pointed further down the street, where Jim had just been. "I saw you walking around earlier. You walked past my home. You didn't appear interested in that, but I'll tell you what I know. Unlike some of the bums around here, I prefer to earn my money."

"Good for you. I respect that." Jim stood up straight. "You notice who rents rooms in this place a lot?" He jabbed a thumb toward the run-down motel nearby.

"Not many people actually stay the night if you catch my drift. It's mostly whores, their clients, the occasional drug deal, and Lord knows what else. I try not to get involved with that lot. There's only two people I've ever seen that actually sleep in there though."

"Oh? One moment please." Jim opened the door to the passenger seat and pulled out the backpack. He put it atop the car and started digging around inside before pulling out the manilla folder from before. He opened it and removed the picture. He stuffed the rest back inside the pack before moving over to the old man. "Is this one of them?"

"Yeah. He's the jackass. One's real nice, and this one," the old man poked the picture with his index finger, "is a royal asshole of biblical proportions. His name's Walter."

"Tell me more about him."

"I don't know, man. You aren't a cop, right? I don't want to be seen ratting people out, even if I do hate them, My street cred's all I got left."

"I can assure you I am not a cop."

"You have to tell me if you're a cop, right? I think that's a law."

"Yes," Jim answered with a friendly smile, knowing full well that was a myth. "That's the way it works. I am not a cop."

"Alright then. I don't know what you want with captain douche canoe here, but he always comes back after three pm. Usually stays in his room afterward except for grocery shopping. One thing does bother me though."

"What's that?"

He scratched his graying disheveled beard. "His folks must have a lot of kids that need babysitting because every so often a kid will come to his room. I've seen like three or four now."

"How long do they stay?"

"I never really noticed, but not that long. Maybe fifteen or twenty minutes. I always thought his family was shopping nearby. He does get them in a car and drive them away. I figured he was dropping them back off."

Jim's eyes lit up. "Did you ever see the same kid twice?"

"Come to think of it, no. I hadn't. He's only been here about a month though. I did ask him once why he came to town. You know what he answered? Just passing through."

"Ah, well thanks, old timer." Jim fished out the wallet from his back pocket. He pulled out another twenty dollars and handed it over. "You've been a great service. There's just one more thing."

"Go right ahead. This is more than I make in a month. I'll answer anything," he said grabbing the bill.

Jim put the wallet back into his back pocket. "You know what room his is?"

"Sure. It's 108. Right over there. Word to the wise, the security in that place is pretty lax. That is, if you were thinking of paying that jerk ass a visit. The back door works. Just don't go to the front desk, and you'll be good. His room is also right by it. Now getting into his room, that's a whole different thing. I can't help you there."

"You got really helpful all of a sudden."

"I said I wouldn't help cops."

"For all you know I'm his friend though."

"Nah." The older gentlemen shook his head. "I see that glint in your eyes. I can tell you have ill intentions toward him. I don't know to what severity, but I can tell."

"You know you never spoke to me or even saw me today."

The old man ran a finger over his lips. "My mouth is zipped. You think I want to be dragged into a police station again? Hell no. Besides, you'd be doing a community service."

"You want to know something? He's not babysitting

those kids. He works at a nearby arcade. I saw him give one his address and room number. I assume the excuse he gave is free quarters or some crap."

"You mean?"

"I do. He was not babysitting. I'll leave it to your imagination why he is luring children in there for such a short time."

"Oh, then go ahead. I don't give a shit then. I knew he was a rude shit, but children? Ugh, good riddance to whatever happens to him. And I don't even know who you are. My memories failing me. I've also gone spontaneously blind. Feel free to do whatever you do."

"Appreciate the support, old timer."

"Call me Ray."

"Thank you, blind Ray." Jim winked at him. "Now get moving along. I have matters to attend to and prepare for."

"With pleasure. You ever need anything else, you let me know. Oh, and the receptionist owes me a favor. I normally wouldn't call it in, but this is a special case. I helped her get rid of some riff-raff who refused to leave on time. Tell her Ray sent you and to give you his room key's spare."

"I will remember, and I'll find a use for that."

Ray started pushing the squeaking cart along. "Good luck, young man."

Jim watched the old man hobble off down the sidewalk. "Good shit. I'm beginning to see why they want him. The only question left is, where is he taking the kids afterward? I doubt it's anywhere good. No one's accused him of anything. He probably makes them disappear afterward, or possibly keeps them locked up. Lord almighty, I've stumbled into something horrid."

He turned back to the car and patted the black roof. He shrugged and shook his head. "Guess I still have some time before he gets back." He climbed back inside and started the engine up. "Can't be seen standing here all day, then donning a mask, and then a guy ends up dead. A toddler would be able to put that together, never mind any wannabe good Samaritan."

12

J im pulled the face mask up over his mouth and put the hoodie up above his head. "Just a cough should be enough to convince her I need this thing." He looked up over toward the hotel and saw a car pull in. It stopped in front of Jim's car.

He reached down and pulled the lever with his gloved hand. His seat leaned back until he was almost perfectly horizontal. All he could see was the aging top of his cabin. *I should really clean this up soon.* His eye wandered over toward the sun visor. *That stain wasn't there before.*

He slapped himself and snapped out of his irreverent reverie. He elevated his position to see his quarry with his back to him in front of his door. The door opened. He looked left and right before heading inside in a hurry.

"It's a little after three. Which means I probably only have a little time left before the boy gets here."

He jumped in his seat when a bump came from the window directly to his left.

Ray stood just outside.

Jim rolled down the window. "Look, I appreciate the

info, buddy, but you may want to head off now. This isn't someplace you want to be soon."

"Sure you don't need help taking down that monster?"

"How about this? If you see a kid headed toward that room, you give him this." Jim handed him a ten dollar-bill. Tell him to use it at the arcade. Say the guy gave it to him since he couldn't see him today. He doesn't need to see this. You get me?"

"Roger that. Just don't take too long in there after you do whatever it is you're planning."

"Now head out and keep your distance. I'm heading in within a few minutes, and I don't want to draw attention."

"Good luck." Ray nodded and hobbled off toward a nearby street corner. He lowered himself gingerly to sit on the sidewalk as he surveyed the street.

Once he was sufficiently far away, Jim got out of the car and exhaled a deep breath. "It's now or never. Just be cool." He placed one hand in his hoodie's pocket and approached the front door. He pushed open the door and coughed into the mask before clearing his throat and approaching the desk, but not coming too close to the young clerk waiting there.

"Can I help you?" The girl's dyed blue hair clashed with her relatively normal clothing and chubby frame.

"Yeah. Ray told me to tell you to give me the key to 108."

"That old coot said that? That's against policy though." She fidgeted in place and adjusted her glasses. "But fine. Just so we're clear - I did not give you this key. I lost it. I don't want it back for deniability reasons. Toss that shit out or whatever. They'll just make another one after changing the lock anyway. You got me?"

"Sure."

She turned around to the wall of keys hanging there and

chose one before turning around and tossing it on the desk in front of Jim. "Also, tell the old man we're even now. I'm going to go on break for fifteen minutes across the street at the diner. I don't care what you do, but leave me out of it." She let out a disgusted exhale and kneeled out of sight before returning with an out to lunch sign. She placed it down and circled around the desk. She pushed open the door, flipped the sign on the door to closed, and left Jim alone in the grungy lobby.

"Will do." Jim followed her out once he saw her enter the nearby diner across the street. He flipped the key in his hands as he walked. His eyes kept watch on the door numbers nearby until he found the right one. His hands shook as he approached it. *Easy now. It's not your first time. It's just the first time you've done it face to face in an ambush.*

He pressed his ear to the door and heard nothing and shrugged. He stuck the spare key in the lock and unlocked it. He pushed open the door and hurried inside, closing it behind him.

"Who the fuck are you and why are you in here?" Walter jumped off the bed and marched up to Jim. His hands at his sides balled into fists. "Get out right now before I force you."

Jim smiled behind the mask. "Try it, kiddie diddler."

A look of shock crossed Walter's handsome features before turning to rage.

Beating him to the punch, quite literally, Jim launched a fist into Walter's throat causing him to stumble back holding his windpipe. He quickly recovered and rolled off the bed onto the carpeted floor below with a thud.

Jim wasted no time in giving chase. He threw himself onto Walter's still recovering form.

"What the fuck is wrong with you?" Walter's elevated voice asked.

"Sorry about this." Jim wrapped his hands around Walter's throat and squeezed. "Can't have you making too much noise, can we? With just that, the locals here will just think you're having a go with some hooker. We're still good."

"Why are you," Walter grasped the wrists of Jim and tried to remove them to no avail, "doing this? What did I do to you?" As he spoke, his tone turned quieter, raspier. "I never wronged you."

"You are correct, technically speaking." Jim leaned down, holding his iron grip steady and whispered, "but I'm not here for me. I know what you do with children, I saw you today at the arcade, luring the boy here. I will not allow it to continue."

In a last bid of desperation Walter let go of Jim's hands and reached up to Jim's face. His fingers jammed into Jim's eye sockets and ripped as best as his rapidly asphyxiating form could manage.

"Good plan." Jim said, raising his form up, buying a momentary reprieve, "but too little too late. Your lips are turning blue already from all that kicking you're doing to my back. Bad move there, bud. You should have conserved what little oxygen you had left."

"Not yet." Walter's hands fell to his belt line. "Fuck you." He whipped his hand around along with a metallic sound. He mustered as much force as he could and swung it toward Jim's side.

"That's it?" Jim smirked. "A little love tap? I expected more."

Walter bared his teeth as his eyes rolled back into his head until all his limbs went limp.

Jim held the hold on Walter's neck for a few minutes more, confident he was going to stay dead. "I guess I'll just hold for a few minutes. Don't want him waking up. Hm? My side hurts like a son of a bitch." He glanced down to see a pocketknife stuck in the side of his abdomen. "Got cocky. Shit. At least it's not bleeding through yet. I need to hurry it up so my DNA doesn't get plastered here." He reached to his own belt line and stood up. He moved beside Walter's body and jammed the knife in his throat, slitting it. Blood rapidly escaped from his newest victim. He held his side and rushed back to the door. He opened it calmly and exited. He removed his hand and sprinted back to his car.

Hopping inside, he immediately looked into the rearview mirror. "No blood on the pavement. Good. Now to get this patched up." He looked down at the handle. "Doesn't look like a big knife, but you can never be too sure. I'll leave it in for now."

"How did it go?" Ray's brittle voice asked. "Oh criminy, son. You need a doctor."

"Should see what I did to the other guy."

"No time for wisecracking. I know a street doctor. Now he ain't exactly licensed, but he can fix that - no problem."

"Get in, now." "Jim unlocked the passenger door.

Ray hurried as fast as his aging form allowed him and got in the passenger seat.

Jim got the car in motion as soon as the door closed. "You're going to tell me where he is."

"Hang a left," Ray said. "So do I want to know what happened in there?"

Jim rotated the wheel left and answered with a grunt. "No."

"Fair enough. Keep going straight until I say and turn right. Say, are you alright to drive? Not feeling woozy or anything?"

"My side hurts, but no. I haven't lost too much blood I think."

"Probably because you didn't remove the damned thing. Smart thinking."

"Still hurts like a son of a bitch though."

Ray inspected it closer. "I bet. Looks like he got you flush. I don't think it hit you anywhere vital."

"I appreciate the confidence but doubt your qualifications to say such."

"Turn right up here, and it should be the first place on your left. Nondescript place that looks like it's closed. Park in the alley. I never told you this, but you learn a surprising amount of first aid on the street."

"No formal training though?" Jim followed Ray's orders and pulled onto the new street.

"None. My dad was a medic though in the marines if that helps."

"Not really." Jim pulled into the alley and put it into park. "Anything special I should know about this guy?"

"You do have cash on you, yes? He'll charge a few hundred for this."

"I have it covered."

"Then if you want painkillers, they run a pretty penny. I doubt you have enough."

Jim groaned and opened the door before looking back to Ray. "Don't need them."

"You say that now." Ray opened his own door and circled around. "Now take it easy. No need to make it worse. Just go slow. I'll go in with you, just to be sure."

"Thanks, I suppose. I don't really know this guy and you do, so it'll be easier."

"Not like I got a job to get to, you young buck."

Jim carefully got out of the car. He flinched when he stood up and his hand reflexively moved to his side. "It's starting to soak through now."

"Not too bad if it took that long. More of a flesh wound I bet." Ray pointed to a nearby door in the area between buildings. "There it is." He quickly made his way over and knocked three times, leaving a few seconds between each pound. "Now be polite. He's a real stickler for manners."

"Far be it from me to be uncouth," Jim grit his teeth.

"Hope you're telling the truth, kid." Ray backed away from the door as loud thumps came from behind the sturdy metal door.

A towering man opened it. "This better be good." He noticed Jim clutching his side. "Is that a gunshot wound?"

"Pocket knife I believe, sir."

"Good. I can't deal with ballistic wounds with this rag-tag setup I got here." His gaze turned to Ray. "Raymond, what are you doing with my newest potential client?"

"Edmund, this is one of the good ones." Ray looked toward Jim. "Trust me."

"If you're friends with Ray, get in here, and try not to bleed all over my floor if you can." He moved to the side and gestured inside. "Just hop on the nearest table, and we'll get started."

Jim hobbled past the dark-skinned stranger and jumped up onto the table. Ray followed him inside and stood a fair distance away from the injured man's new resting site.

Edmund slammed the door shut and locked it before coming back over to the pair. "Before we start, you do have money, yes?"

"Of course I do."

"Good." Edmund invaded Jim's personal space and inspected the wound site. "Judging from this, it should run about three hundred."

"Got it covered, Doc."

"That's what I like to hear." Edmund wandered off and

brought back a rolling table with a variety of medical implements perched atop. "Money first, treatment after." He put on a face mask, applied hand sanitizer, and put on some latex gloves from the nearby tray.

Jim grimaced and got his wallet out. He pulled out the required amount and handed it over. "We good now?"

"We're good." He pocketed the money. "Just let me get everything ready before we extract the offending foreign entity. Don't want you to bleed too much. I assume you want to drive away. I know your friend here can't."

"You're still a dick I see," Ray chuckled, helping Jim out of his hoodie.

"Enough of a dick to allow you in when I know you can't pay, yes. Now we need to get this shirt off too. Do you have any attachment to it?"

"Not really."

"Good, I'll dispose of this later." Edmund sliced a circle around the cloth, and helped Jim out of the flimsy fragment, leaving him bare from the waist up.

"You two know each other?" Jim watched Edmund's hands dance across the tools as he sat beside him.

"Hold still. This is going to hurt like hell."

"At least you're honest, unlike other doctors."

"To answer your question," Edmund grabbed hold of the pocketknife, "yes, we know each other. Have for a few decades now."

Ray spoke up, watching the procedure. "I've gotten him a lot of referrals, kind of like you. A guy on the streets sees a lot of stuff go down. Not everybody has insurance, or they want privacy, like you. He specializes in just that."

"I have a strict no questions policy. I'll let that one slide since you didn't know." Edmund jerked the knife out. "Just don't do it again, and I'll show you the same courtesy."

"Damn." Jim winced.

Edmund set to work disinfecting the wound. "It's not too deep. You'll be sore for a while, but fine so long as it doesn't get infected. You're lucky it wasn't a big knife. This thing's barely two inches."

"First time I've heard that one."

"This is probably the best one I've sent your way," Ray said, trying not to laugh.

"Best you say?" Edmund's eyes momentarily went up to Jim. "I've never heard you say that before. I won't ask how you know that, but I trust you have good reason."

"Indeed, I do. Oh, and by the way, kid, that child got home safe thanks to you. You did a good thing today."

"And you, I presume." Jim looked away from the treatment. "Thanks for handling that."

"Sounds like you've had a day and a half." Edmund's hands moved with clinical efficiency as he spoke, patting the now bubbling wound with a dry cloth. "It won't need stitches, just some gauze and bandages. I don't know what you did today, but you need to tone it down a touch, or this could reopen when I'm done."

"I understand. I am hoping you won't be talking to anyone about my being here."

"If you promise not to speak of you being here, we're golden. My business dictates I keep my mouth shut about everything I see. I'm guessing yours does as well. Keep that in mind, and we'll get along great."

"Deal."

"Tell you what, since Ray here has vouched for what you may or may not have done, I'll do something special for you."

"You never did anything special for the other good ones I sent here."

"You never let it slip they helped a child either. I may be a gruff, sarcastic asshole but someone who helps children is a cut above." He looked up at Jim. "Pardon the pun."

"I'm honored," Jim's deadpan voice said. "What does that mean?"

"It means," Edmund applied the gauze and pressed it against the disinfected wound, "that once you get home, you won't be in so much pain. Tomorrow will suck, but unless you want to pay, it's the best I can do. I still have a business to run. You'll get two of my highest caliber pain pills. I recommend taking one at a time only when you know you're not going anywhere for the next eight to ten hours."

"Kind of hard to find a time like that with my schedule, but that would be helpful."

"You could just take it before you go to bed. Falling asleep in pain is difficult." Edmund stopped applying pressure. Now for the bandage wraps. You know you will have to change these dressings every day, right? I don't suppose you have anyone that can help besides our mutual friend here?"

"What's wrong with me doing it?" Ray asked.

"Besides the fact I can smell you from here, and you would probably cause more harm than good?"

"You don't have to be so blunt about it. Fine." Ray looked away and down toward the floor.

"I have a couple options, but I'd rather do it myself if possible."

"Secret huh?" Edmund asked. "Not really possible here. If you tried to twist and stretch like you'd need to, you'd tear it open again and have to come back. Which would be great for my pocketbook, but I doubt you want that."

"Shit." Jim's eyes followed his caregiver as he circled around. "Yeah. I just need to come up with a believable story. Don't suppose you can help with just why I need the help."

"I am not a creative man, but if I wanted to con someone into changing these, I'd say you pissed someone off." Edmund chuckled. He finished up the wound dressing. "Not an option?"

"If at all possible, no. She'd kill me herself if I said that."

"Oh, lady problems? No, don't have her do it. You'll scare the poor girl half to death and open a can of worms you really don't want to," Ray said. "Don't you have any male friends? Get one of them to do it. He won't ask many questions."

"How could you possibly know that?" Jim asked. "You don't know him."

"We men as a gender will ask the bare minimum. Haven't you noticed? He'll ask how you got hurt, and you tell him you had an altercation. Make up something believable. I bet you he'll ask if you won. You say yes, and that'll be that."

"Or find a nurse off duty," Edmund rolled the tray off and elevated his voice to still be heard, "they'll usually do it pro bono. Something about human decency or some such." He dumped the tray into a nearby sink and moved to the adjoining cabinet. He reached into his white lab coat and pulled out a key. He unlocked it and pulled out a bottle. He twisted open the bottle and dumped out two capsules before putting it back on and placing them back inside. He closed it and relocked the cabinet. He picked up a nearby bag and dumped them inside. He sealed it, then walked back to the pair and handed it over.

"Appreciate this." Jim hopped off the table and took the bag. "Now what to wear home?"

"Your undershirt is ruined," Ray said, holding up the

tattered remain. "The hoodie is relatively clean. Just a bit of blood here." He pointed to a red stain on the side. "Say you spilled some donut filling to your filly if she asks. Oh, and take this." He reached into his shirt pocket and handed Jim a folded piece of paper. "The kid gave it to me. Figured you may want it."

"Not remotely the same consistency, but so long as she doesn't do your laundry, you'd be fine," Edmund piped up. "Take it from me, they're not stupid, kid. Try not to lie to women. They will catch you in them."

"Speaking from personal experience?" Jim asked, putting on the hoodie and stashing the paper in his pants pocket.

"You could say that."

"You need a ride back to your corner, Ray?" Jim asked.

"I can walk. It's not that far. Take off without me, kid."

"If you say so." Jim looked to the exit. "Guess I'll head home then." He stuck the bag into the pocket in the front of his hoodie. "Take it easy, fellas."

"You too. No more hijinks for at least a few days - doctor's orders," Edmund called out to the departing Jim.

Once Jim was out of the building, Ray looked over to the large man. "We both know you're not a doctor anymore."

"No, but this is the first time in a while I feel good about treating someone. So, what did he do?"

"You expect me to blab about the guy? What happened to no questions?"

"No questions while the patient is here. This is called gossip - it's totally different."

Ray shifted his feet. "He found out a kid was being lured to some seedy motel by a molester. He didn't allow it to happen. Apparently it wasn't an amicable discussion as we saw. The kid damned near walked in on them a minute or two after he went in. I managed to get him to go back to the arcade with a ten the kid had slipped me. I was just in time too. The guy came out like two minutes later with that knife in his ribs."

"You? Must have scared him half to death from the smell alone."

"Possibly, but better than him finding the guy and being scarred for life."

"Along with God knows what else if our little hero hadn't been there." Edmund tore off the latex gloves, balled them up, and tossed them into the nearby waste basket. "Makes me almost wish I didn't charge him as much."

"Alright, now I know you're joking."

"You got me there."

13

"Where have you been?" Cynthia laid with her head on the end of the sofa. She angled herself around to look at Jim near the front door. "Because I couldn't help but notice the near full charge on the laptop when I got back. Have an eventful day today? You left your phone on the table too." Her eyes narrowed. "That's mighty suspicious."

"Jealousy is cute, but don't let it get out of hand."

"Cute deflection, but answer me. I want to know where you were." She got up from the sofa and eyed him up and down. "Not to mention why you're favoring your side."

"I tripped."

"You tripped? You tripped and what? Fell with your arms up, landing on your ribs?" She approached him and looked closer.

"It's nothing, just a scratch. Which if you want to be pedantic, it wasn't a trip and wave my arms around kind of fall. It was more of a fall onto a handrail after losing my balance thing."

Cynthia laid a hand on Jim's left arm. "Then you won't

mind letting me inspect it? Can't have you injured under my care, can we? Your mother would never forgive me." She tried to pull it away only for it to not budge. "Come on already. Don't be stubborn. You know I'll be on this all night. This will go quicker if you just play along." She pulled again and met with the same resistance. "The more you fight, the worse it looks. You weren't doing anything you shouldn't, were you?"

"Fuck." Jim grit his teeth and hissed before finally relenting.

"There's blood here. You got something you want to tell me before you strip down and show me exactly how bad it is?"

"I plead the fifth?"

"Not in court, jackass. Try again. You know what? No, don't. You're doing this, and that's final. You're under my roof, so take it off."

"Did I just hear the same argument parent's make but insisting I take my clothes off? Yes, mommy, please."

Cynthia glared at him. "Not the time." She unzipped the hoodie for him. "What did you do?" she asked. She took off the hoodie and tossed it aside.

"It's not as bad as it looks."

"Not as bad as it looks? It looks like you already went to a hospital. What happened? You tell me right now."

"If I tell you, you promise not to be mad?"

"No, I'm already mad."

Jim sighed. "You promise not to kick me out?"

"You dumbass, of course I'm not going to kick you out. Why? Did you go back to your cat fishing or something?"

"Or something."

"Don't be too specific now. You know I'll stay up all night needling you about this, so just come clean." She led the now shirtless Jim over to the couch and sat him down. She took a seat next to him and lifted his left arm. "I see bandages, probably styptic underneath. Whatever this was, it wasn't just a fall."

"I may have been involved in an altercation today."

"An altercation? About what exactly? Also, with who? Who would do this?"

"You're stubborn as a mule. Fine. You want to know, do you? I went to the old arcade today."

"So what?" Cynthia asked. "What's that got to do with anything?"

"You remember the old man that used to tend the counter?

"Sure."

"He's no longer working there. It was news to me too. Anyway, I was minding my own business playing, clearing my head as one does, when I see a child walk up to the counter without any tickets."

"Get to the point already."

"The guy slipped him a note. You know what that note was? It was inviting him back to his cheap motel room in the bad side of town. What do you think he was trying to do to him?"

"You confronted him, huh?"

"Maybe."

"There is no maybe - you did. This," she hovered a hand over the dressed wound, "is all the evidence to prove that much. What did he do to you? For that matter, what happened to him?"

Jim looked away. His voice turned somber and serious. "I can trust you, right?"

"Obviously. Wait," her eyes widened, "you don't mean what I think you do?"

"He did not appreciate my candor. Forced my hand so to speak."

"I did hear of a guy getting found in a motel with his throat slit earlier. Tell me that wasn't you."

Jim did not answer.

"It couldn't have been, right?"

Jim turned to look at her. "He stabbed me here." He took her hand and placed it over the puncture site. "I didn't feel pain for the first few minutes. It didn't even bleed until I got back in the car. I left it in until I got it attended to."

"It was self-defense then, obviously. We should tell your father. He can put in a good word with the cops, and it'll all go away."

"No. You don't understand. You remember when Dad was here last?"

"Yeah? He got riled up about some case."

"I have some things to tell you. You're not going to like them, and I wouldn't blame you if you kicked me out on the spot and called the cops yourself."

Some time later...

"Jesus fucking Christ." Cynthia laid back on the sofa and covered her eyes with her arm. "This isn't a dream, is it? Tell me it is. Please."

Jim didn't vocally answer, instead pinched her other arm. "That answer it for you?"

She didn't respond. She simply leaned her head back and groaned.

"Guess so."

"You have no idea the shitstorm you're walking into, do

you? I'd be well within my rights to have you arrested. Do you know why I'm not going to do that?"

Jim held his answer for a moment and thought. "Honestly, no. I have guesses, but I don't know."

"I'm not turning you in because, while I think what you did was wrong, abhorrent even, I know you wouldn't have done so without reason. Now do not get me wrong. I do not support your little vigilante streak of sorts. You said the kid got away clean, yes?"

"Yes. He never saw anything. I made sure of that."

"Then good. It wasn't all a senseless felony. You promise to not do this without my input again?"

"If I must, but I need to tell you something else."

Cynthia removed her hand from her face and lifted her neck up. She looked at him with bloodshot eyes, tears dripping down her lithe face. Her voice cracked and shook. "I don't know if I can take many more surprises tonight."

"The powers that be at the law firm are targeting you now."

"How would you possibly know that?"

"I didn't tell you where I went when I snuck out the other night."

"I didn't know you had."

"Anyway, I got a text to meet them."

Cynthia punched him in the shoulder. "You do not meet random ass people in the dead of night. God, did you want to be murdered in an alley?"

"There I met someone who was an envoy for an organization that wanted this new guy. He said they knew you were linked with me. Since they officially know I ended their lead lawyer, they're trying to go after the next best thing. Which reminds me, I should be getting another request for a meeting soon. They said they knew who they were sending after you and would tell me only after I dealt with this guy."

"And you believed them? Why?"

Jim gingerly got up and moved to the door, knelt, and picked up his backpack. He brought it over and took his seat again. He pulled out the manilla envelope. He handed it over. "They made veiled threats against you if I didn't."

She wiped the tears out of her eyes and sniffled. "Who-ever did this was thorough and did their research. They just handed this to you?"

"With the understanding that if I didn't, they wouldn't tell me who was hunting you."

"Holding me as hostage, huh? Doesn't sound like too good of a group either. I have a hint as to who they may be too."

"You do?"

"I spend way more time online than you do, even if you do work online. Yes, there's a group of pedophile hunters spread across the entire country. No doubt they saw you had snapped, and don't sass me. You've snapped, at least a little, and they figured they could use you. Possibly even try recruiting you if my guess is correct."

"Now when you say hunters..."

"I mean they track them down, and they end them permanently." Her head tilted as she spoke. "Kind of like you now apparently." She crossed her arms in front of her. "Getting off that, they're not people you want to get involved with of your own volition. Beyond their little goal, they also manipulate, murder, and do anything to accomplish their goals. On second thought, maybe they do remind me of the new you. You did lie to my face, your parent's faces too, and then had the audacity to come back."

Jim looked away.

"You look at me when I'm talking to you." Cynthia dropped the folder on the other end of the couch and grabbed the sides of Jim's face. She turned his face back toward her. "You did lie to me. I know you thought you were trying to protect me, and maybe you even did. Not anymore though. Now I'm either an accessory, or I rat you out. Do you understand what you've done to me? If I don't turn you in, I'm on the hook now - and I didn't even do anything."

"So turn me in. I fucked up. You don't deserve this shit."

"I'm not going to do that."

"You should. Hell, I'll do it myself." He got up until his hand was grabbed. He looked down and back at her.

Her voice wavered as she spoke. "I didn't get a choice when you got me into this without my consent, nor am I giving you consent to take away my best friend because he wants to have his own mea culpa to assuage his conscience."

Cynthia pulled him back down to the couch. "Now sit your ass down here until I'm finished with you. I may be yelling at you, I may be pissed off, I may feel a bit betrayed right now, but that doesn't mean I want you to go away for the rest of your life and never see you again. You've put me in a no-win situation, but I don't want to lose you all the same. I'm not going to tell you that you did the right thing. I'm not going to say I like it, but you did keep the kid safe. That's not a terrible thing, but you went about it the wrong way. Do you intend on keeping this up? Answer me that."

"I intend on keeping you from harm's way." His phone chirped in his pocket.

"Don't even try and use that as an excuse to get out of this conversation. I don't care if it is the PHR or your mother."

"PHR?" Jim asked.

"Pedo hunting republic. That's their grandiose name

they came up with. The only way this whole thing works from here on out is if you consult with me before you go on your little adventures. Do you understand? I won't have you going off on half-cocked adventures because your gut tells you it'll work out fine. I'll try and keep you from committing anymore felonies while going about your business. So that means no more mid-day operations."

"I can work with that."

Cynthia exhaled a large breath. "You didn't leave any DNA at your latest crime scene, did you? Because if you did, this gets a lot worse."

"I told you I didn't bleed until I got in the car. I made sure of it."

"You got lucky then. I have one way of confirming it though. You up for your parents coming over tonight?"

Jim leaned back and stared at the ceiling. "You want to talk to my dad again."

"Bingo. What better source of intel can you get than a guy with inside sources familiar with the investigation. If they do have DNA, then you're screwed and may well have to turn yourself in. If you're right, then we're clear to proceed. May as well see the blade before it falls, right?"

"Not very comforting, but I see the point." He grunted as he got to his feet.

"Where do you think you're going?"

"To put on a shirt, unless you'd rather I be shirtless when they get here. They would so love a new topic to gossip about and tease us about. Your choice."

"I'll call them then, shall I?"

Jim picked up the discarded hoodie on the floor, left the door to his guest room open, and found a new shirt. "How are you planning on getting them here?" He threw the old hoodie on the bed and took the bag from the pockets.

"That part is simple. Every mom wants his son's girl-friend to learn their favorite dishes. She'll drag your father over here guaranteed."

Jim smiled and pulled the new shirt over his head with a stab of pain as he stretched his arm up. "Clever girl." He meandered back into the main living room to see Cynthia pacing behind the sofa. "Yeah. I offer to make dinner, and the big lug won't tell me what his favorite dishes are. He's a quiet one sometimes." She gave him a pointed glare. Her sweetened voice continued unabated. "Yeah, I guess you could call it considerate, but it makes it hard on me sometimes. Oh yes, I would appreciate it. You're too kind. Uh huh. I'll see you tonight then. Bye bye." She hung up and placed the phone back on the table beside the sofa.

"I'm going to be getting shit for this forever, aren't I?"

"That is putting it mildly. Jim, you've killed people - not just the one guy anymore. What is it, three now? One just for not reporting molestation rumors and one for attempting it. In the eyes of the law, the second isn't justifi-able in any circumstance. You played judge, jury, and execu-tioner on the word of one office intern. You don't see the problem with that? I know you hadn't slept in a while but that's no excuse. I like to think it wasn't a burst of anger, but at the same time, premeditated? It's not much better. I'm still trying to wrap my head around all this."

"In my defense, the guy said he knew it was going on and decided to let it continue on unabated."

"That doesn't make it okay!" she stomped.

"Yeah, maybe."

"There is no maybe. Now you're going to sit down the entire time they're here. So get a seat somewhere and get comfortable. We cannot allow them to find out about your injury. If they do get an inkling, say you have a bruise from tripping. Is your mom as insistent as me?"

"Not usually, but I do have something to make it a non-issue."

"What's that?"

Jim produced the baggie containing two pills. "Painkillers, courtesy of your local friendly street doctor."

"He was licensed?"

"At one time."

"Christ. How did you even find an unofficial medical technician anyway?"

Jim scratched the back of his head with his uninjured side's arm. "Through an acquaintance."

"Give me that." She came over and swiped the bag. "I'm going to look up these pills and make sure they are what they say they are. They do look legit."

"The dude knew how to remove a knife, disinfect the thing, and dress the wound. I'm pretty sure he really was a doctor."

"I presume he didn't tell you why he wasn't still?" She plopped in front of the laptop in the kitchen.

"Not as much."

"Of course not." Her fingers danced across the keys. "According to a cursory search, these are in fact pain pills. Quite good ones at that. You will take one, and only one. You haven't drunk anything today, have you?"

"No."

"Good." She removed one pill and beckoned him over before placing it in his open palm. "Now take it, and try to remain lucid. I can't explain you stoned off your ass. Or if not possible, go lay down. I can always say you're not feeling great today."

He popped the capsule in his mouth and swallowed

with a grimace. "They should be here soon. I'll just take a seat then." He moved back to the recliner and lowered himself into it carefully before pulling the lever at the side and extending the footrest.

She sauntered over and leaned on the top of the chair. "This is not over. You best savor this reprieve of your parents being over, because I'm going to yell at you all night long."

"Not a fun promise, but I deserve it."

"Yes, yes you do. Probably more if I'm being honest, but this is all I can do for now."

14

"No evidence left there either." Cynthia waved with a sweet smile out the window at the departing vehicle. "You must be a regular at this whole murder thing."

"I don't know how to feel about that."

"You should feel happy you're probably not going to prison." She paused. "Not yet anyway. You're just lucky that didn't bleed while you were inside. Blood on the carpet or pavement would have had you dead to rights."

"Thank God for rudimentary medical knowledge."

"Sure, whatever." Cynthia moved away from the window after closing the blinds and went back to her laptop. She picked it up from the kitchen bar and carried it over to the sofa. She plopped down and put it on her lap. "Get over here. You didn't forget about what I said earlier did you?"

"Yes, dear." Jim placed a hand on his head and stopped for a moment. "That pill's kicking in." He slowly made his way over and eased into the couch. "Yeah?"

"Hand me your phone."

"Why?"

"Follow my order." She held a hand over toward the seat.

He took it out of his back pants pocket and dropped it into hers. "Fine."

She started pressing on the screen. "You need to change your password by the way. My birthday? Seriously? Why'd you pick that?"

"Better question is why you tried it so fast. Narcissistic much?"

"Sure, whatever you say. Oh crap. That message you got earlier - it was from the PHR representative you met earlier I presume. They want another meetup tonight." She glanced up at Jim's form. "You think you can make it if I drive?"

"You want me to go?"

"If someone's hunting me, I'd rather not die; so we should hear what they have to say. Their intel was good before, however misguided their aims. The only thing is it says come alone, which is not possible. You can't drive under the influence, so they'll get a nice surprise."

"Always a good idea, surprising a clandestine group known for killing folks they don't like."

"Even stoned you keep the sarcastic remarks coming, huh? Look, you can't show these guys you're feeling loopy. Can you manage that, or shall I text back asking for a reschedule?"

"I'm fine."

"Good." Cynthia squinted at the screen. "That address looks sketchy. It's in an empty lot."

"Similar to last time. Probably the same place. They got out of there quickly, and the place isn't high traffic. It's a double-edged sword. They couldn't see my car from there before, so they should be none the wiser you're even there."

"Good. This time you're going to be wearing a wire of sorts."

"A wire?"

"Simply have your phone on your person. We'll have a call connected, so I should be able to hear most of what's said."

Jim looked over at her. "They use a voice changer. Would that hinder it at all?"

"Possibly. I've never tried this before, but it's better than wearing an actual wire. If they found that on you, they could kill you. Carrying the phone they message you on is expected. If they somehow notice, just hang up and apologize saying you thought it was off. An honest mistake. They won't notice if it's hidden though. Well, unless they have some tech wiz with them, and I doubt that they've convinced one to join them, given their methods. Unless it was with blackmail they're likely just good at staying undetected - careful, but not overly tech savvy."

"That's a lot of assumptions about people you don't know. I find it better to overestimate rather than under," Jim said. "What time do they want me to be there?"

"All it says is same as last time."

"If it works, don't change it I suppose," Jim said. "It was one a.m. Can you stay up that late? Don't you have class tomorrow?"

"It'll be fine. Extenuating circumstances demand it this time." Cynthia opened her laptop.

"Doing last minute homework for tomorrow?"

"No, scouting out this place they sent you to last time. According to your previous message, it was right about here." She clicked on the local map on the screen. "Yeah, this is sketchy as all get out. You actually went there alone and talked to some random guy?"

"With a mask and voice changer to boot, yeah."

"Sometimes I forget how rash you are. Tell me you were

at least armed. Who am I kidding? Of course you were. You're brash, arrogant, and foolhardy, but not stupid."

"I appreciate that."

"Don't get used to it. We're prepping before we leave tonight. I'm going to go over every single minute detail before we head out."

"Sounds as fun as preparing for finals was in high school."

"I will endeavor to make it worse."

———

That night...

"How are you feeling? Sleepy?" Cynthia asked her passenger. "You can still walk I hope."

"Just sleepier than usual, and my injury doesn't hurt as much. I'll be fine if I take it slow and focus."

"Good." Cynthia put Jim's car into park a block away, around the corner from the meeting place. "Now I'm going to sit here and listen in." She punched a number into her phone causing Jim to answer it. "Now keep the line open and in your pocket, and we'll be golden. Do not turn it off unless they direct you to. Got it?"

"For the twentieth time, yes." He stuffed it in his hoodie's pocket.

"Don't back talk me after the bombs you've dropped tonight," Cynthia scoffed. "You're lucky I'm still here by you. Recognize your good fortune and don't bitch." She huffed. "We have a few minutes before you head out, so remember the plan. Ask all about who's coming after me, and let it be known you're finished with them. You're not their pawn, you're not a killer for hire, and you're damn sure not interested in joining them."

"You really don't trust me anymore, do you?"

"Have you given me reason to lately? All I've gotten are lies, and then finding out your recent hobby doesn't make it easy."

Jim raised a hand and knocked on the window. "Yeah. I've screwed things up again. It's what I do after all. Just like when we were kids."

"Spare me the pity party, and get your game face on. Whatever you did before, do it now."

Jim reached down near his feet and pulled up the backpack. He took the mask and donned it along with the leather gloves. "There, how do I look?"

"Like someone about to rob the local gas station. Is this what you use?"

"Normally I use a hairnet under the mask. It's not really needed this time around though."

"Regular criminal genius huh? Noted."

Jim tossed the backpack down to the cabin floor and took a deep breath. "Guess it's go time." He pushed the door open and placed a shoe on the pavement.

"Just be careful."

Jim got to his feet. "I always am." He shut the door and headed for the meeting site. The balmy night air brushed against his skin as he ambled forward. "I look like a crazy person right now I bet," he muttered to himself. He saw the familiar buildings along with the empty lot between them after he turned the corner. He only saw one car pass by him on the road along the move to the lot. He got to the front of the empty lot and looked both ways on the road before jogging across.

"You're later than last time." A figure in the nearby

shadows emerged with his arms crossed. He had a mask covering his face along with the tried and true voice changer. "Any reason for that? No problems I hope?"

"Problem? Not so much. Your target is taken care of. He won't be taking any more children and touching them. I made sure of that."

"And no doubt you're here to find out who's going after your little live-in girlfriend. I'll tell you. You've pissed off some powerful locals. Powerful by this yokel town standard anyway. The point is, they're trying to find the best way to strike back without repercussions. They reached a conclusion today and are implementing it tomorrow."

"You're going to tell me then?" Jim asked.

"Of course. We always keep our word, especially when you do such fine work. I'll say! The strangulation was one thing, but the slitting of his throat afterward," he brought a hand up to where his mouth would be and made a kissing sound, "was a perfect end to his miserable excuse of a life. We approve of your work."

"Imagine what that means to me, Mr. Random."

"Call me Casey."

"Alright, Casey. I want to make one thing clear here. I'm not looking to be recruited, though I appreciate the sentiment."

"That's a real shame, but understandable. We won't be forcing the issue, but merely wanted to extend the offer. Rest assured we hold no ill intention. We are in the same righteous business after all. We all stick up for one another."

"Sure. Now about those hunting my friend?"

"Right." Casey snapped his fingers and reached inside his coat, producing another manilla envelope. "I do wish you the best. If they want your girl dead, then we want her alive. Pissing those kinds off is a wonderful delight."

"Couldn't have said it better myself." Jim extended a shaky hand and accepted the intel.

"Are you feeling alright? My sources say you sustained an injury. That shaking hand doesn't look too good either."

"What? What injury?"

"Come now, you need not lie to us. We know you were stabbed in your little disagreement."

"The only people who know that are a small group."

"Oh dear. I may have said too much in my giddiness. Rest assured, you're among friends. Now onto your girl's business. Normally they would stonewall her after she graduates and put out the word that no one should hire her, but they are not doing the normal routine. They really hate you. They can't prove it yet, but they suspect you are also the newfound vigilante. I'll give you a hint. They have no plans of going through the law."

"Don't tell me they're hiring hitmen?" Jim secured the file under his arm. "They wouldn't go after her, would they? They'd go after me."

"Depends." Casey shrugged. "If they wanted you dead and broken, sure. But since you've done so much damage, they could just want you to suffer before they turn their attention to you. I do not care for their motivations. I will give you a piece of advice since you've been so compliant and are efficient at what we do. Do not get complacent. Word is they are calling for a professional from out of town. The details are in that folder. He is the best at what he does. As competent as you are, I do not believe you stand a chance in a straight fight. Do with that what you will."

"Gee," Garret flashed him a wide smile, "thanks."

"There is one more matter to attend to before I leave. Did you forget the meaning of alone?"

"Pardon?"

Casey chuckled. "Not this time. Did you think I came out here alone? When you get back to your car, your Cynthia will have an interesting story. Suffice it to say, when I say come alone, I mean alone. I let you off with a warning this time because we like you. Do not test us again."

"I understand."

"Good boy. Now go plan and figure something out. We would hate to see such a promising law student get blindsided. She's wanting to be a prosecutor or a defender? It matters not. Ignore my ramblings. Farewell, and remember what I've said." Without warning, Casey took off in a dead sprint down the same alleyway and disappeared into the night.

"Guess that's all then." Jim turned and made his way back to the car. When he turned onto the street, he saw Cynthia out of the car, sitting on the top of the hood with her hands behind her. He could see tape over her mouth and moved as fast as he could.

"Oh man." Jim stopped and immediately got the tape off her mouth. "What happened?"

"Get me untied first, and I'll tell you on the way home. You did bring your knife I hope, because I think they used tape for it."

"Always." Jim transferred the file into his left hand and pulled the knife out of it's holster at his side with his right. He circled around her. "Don't move." He sawed through the mound of tape until her arms pulled apart.

"Get in the car, now," were her only words.

Jim followed the order and closed the door behind him.

The car started up and Cynthia wasted no time getting out onto the road. Her voice was even, "You wanted to know what happened?"

"He did say you'd have something to tell me."

"While I was listening to your little conversation, someone in a mask managed to unlock my door, and pull me out."

"Did he hurt you?"

"No. He did ask me a few questions though, like why I was here. You know what I told him? Because while you may be a moron, you need my help. All he did was chuckle and mention how lucky you were before tying me up and sitting me where you found me. But it didn't end there. He started asking me a bunch of questions like why I accompanied you here, or if I had figured out your little secret. Then he put it together and asked if that was why I was here - to keep an eye on you. He basically told me to mind my own business and let you deal with them alone. He went on about how I was an interloper, a pretty one, but unwanted all the same. That is, unless I was your partner."

"What did you say?"

"I said I was. Because, essentially, I am. I'm party to your crimes. What else does that make me? An accomplice maybe, I guess. I have a suspicion that's why they let me go with just the ties. Leave it to you to get me in these messes."

"I was the one who said turn me in. You can't blame this entirely on me."

"No, I suppose not. It doesn't mean I can't be annoyed with you." Cynthia shivered. "Those masks and the voice changer were creepy. How do you talk with them so nonchalantly as if it were natural?"

"So, they heard your listening in? I'm lucky they didn't get angrier. Though I suppose if they also had two, it's not totally unheard of to want backup."

"We're just lucky they like you. As weird as they were, they were not as cutthroat as I thought they would be." Cynthia stopped at a red light and took her hands off the wheel. She massaged her left wrist with her right hand. "They're not the type of people I want to get on the wrong side of. Changing the topic - what did he give you? I heard him give you something right before I was interrupted."

"Oh." Jim pulled up the folder. "I hadn't looked inside yet on account of the darkness. He said this was who was coming after you, and it wasn't good."

"Define not good."

"They're sending a well-known hitman after you or me. We're not sure yet. They're coming after one of us."

"All this because you took out..." she paused. "I guess you did take out two of them. Shit. Wait. Why did you go after the second guy?" She snapped her fingers, "You overheard me and Charlie talking about them while we thought you were asleep. You sneaky bastard. I hope it was worth it. Was that the guy who was complicit?"

"That's the one. He wasn't the least bit sorry, regretful, or anything - just scared. He was like an open book. Told me anything I wanted to know."

"He does everything you want, and then you still kill him? Must have made a hell of an impression on you. It doesn't sound like you."

"We're getting off point now. We're going to have to pore over that folder all night. You realize that?"

"Damn the class tomorrow. I can call in sick. Fuck it. I've never missed a class, but I've also never been targeted for assassination before either. Thanks for that by the way."

"Sorry about that. My bad."

"That's a hell of a bad. Normally that's for when you spill a glass of water on someone, or maybe if you drop something on the carpet. This? This is in another ballpark. Anyway, we're almost home. Hope you're ready for tonight."

Jim leaned his head against the head rest. "As I'll ever

be." He watched the lines of houses pass by as they slowed down. He hopped out as soon as they came to a stop. "At least I'm not feeling as woozy now."

"Thank God for small miracles. Head inside and put it on the kitchen bar. We'll set up our operations there." Cynthia looked around at the dark neighborhood. "You don't think they are still following us, do you?"

"I doubt we'd know if they were." Jim placed a hand on the doorknob. "They may be psychos, but they're good at what they do."

"These are the people that want you to join them - keep that in mind before name calling them." Cynthia followed behind and closed the door behind them.

Jim tossed the envelope on the marble surface and pulled a stool over. He took a seat and flipped it open. He pushed the folder over to the nearest seat. "You should take lead given my condition tonight."

"Sure. Just push the hard work on me too." She filled the spot and glanced over at him. "That one was actually a joke. I can't be mad at you all night all the time."

"Good to know."

"To be expected, I've never heard of this infamous assassin. Almost like that's part of his job or something." Cynthia pulled out the first page and placed it between them. "Alfred Jones is our hunter it seems. He's bald."

"No chance of hair at his crime scenes."

"You think he burned off his fingerprints?"

Jim shook his head. "Gloves work just fine without the horrific pain. Ooh," he pointed an index finger at the paper, "it says here that his weapon of choice is either poisoning or, if that's not an option, knives. He's been known to employ a crossbow at times."

"He's a silent killer it sounds like." She pointed to

another passage. "You don't get two hundred confirmed kills by being loud and dumb. Oh, fantastic. He's ex special forces, meaning he knows how to sneak around and find people off the grid. What the hell can we do against that?"

"We can get you armed for a start. Do you have a weapon in this place?"

"I have a golf club."

"So, no." Jim reached behind him and extracted the firearm he recently purchased. He placed it between them. "Until this all blows over, use this."

"Where did you get that? Also, why is there a bunch of scratch marks on it?"

"No serial number on it."

"I'm not carrying that thing around then. That's illegal. Fucking hell. Let me search my room later. I think I might have a registered handgun my dad forced me to get before moving out. You keep that away from me. Why did you even - oh right, I know why you bought and probably used that."

"Fine." Jim put it back in place. "Besides that, we can possibly move about and stay in different places I guess."

"Along with what? Me not going to class for weeks? I can't do that, or I fail. That's not happening to me after all the work I've put in."

"Then I can accompany you to class if need be. Maybe not into the classroom, but who's going to care about me going into the building and escorting you? If anyone asks, I'll take care of it."

"Then what? Stand there for two whole hours outside looking suspicious?" Cynthia looked over to Jim. "You can't babysit me all day every day."

"The hell I can't. Look, he's not going to waltz into your classroom and shoot you in front of everyone. Public spaces will be your friend. I can be back up there by the time your class ends and get you back to wherever we call home easily." Jim hovered a hand over her unattended left one and covered it. "Don't you trust me at all anymore?"

"In some ways, yes. In others, no. I do to keep me safe. So fine, class is figured out; but home is another matter entirely. For now, let's learn more about our potential murderer." She did not move her hand from under his. "It says here that he has known connections to numerous crime families. Apparently he's not picky about who he gets jobs from. A real freelancer."

"That's rare."

"Really?"

"Yeah. I'd imagine criminal organizations would want total loyalty, not someone who could theoretically be setting them up for their rivals. Which means this guy is old school, has connections, and is savvy."

"It gets better by the minute. It says here he charges one hundred thousand per body. Great, at least we're valuable. It also says that he normally operates out of New York and Chicago. It says he left today by car at six. The earliest he could get here is in the wee hours of the morning I think." She tilted her head, "Right?"

"Chicago to here by car would be something like sixteen hours. It is almost two now, so it's been eight hours. Meaning he's approximately halfway here, given optimal traffic conditions."

"So we can get a few hours' sleep and move out. It's a pretty safe bet he has this address too."

"It's likely he has my license plates though. It should give us a control of the battlefield if we stay in a local place until we can pinpoint him and neutralize him."

"You mean kill him," Cynthia said. "Just to be clear."

"Yeah, or we can pack up now and go to a local place. It

would allow us to get a fuller night's rest. It's the same difference as here really, seeing as you don't have an alarm system. Not that I believe it would stop someone of his caliber." Jim removed his hand from hers and patted her shoulder. "I may have an idea that could help."

"I'm willing to listen to any suggestion at this point."

"We could make our makeshift new base a little more secure if we have some pocket cash. You know, buy some digital cameras, connect the feeds to the laptop, and then at least we'd know he's coming. It'd give us a much-needed leg up. It'd only cost something like a couple hundred. We want something that can at least let us tell faces apart."

"Good idea. I can chip in for that." Her right index finger trailed down toward the bottom of the page now, "He is proficient in close quarters combat as well. Martial styles are unknown but effective. Not that it matters to us since neither of us want to get into mortal combat with the guy up close anyway. At least with all that history, he's got to be getting up there in years."

"His date of birth is September 9, 1970, so he's fifty now. There's plenty of fifty-year-olds in better shape than me. Especially if they work out every day. We can't count on that either, because something tells me the guy takes care of himself."

"So to summarize, we're facing a guy with military experience, in better shape, more training, assassination experience, and connections." Cynthia blew a strand of red hair out of her face. "What the fuck are we going to do? We can possibly delay, but he will find us."

"I may have a few people who would be willing to help us. Not sure on the one, but it's better than nothing. We'll have to pay a little extra, but it should give us an extra set of eyes on top of the surveillance we're planning." He stood up. "Time to pack."

"Already?"

"We have around eight hours left to prepare. I'd like to get some sleep tonight, and we can't stay here. Remember your chargers for your phone and laptop. Those will be key for our survival. Also remember your firearm. Hopefully you won't need it with me around, but it's better to be safe."

She closed the laptop and got up. "I'll need to find my bags and everything, but yeah. Time to get to work. You have an idea where we're going to stay? It can't be anywhere he'd expect - meaning your parents or mine."

"I have an idea..."

15

"This is your idea?" Cynthia looked at the run-down building in front of them while leaning against the hood of her car. "This dump? Hey, wait a minute. Isn't this where that guy was?"

"As evidenced by the signs of police presence previously." Jim stepped out of his car and slammed the door, "Yes. Now you go get us a room, and I'll set everything else up." He opened the back door and pulled out a full plastic shopping bag. "If all goes well, we'll have a solid six hours of sleep ahead of us."

"I can't believe I'm going to be staying in this sketchy ass motel," she grumbled and hurried toward the front door.

"Now to set up everything. We need all the angles covered to be safe." He wandered around the lot. "At least I know there's no cameras here to see me do this." He pulled out the rubber cement from the bag and prepared it for use, along with one of the already removed cameras. He put some on the bottom of it and angled the device so that it could watch the entire back of the building. Pushing it firmly high up on the wall, he pulled his hand away to have it stay there. "Perfect. Now to repeat that three more times."

"Hey, young man," Ray spoke up as he approached from down the street. "What're you doing here again? If I'm not mistaken, I saw you with a young filly too. I can only imagine."

"Whatever you're imagining, you're wrong." Jim continued along his route. "Come on, old timer, and I'll explain."

"Got nothing better to do, and it's warm out tonight. Sure." Ray followed behind a few feet. "Didn't expect to see you back here after earlier today. How's the side?"

"Aching, but not that bad. Look, we're not here for the sights, privacy, or luxury. We're here out of necessity. I can't explain why, but we're going to be hunted by tomorrow morning." He prepared another camera with the cement and stuck it on the wall. "I'm doing this so we can have eyes on our surroundings."

"Hunted? By who?"

"An assassin hired by those who hate me. They're going after people close to me, so I brought her along."

"Doesn't seem like much of a long-term plan, hiding out in a motel."

"I am aware of the situation," Jim said in a tense voice. "Sorry, not trying to be a dick, but I'm tired, sore, and pissed off."

"I can keep a look out if that would help, but I can't help directly. Not against an assassin anyway." Ray rubbed his hands together. "Distracting him would be easy though."

"You sure?"

"He wouldn't blow his cover to kill a random bum on the street would he? He'd be awfully dumb to do that."

"He is the best." Jim reached into the bag and pulled out

a photo. "Here, keep it. We made copies while we were preparing earlier. That's him."

"An old guy?"

"An ex special forces assassin with over two hundred kills."

"Shit." Ray plucked it from Jim's grasp. "He's not much younger than I am. Fella looks like he's in shape too."

"Just keep in sight of these cameras and keep him busy. I don't know, ask him for change or something stupid."

"You underestimate someone who does this for a living. I can keep him for at least five minutes. It's up to you to figure out what to do with it. Whether that would be to run or otherwise, it's all I'll be able to do."

"Any edge we can get, we'll take. I owe you for this." He reached up to apply another camera with a wince. He dropped the bag and his now free hand raced to his side. "Son of a bitch."

"Sure you're in shape for this showdown?"

Jim hissed through his teeth. "No, but the time is hardly of my own choosing." He picked the container back up and kept walking to his last destination. "Apparently no good deed goes unpunished, as the saying goes."

Ray rubbed his graying beard, "True. Do you have a plan for when he does show up?"

"End him before he ends me."

"Simple plan. I like it. Just make sure I'm out of the line of fire before you do it, eh?"

"Obviously," Jim said through gritted teeth.

"Oh, there's your girl now." Ray pointed ahead at Cynthia jogging up to the pair.

"Got the room." Her eyes wandered to Ray. "Who's this old guy?"

Jim took a deep breath. "He helped me out earlier today

by showing me to a doctor. He'll also be our lookout. Meet Ray. Ray, meet Cynthia."

"Hello, Miss Cynthia."

"Hi, Ray." She turned back to Jim. "So, about the room. I could only get a single."

"It's fine." Jim retrieved the last camera and glazed the bottom with the rubber cement.

"Maybe you should take care of this one, lassie. He hurt his side on the last one."

"I'm fine."

"You're as stubborn as always." She grabbed it and held it up to the wall. "You want it here?"

"Close enough, it's angled correctly so it'll work."

She pressed it against the outside of the motel and looked back at Jim. "Now get back inside. I need to take a look at that injury.

Ray grinned. "Take good care of her. She's a keeper."

"Gee," Cynthia said, "thanks, random old guy - I guess."

"She's actually very nice, just sarcastic and cranky."

Cynthia's voice turned tense. "Especially given our current situation." She slapped his shoulder. "I can speak for myself you know."

"Yes, yes."

"You two be careful and uh, have fun in there tonight."

"Sure." Jim watched Ray head back the way they'd come - back toward his makeshift home. "Now to get the inside set up."

"You're going to help me move everything in first." She led the pair back to the car. "I've got the key here, so start taking bags. We'll be done in no time."

Jim followed behind closely. "At least it's only a few bags along with the electronics."

Cynthia reached the car first and flung open the door.

She took two bags and handed them over to Jim. "It's 103. She said it was just over there." She pointed over Jim's shoulder. She grabbed another two of the remaining four bags and walked side-by-side in that direction. "Who was that old guy? You didn't strike me as the type to chat up hobos."

"He's a good guy. He helped me get patched up instead of bleeding out."

"Guess I should have been nicer." Cynthia's face fell. "I'll make it up to him later."

"That's the right attitude. We'll get through this fine. What's one assassin got on us?"

Cynthia unlocked the door and pushed it open. "Right?" She led them inside the cramped room. "Just toss them on the bed, I'll organize everything after we're done moving them in." She placed hers down first and watched as Jim did so. "You sit down, and I'll finish bringing them in. Try not to pull anything else, alright?"

"Sure." Jim sat near the head of the bed and removed his shirt as she closed the door. He raised his arm and looked down at the covered wound. "Yeah, it's bleeding. Damn." He placed a hand over the wrapping. "Just my luck." He looked around at the inside. "A tv, a bathroom, and a bed. Looks about right. It can't be more than a hundred square feet."

The door opened, and Cynthia came inside. "Couldn't wait to get your shirt off, eh?"

"Something like that." He lifted his arm to show the damage.

"Ah hell." She dug through one of the bags in her grasp. "I can probably fix this."

"I sure hope so. I can't afford to pay the guy again."

Cynthia tossed the other bag down and placed her supplies on the other side. "It should be said that I've never treated anything bigger than a scrape before. This should be a fun learning experience."

"Define fun."

"Fun for me. Not so much for you. Now lay down on your side and keep your arm above your head. That should give me enough access. I'll just disinfect it, apply another styptic, and redress it. That's right, right?"

"Sounds like it. I'm not sure." Jim followed her instructions and exposed his bare side to her. "Don't start drooling now at the view."

"Always with the quip. I'll allow it to pass this time because this is going to hurt. Just don't get used to it." She started the process of removing the bandages. "Can I ask you a question?"

"Besides that one? Yes."

"Smartass. If I wasn't involved, would you have told me eventually?"

"Possibly."

She removed the last of the bandages. "That's not much of an answer." She looked closer. "Okay, good news. It hasn't gotten worse, but it's dribbling a bit." She removed the bloody styptic and tossed it in the nearby trash bin near the bed. She unwrapped another styptic and prepared it. "This could hurt a bit."

"I've been through worse today. I guarantee it."

"I bet." She pressed it against the now exposed wound site. "Has the whole vigilante thing been worth it to you?" She glanced up to his eyes and back down to her work. "From where I'm sitting, you've been stabbed, had your house broken into, and now we're being hunted, on top of all the emotional trauma you've had to endure ending their lives. I know you can't be handling it as well as you're projecting."

"All I know is I've kept two small boys from directly being molested. Is my emotional state more important than that? I like to think not."

"Maybe it is to me." She removed her hand and paused, making sure it was stuck. "You're not a superhero. You're a random guy that grew up in a suburb across the street from me. You've never been the expressive type, but you do know it's alright to show those occasionally, right? I don't mean be a crybaby, but suppressing those has a nasty effect." She grabbed a roll of wrapping. "Now sit up for me."

Jim got up with a groan. "Maybe, but what if I told you I don't feel bad about who I did it to? Only about what I've done."

"Logical, but the human brain and heart isn't logical. So, you do feel bad about killing?"

"Of course I do. I'm not a machine or a psychopath. I just don't feel bad about who I did it to. Does that make sense?"

"Yeah." Cynthia wrapped the cloth around his torso and kept adding layers as she spoke. "You've always been the type to stand up to the bullies. Like when I was a kid. Everyone always called me the teacher's pet and ostracized me. You were the only one to stand up for me. I noticed, you realize."

"It wasn't right. Someone had to do something about it. I figured it may as well be me. It's the same thing with these kids. They don't deserve it, and I can do something about it."

"Just let the police know. You're not qualified for this."

"They'd just open a file and maybe get into it in a few weeks. In that time the kid's either missing, traumatized, or dead. Isn't that worth risking my life for? Saving a kid's life seems like it."

"You've always been a moron. A well-meaning moron, but an idiot all the same. I both love and hate it about you.

What about people who care for your dumbass though? You know this can't last forever. Eventually either you're going to slip up and get sent to prison for premeditated manslaughter, or you'll lose a fight and end up dead. What then?"

Jim looked away and kept silent.

"I asked you a question, and I expect an answer." She slapped his back eliciting a wince from Jim. "I do not like to be kept waiting. What about me? You know what that would do to me and your parents? You have the slightest inkling? I'd be disbarred if they ever found out I knew. Your parents would be shunned, all because of you and your crusade. The ends do not always justify the means. You realize that, right? Even if it did, where would it end? There's always going to be children getting exploited." She stopped wrapping the cloth around his torso and ripped it, finishing the job. "Are you just going to keep going forever, pressing your luck? It will eventually run out."

"You think I don't know that? I don't..." Jim paused and turned to look Cynthia in the eyes. "I don't know what I'm doing." His eyes fell. "You happy now?"

She tied off the dressing and tossed it aside on the bed next to the other supplies. She leaned forward, enveloping him in her arms. "No, not really."

The two sat in silence for a few minutes until Jim spoke up. "We should focus on our more immediate concern instead of playing psychologist for me. I do appreciate the sentiment though." He gave her a smile.

She backed off and cleared her throat. "Don't make me do that again."

He lunged forward and returned the favor. "I didn't say I wanted that part to end though." He gave a gentle squeeze.

"Also, I can't help but notice there's only a single bed in here."

"It's a double, but yes, a singular bed. This isn't exactly a luxury motel you found us here." Cynthia blushed and turned away. "I figured we could - you know."

"What? You need to speak properly, or people won't understand."

"You already know. Don't make me say it."

Jim released her then raised a palm and frazzled her hair. "Still so adorable. You need to be honest. Yes, I understand."

"Good."

Jim hefted himself to his feet and bent down to pick up his shirt. "Now to finalize our plans before tomorrow."

"Can't we sleep yet?" Cynthia whined as she collected the assorted medical supplies and dumped them back in the white plastic bag. She placed it back on the floor beside the bed. "I'm beat, and we'll need our energy tomorrow."

"Half right. Unfortunately, the guy probably has my license plates number, and there's a very real chance he can find us. We need to know what we're doing if that happens like see if there's another way out of this room and try and surprise him." He threw the cloth over his head and got one hand through before stopping in place. "Ah."

"Let me help you, doofus." Cynthia got up and helped him into his shirt. "Let's go see." She led the pair deeper into the room and opened the door at the end. "Just a bathroom. There is a window up there, but it's too small for you I bet."

Jim put a hand to his chin. "You could fit though."

"Surely you're not expecting me to do anything to him."

"No. Not directly anyway."

"Explain."

"This takes you to the other side of the building. You

could use it to flank him if it comes to that. It'd be quite an ingenious plan actually."

"You want me to shoot the guy? What happened to not directly?" Cynthia asked. "I can't aim for beans."

"Look, the guy will be coming for the front door. It's his only way in as well. We know how he has to approach it, right? The only other option is to get up early and have us outside already. Would you rather do that?"

"If it means me not shooting at someone, yes." Cynthia leaned back against the nearby wall. "It's not like you can take him on anyway. Why don't we just keep moving?"

"Forever? How about this? Assuming we can get to sleep and wake up before he gets here, we head out and go a ways off?"

"To serve what purpose? Make his job of disposing of our bodies easier?" Cynthia asked.

"It goes both ways. Plus, if we get there ahead of time we have the drop on him. I'm not saying hide in the woods - he'd be at an advantage there, but somewhere where we have the advantage."

"Where would that be?"

Jim paused a moment before returning back to the main room and sitting on the foot of the bed. "How about we improvise a bit instead?"

"So, you couldn't think of a place. Wonderful."

"You can act like a ditsy girl, right?"

"Probably, but I don't want to go near the guy."

"If it works, we'd be set." Jim grinned. "All we'd need is a little favor. You get to bed, and make sure to set your alarm. I'll go see if I can collect. Just in case, I'll need a bit of money. A few hundred should do." He whipped out his wallet and thumbed through the bills inside. "Got a hundred I can borrow?"

Cynthia rolled her eyes and reached into her side pants pocket. "Yeah." Her hand emerged with a fist full of bills. "Give back what you don't use. You want to enlighten the class on what your plan is?"

"I'm going to get something to knock him out with. I'll get his attention, and you'll cover his nose with a cloth dipped in the stuff I'm about to get. Surprise is about the best we've got against this guy. That means you're required, unless you'd rather I try to take him on."

"God dammit." Cynthia pulled out her phone and set the alarm. "Fine, but this better work. Any plan for when he's unconscious?"

"Of course I have one. I'll leave that bit as a surprise if we get that far. I'll park right by our room when I get back, and make sure the trunk is ready tomorrow."

"Fantastic, I'm about to be party to kidnapping and unlawful detention."

"Kidnapping and unlawful detention to an assassin." He flicked her nose. "Important distinction there. Where's the key for the room? I'll need it to get back in."

She reached into her other pants pocket and deposited it in his hand. "Here. Don't lose it."

He placed it in his wallet and returned it to his back pocket. "Surely. Now I'll be back in hopefully a little bit. I sure hope he's still in the office at this hour, or I'll have to concoct something myself."

"Lord willing. Now hurry up." She pulled the sheet down. "I'm going to bed."

He opened the door and waved. "Be back soon, honey." He shut the door, making sure it was locked before continuing back to his vehicle. "This should all work out if all goes to plan," he muttered to himself walking across the vacant parking lot. He got in his car and started it up.

Thinking back to earlier in the day he remembered the path to the office he'd got patched up in and was on his way. "Been a hell of a day already." He noticed the familiar cityscape from earlier and slowed down. "It was this alleyway I believe." He pulled into the narrow entryway and put it into park. He had just gotten out of it when the familiar door swung open to reveal his attendant from earlier.

He shut the door behind him, turned around, and clutched his chest. "Jesus Christ almighty, don't scare me like that. Wait, you're from earlier. What are you doing here at this hour? I just finished my last client for the night. Did it open again?" Edmund asked.

"No, but I am in need of your unique services."

"Someone's hurt?"

"Not quite."

Edmund furrowed his brow. "I don't follow."

"Let's just say I want to subdue someone without hurting them. You strike me as the kind of guy who could help with that. Say, with a cloth over their nose and mouth."

"Don't tell me this is for your lady friend? I will have no part of that."

"No! God no! In fact, this person is hunting her specifically, and I don't fancy fighting him in my state. I'd rather he just take a nap. It'd make him much more manageable."

"Provided you could get near him. I have an idea. It's not too complicated." Edmund rubbed his eyes. "You do have money, right?"

"What do you take me for?"

"Right. I can whip something up real quick. Only if you promise it's for a ne'er-do-well though."

Jim took a step forward. "The guy is going after my best friend. Can you help me or not?"

"Fine. Come on into my office, again." He put the lock in the slot and twisted it, unlocking it. "I warn you," he said leading the pair inside, "I'm not a chemist, but it should work for what you need. I admit," he said, wandering over to the far side of the room near a table with assorted bottles lining the shelf above, "I haven't had a request like this before. I'm not sure how much to charge. Let's see," he said grabbing a bottle from above along with a beaker, "if I add the components together, and add the processing fee, I suppose it would come to another two hundred."

"That will work." Jim stopped a good ten feet behind the man and watched his actions.

"What the hell have you gotten yourself into, kid?" Edmund asked.

"Aren't you supposed to not ask questions in here?"

"During normal work hours, yes."

"Let's just say I pissed off the scum of the earth and they don't like getting pushed. So they're retaliating."

Edmund stopped in his tracks. "You weren't followed, were you?"

"No. He won't be in town for at least another seven hours. You're good."

Edmund continued preparing the concoction. "You better be right. Now this stuff will get him down if you get him to take a good lung full of it. He might stumble a bit if he's particularly hearty, but may I ask what you'll do afterward?"

"The man has killed over two hundred people. He ain't a choir boy. Let's leave it at that."

"Fucking hell." He poured the mixture into a final bottle and screwed the top on it. "Here. I'm not sure how you're going to get a guy that dangerous to breath it in, but that's your problem, not mine. You figure it out." He held his empty palm out along with a syringe.

Jim paid him and took the bottle. "So just pour it on a rag and shove it over his mouth and nose?"

"Pretty much. It's not an exact science, but I guarantee it'll get him sleepy. I don't care who you are, you're passing out if you breathe that in. Once he's out, stick him with this needle. It's a sedative. It'll keep him asleep. Be careful with them. Even inhaling the fumes for any length of time can be bad. Now I don't mean to be rude, but I'd like to get home and sleep before tomorrow. It sounds like you'll have a full schedule tomorrow as well. So, if you'll excuse me." He gestured over to the door.

Jim obliged and moved back the way he came with his prize in hand. "Don't suppose you had any unique visitors besides me lately?"

"Why do you ask? I don't give up client details."

"Because a dangerous group somehow knew I'd been injured. The only people that knew are you, Ray, and my friend. I know my friend didn't talk, and so it falls to you or Ray. You have something you want to tell me, Ed?" Jim stopped at the door and turned to him. "Did they threaten you too?"

"Look, kid," Edmund's tall form bent down, and his voice lowered, "I know who you're talking about. They came in about an hour after you left, asking after the vigilante. I assume that was you. They said they'd report my ass to the authorities if I didn't answer. I have a kid to feed. I can't be in prison - my baby would go into the system."

"So you told them. Right." Jim shook his head. "Was just wondering how they knew. What did you tell them?"

"Just the facts. That you were stabbed, it didn't bleed much, and how you paid. Speaking of which..." He reached into his coat pocket and took out an envelope. "They said to give this to you. I don't know what's in it, and I don't want to know. I was actually stressing on how I was going to find you, so I suppose this was a fortunate meeting. Now leave me out of this crap from now on unless you're bleeding out, eh?"

Jim took it in his free hand. "Got it."

Edmund opened the door leading to the car, and tilted his head. "Now get going. I've had enough of you for one day, kid."

Jim took the hint and headed out. "Noted."

"Good." Edmund shut the door behind them again and walked off down the alley toward the open road. "Now to get some sleep."

"Bye then." Jim opened his door and deposited the envelope in the passenger seat and the bottle in the cup holder. Ensuring it's snug fit, he started the engine and backed out after Edmund was clear. "What would they want me to have?" he asked, jolting the car forward back to the motel. "How did they even know I went there? They must have someone watching me. Phenomenal. One more thing to worry about. Though now that I think about it, they probably wanted to be sure I did what they wanted. No sense in them still following me at this point. I'm probably in the clear." He sped through a yellow light. "Not like I can rely on them to help me through this shit though." He saw the motel in the distance. "It's all on me and Cynthia now. All because of me." He frowned and approached the vacant parking lot.

He pulled in and backed into the parking spot in front of their room. He pulled out his wallet and took out the key before grabbing the two other items and getting out of the car. He opened the door and shut it behind him to see

Cynthia laying on her back with the tiny television in front of it on.

She looked over to him. "I couldn't sleep. What's that extra thing?" She sat up and swung her legs over to the side. "An envelope?"

"Bit of a long story." He placed the bottle and needle on the windowsill. "These babies are the answer to all our problems tomorrow. This," he held up the envelope, "I have no clue. Apparently, the hunters left it for me at the doctors."

"You went to a doctor this late?"

"An unofficial one, yes. Let's find out what they wanted to give me." He sat down next to her and tore open the back of it. He reached inside to find a fist full of hundred-dollar bills along with a note. "Hope this covered the medical costs." A smiley face was drawn in blue ink underneath the text. Along with an extra bit of text. "Good luck with your new problem. Best regards."

"They like you," Cynthia said grabbing the paper. "I'm not sure that's a good thing."

"They see me as a sort of kindred spirit I think. Not like I mind the cash."

"Sure you want to take it? You've no way of knowing what they did to get it. It could be blood money off some poor sod they blackmailed. Don't you even start to say he may have deserved it either."

Jim shrugged. "It's not like I can give it back anyway. May as well put it to good use."

"Putting aside your lack of moral fiber in the face of money, what is that bottle for?"

"Remember when I asked if you could play the ditsy girl?" Jim patted her shoulder.

"Yeah."

"You're going to do just that. I'll wake you up early, you'll take the car around the block, and when I call, you'll take a little walk. You know what he looks like, so you can identify him. Then when he gets near the door, distract him a little. I'll open the door, he'll no doubt turn, and then you shove a rag with that stuff over his nose and mouth. He'll fall over asleep, and then we're home free after I jab him with the needle."

"How is rendering him asleep going to make it home free?"

"Because having an elite assassin incapacitated is better than not? I'll take care of him afterward. All you worry about it knocking him out."

"Using yourself as bait then?" Cynthia asked. "That would work. He's not going to have a crossbow or some such out when he's walking about. Could have a knife, but if we do it right he'd never get a chance to use it. It's the best chance we've got. May as well try."

"Glad I have your approval. It'll be better than taking him head on anyway. Now help me remove my shirt."

"Why?"

"I need to sleep too you know. I always sleep shirtless."

Cynthia shook her head no. "Not tonight you don't. Put up with it for one night like me."

"Didn't know that about you?"

"What are you talking about?"

"That you sleep topless too. We could match if you like."

Cynthia pushed him, causing him to tumble backward onto the bed. "No. Now scoot over." She fell down beside him and adjusted herself so she was angled properly. "Now sleep."

"Fine. If you're going to be such a killjoy I guess I will."

Cynthia reached over to the lit lamp and turned it off. "Do you want to know why I couldn't sleep?"

"I assumed you'd tell me."

"Because you want me to walk right up to a serial killer and distract him. My mind keeps playing through this scenario over and over. None of them go very well."

Jim rolled over to face her back. "He's not going to kill you in broad daylight on a public street in the morning. He's going to notice the cameras. If he does, he'd be stupid to do anything in front of them. Remember he's gotten away with it for decades. He might be short with you, but that's okay. In fact, it's desired. All we need is for him to turn away when I open the door. Be quick with the rag, and we'll be fine."

"So be quick, or he'll possibly kill you. No pressure, huh?"

"At worst, he'd try to invite himself into my room before killing me straight up. He wants to get away with it. Having the whole world see him is not conductive to that. You'll be fine. Just act like that one girl in high school that pissed you off all the time. You know the one that always kept talking and talking." He laid a hand on her arm. "You'll have your phone on the whole time, so I'll know when to distract him. It'll be fine."

"So you keep saying. I've just never had a life hanging on my ability before."

"Good practice for your future career then. You think it'll be easier in a courtroom? Except this time you won't have to convince twelve people. You just need one to look a certain direction, and then reach around his face. Easy. Besides, I'm the one that has to load him up without anyone noticing, and then take care of him."

Cynthia rolled over to face him. "You're going to kill too?"

"It's a him or us situation. I can tell you he won't give up. His reputation would be in tatters. He will keep coming at us if we leave him alive. You know that as well as I do. Now I won't ask you to do anything. You can stay here or hell, go to class if you want."

She brought a hand up and cupped his chin. "Life just sends you surprise after surprise. I trust you have a location in mind for your little disposal?"

"Of course I do."

"Good."

"Really?"

"You think I want a pissed off assassin coming back for revenge? You do whatever you have to. To keep us safe is all that matters right now. You get me?"

He placed a hand on her forearm. "Yeah."

"Good." She leaned forward and planted a peck on his cheek. "Now sleep, you bastard. I have the alarm set for an hour before he arrives to be safe. I need my beauty sleep."

"Not really."

"No one likes a flatterer, except me sometimes."

"I know. It's always worked before."

She kicked his legs and rolled over with a chuckle.

They closed their eyes and drifted off.

16

Cynthia fiddled with her phone as she leaned against the front of the car. She yawned and brought it up to her ear. "Anything yet?"

"Ray isn't moving yet. If he sees anyone suspicious, he'll be all over it."

"You trust he's awake at this hour? Does he make a habit of getting up at seven am?"

"I don't know the man's sleeping habits, but I don't see anything on the cameras yet."

"I feel like a jackass standing out here you know."

She could hear Jim laugh. "I'm sure you can deal with it. I'm the one about to be targeted. Besides, you're on the side where I told you to be, right?"

"Yeah," She looked over her shoulder at the man on his porch and turned back, "He's looking alright. Must be retired to get up this early and just people watch. He certainly looks old enough."

"Then you're safe. Witnesses are not okay for our assassin. You're safer out there than I am in here."

"If you say so. I just hate being watched."

"He's harmless, probably. Now pay attention, keep the phone on, and hide in plain sight. Should be easy for you."

"You saying I' m plain?"

"No. Wait a second now. I see something. Ray's on the move. You see anyone?"

Cynthia looked up from the phone and scanned left and right. "Not really. I see your friend moving, but no one else. He's probably just stretching his legs."

"Be sure."

"Fine." Cynthia walked down the sidewalk. "You better pay me back for this crap later."

"You have my word."

She stopped halfway down the curb and turned off the speaker option. "Yeah, there's a guy that matches our guest's description. He's talking to him, but I can't make out the face. He has his back to me. Should I get closer?"

"Don't walk up on them, but amble on over to the motel's parking lot."

She did so and looked down at the short shorts she wore. "Were these necessary? I feel like a hooker in these."

"That's the general idea. Cheap hotel, and women hanging around. He's seen it all before. It'll all be business as usual for him. He'll just brush you off. Those star glasses were a nice touch."

"Girls I know that have these are always insufferable. It made sense when you explained it at the store last night." Her voice turned louder, and switched accents to a more bratty pitch. "Oh honey, you know I love you." She approached the pair and saw Ray get shoved out of the way.

Alfred's stern even voice emerged. "Out of the way, old man."

Ray bounced back. "Hey there, young whipper snapper. Is that any way to treat your elder?" He eyed him up and down. "Okay, maybe you're not that young, but I could be your pa. You ever heard of human decency?"

"Overrated," Alfred said without turning to face him. They were now about twenty feet in front of Jim's motel room, in the parking lot.

"Aw, now don't say that. Don't tell me you're too jaded by the world to help the less fortunate."

Alfred's voice became laced with steel. "Go away. Now!"

"Geez, young fella, fine. I see you and this girl have some unfinished business. I know when I'm not wanted."

"Young woman?" Alfred turned around.

"So yeah, baby. I'll talk to you later, hun. Bye." She shoved the phone in her pocket. "Oh, hey there, hunk. How are you doing this morning?" she asked with a wink.

"You're enchanting, miss, but I have business to attend to. If you'll excuse me..." He started to turn away only to be stopped with a hand on his suit covered arm.

"Oh don't be like that, darling," she cooed. "It'd be such a waste for a masculine man like you to be lonely. Are you married, sweet thing?"

"No."

The door to Jim's room opened causing Alfred's neck to swivel to look.

Cynthia's arm snaked around to her back pocket and retrieved the prepared rag. She wrapped one arm around his head and yanked back, securing the cloth around his mouth and nose, the other clutched his shoulder.

A faint imperceptible noise escaped Alfred's lips as he wobbled in place. He tried to elbow her in the stomach, but the resulting blow felt more like a gentle shove. He lost his balance and collapsed just as Jim got close.

"See? Easy." Jim pulled out the syringe and administered the sedative. He dragged him to his nearby car. "All done.

Now pop the trunk, and Ray," he tossed over a roll of duct tape and two zip ties, "use these. Zip tie his hands first, tape after. Think you can handle that? Don't forget his feet either."

"Sure." Ray caught them and got to work as soon as the limp body plopped into the compacted compartment.

Jim stood on one side of the trunk as Cynthia moved to the other, blocking sight of their deed.

"Easy?" Cynthia asked, not raising her voice. She leaned back to see Jim's face around Ray. "The dude is a real stickler. Me and, what was it again, Ray?" She gestured toward the man now wrapping tape around Alfred's wrists and hands, "We were starting to piss him off."

"Ah," Ray started, "if he'd gotten frisky, I'd have been the first one he went after, not you, young lady. I was the really annoying one." He tore off the end of the tape. "There, he's secured." He reached up and slammed the trunk shut. "He's ready for transport. I taped his mouth shut, and hog tied him for you. Don't want him being comfy in there. I don't want to know what you're doing, and don't care. So, have at it. I'm having a bout of amnesia again."

Jim picked out his wallet and took out a few hundred and handed them over. "Be really nice if you never saw us either."

"Spontaneous blindness is a hell of a thing." He wandered off a few steps. "I can't see."

"He's certainly a character." Cynthia scooted over toward Jim. "He won't snitch, will he?"

"No. At least I don't believe so. He has no reason to. I think he just wants a friend." He patted the trunk. "Well, head back inside or to class, whatever you're going to do. I'll deal with our cargo myself. Just if you head to your house, don't go to the basement. Got me? Oh, and before I forget, you did save those feeds onto an external hard drive, right?"

"Of course."

"Then smash them, submerge them in water, whatever - just get rid of them. I'll take care of the cameras."

"Sure. Just realize my basement is not sound proofed, so don't do anything crazy. I'm going to get out of these flashy clothes now." She produced the one key out of her bra and unlocked the door. "Have fun." She disappeared inside.

He turned away and back to the car. He patted the trunk and looked left and right, spotting no one. "Now to take care of the only witness to this." He approached the front door of the motel and moved to the nearby drink vending machine. He inserted a dollar bill and pressed the top button. He shook the can while he walked back toward the room. He raised the can up to the newly cemented camera he'd planted earlier in the morning and popped the top open. Fizzing brown liquid spurted out of the aluminum container all over the electronic camera. "Now for good measure," he swung the now mostly empty can and smashed the majority of the camera. The base was still stuck on the wall, but the majority littered the asphalt below. "There, now for the others." He smiled to himself.

Back at Cynthia's house.

Jim parked back into the driveway and got out of his car. He walked over to the garage and reached down. He hefted the door up with a hiss of pain and a jolting pain in his side. "Fuck." His other arm raced to the wound. "Who would have thought getting stabbed would still hurt?" He turned his attention to the empty garage and hopped in the car before pulling it in and closing the door back. He opened the adjoining door and headed inside, leaving it open behind him. Wandering the halls, he came across the basement door and opened it, again leaving it open.

Coming back to the car, he moved to the driver's side and reached inside. He popped the trunk and ambled back. "Having fun, sunshine?" He kept his eyes on the hands of his prisoner, but saw they were still restrained. "Not thinking of trying anything cute I trust?"

Alfred glared up at him and wiggled in the enclosed space. Not a sound came aside from the movement.

"Playing hard to get, huh? Too bad. Now this won't be pleasant for you. I'm going to drag you out of that trunk. Sound good?" He saw Alfred's unending gaze pierce through him. "Alrighty then. Now unfortunately I'm not in peak condition right now, so it could be a bumpy ride. Do forgive me." He reached inside and angled Alfred's tied together legs out and yanked hard.

Alfred's body was now half in the trunk and half hanging over the back of the car. His hands and feet were stretched at an odd angle as this all went on.

"Ooh, that's got to hurt. No cries of pain? Tough guy I see. Let me help you out with that." He checked the tape to make sure it was still intact. Once he was sure, he kept pulling. A thunk indicated Alfred's head had collided with the elevated exit of the trunk followed by his entire body tumbling to the concrete below with a muffled grunt.

"So sorry about that." Jim's voice dripped with sarcasm. "I'm just so clumsy nowadays." He bent over and grabbed his tied feet with his uninjured side's arm and dragged him inside. "Shut the door behind us, won't you?" He kicked back, smacking both the door and the side of Alfred's face.

"Thanks. Welcome to the last home you'll ever enter." He kept dragging him through the house as he talked. "I know you're used to being the hunter and all, but a change of pace isn't so bad, right? Well, for me anyway - kind of sucks for you. I'm curious to see how you'll react when this all sinks in. Will you start begging? Maybe you'll offer to work for me instead." The pair reached the stairs leading down.

Jim looked down the flight of stairs and back to his quarry. "I'll be honest," he paused, getting back behind Alfred. "I've always wondered how this would work. Guess we'll find out together."

Alfred shook his head. The sound of crinkling tape filled the air as he attempted to roll away.

"Where do you think you're going, pal?" Jim placed a foot down, blocking his escape. "You're going downstairs. He got down to his hands and knees and placed his palms on Alfred's back. "I recommend tucking and rolling. Does that really help? You're the assassin special forces guy, so you'd be the one to know. Well, I'll trust you know what you're doing then." He pushed, inching Alfred closer to the doorway.

Alfred's wriggling body reached the precipice of the stairwell, and Jim stopped for a moment. He angled his neck to look up at his captor and shook his head, sweat dripping down the side of his pale bald head.

"You come after me and mine, this is what you get." Jim stood up and placed a sneaker square in the middle of Alfred's back. "Get fucked." He pushed forward.

Alfred's body tipped over the edge. His body smacked on each step amidst muffled cries of pain and flesh slapping on wood. His arms and legs contorted behind him as he fell in their constraints. Finally, almost mercifully, his body slapped the cold concrete below. He laid still finally after reaching his destination.

Jim skipped down the stairs after closing the door and flicking the light switch at the top of the stairwell, illuminating the unfinished basement. "Welcome home," he said, extending his arms out to either side. "It ain't much, but it's where you'll be staying; so make yourself comfortable." He delivered a kick into Alfred's back. "I'm about to show you some real southern hospitality." He knelt and checked the restraints. "Still holding I see. Good." He stood up and moved in front of the constrained man. Looking down he started again. "I know all about your methods, your connections, and skills."

Alfred sneered and struggled against his bonds.

Jim paced as he spoke. "You probably thought I was just some hick that crossed the wrong people. As you're learning now, that was a fatal mistake. Did they even tell you why they wanted me dead?"

Alfred gave no response other than a blank glare.

"I bet not. You seem the type that doesn't care. You just want the name of the target and your money, right? I'll enlighten you before I start." He stopped a few feet in front of Alfred and sat down so the man could see him easier. He pulled out his firearm from his back belt line and held it up to the light. "It's a bit of a long story, but bear with me, won't you? I put a man down for breaking into my home." He pulled back the hammer and aimed at Alfred. "Pow." He raised the barrel along with the makeshift sound effect. "Why did he break in, you ask? I outed his ass as a pedophile for the world to see. So he got drunk and came back." He grunted and got up. "But that's not the end of this story. Oh no. I guess you could say I took on a personal crusade after that fateful night. The same place my home invader worked was a hive of filth."

Alfred's eyes widened as he listened.

"Yeah, that's right. You're starting to understand now. I put down another that knew of all of it and did nothing. May as well have touched those kids himself the way I see it." He pointed the business end of his weapon up toward the ceiling. "Then I went after who he squealed on. She had invited a little boy to her house and planned to consummate their little relationship. For reference he was around eight years old. I assume they reached out to your little mafioso buddies who called you in." He squatted down and gripped the tape on Alfred's mouth. "Scream, and you die. Get me?"

Alfred nodded.

Jim ripped the tape off. "Did you know who you're working on behalf of?"

"It's not my concern."

"Of course it is." Jim stood up and backed up a few steps. "We are the product of our actions." He gestured to himself and back to Alfred. "We're both killers here. The only difference is who we kill and for what reason. I don't give a shit about your mafia kills, that's whatever. Honestly, man to man, you need to vet your other employers though. You are literally trying to kill me on behalf of the local child molester ring. You don't care about that?"

"Whatever you're going to do, do it already. I am sick of listening to you. Blowing my brains out would be a mercy at this point." Alfred's cool demeanor reflected in his calm voice. "I get paid to do a job, and I do it. It's just business. You take your job too personally, and it will screw you down the line. Mark my words. Losing your temper like I suspect you do, is a good way to either be killed or get someone else killed. I know from experience."

"You sure do live up to your rep. You know that?" Jim chuckled. "The big bad mafia hit man daring his captor to kill him." His voice turned stern. "I'm not going to make it that easy."

"Whatever you're going to do, I've went through worse."

"Is that so? I say we put that to the test." He holstered his gun. "I'm sure you've been stabbed, shot, and all manner of things in the past; but see, I'm creative. I can't cause too much of a mess, but I have some ideas."

"What?" Alfred asked, "are you going to waterboard me or something? You got nothing down here to play with. Not even a bucket to hold said water. At least keep your work shed stocked. What an amateur."

"Keep talking if it makes you feel better. I'm not a sadist, but I do need something to fill the time until dark."

"Going to bury me later? You ever dug a hole, son? Much less a grave? That shit isn't as easy as the movies make it out to be. Trust me. Just dump my carcass by the side of the road."

"You'd like that, wouldn't you? So your employers would know to send another goon after me. How's it feel to be so replaceable?" Jim asked, staring down at him. "You're just another grunt in the big machine of organized crime."

"Same as it was in the service. You get used to it. It's actually comforting in a way."

"You have a screwed up world view." Jim made for the stairs. "Don't worry, old man. I'll be back in a little while. Fun fact - if you'd showed the slightest remorse at working for pedophiles, I'd have made it quick and painless. Since you're so proud of who you work for, I need to teach you a lesson." He climbed the stairs and looked back down. "Just two minutes, and I'll be back."

Alfred watched Jim disappear and started attempting to

move. His hands were firmly locked together, being suffocated from the tape over top of the bonds along with his feet. He wiggled his way toward the stairs and placed his covered feet below the bottom stair. He turned around and managed to put his butt on the bottom stair. "Easy now," he whispered to himself. He angled his body so as to repeat the process up the next stair and barely managed to keep his balance. With every ascension, a small sound came from the creaking wooden stairs underneath.

"Not trying anything stupid, are we?" Jim's voice wafted down from above. "Let's see." He appeared in the doorway. He descended, shaking his head. "Alfred, I appreciate the spirit, but did you really think this would work?" He pressed a palm into his back and pushed him forward down to the basement floor.

Alfred's body slammed into the concrete, his head hitting with a wet slap.

"Hey," Jim ambled down the stairs, "you still awake? Don't tell me a fall down the stairs took down the badass killer now." He inspected the ties. "Trying to escape while everything is still bound? Bonus points for the balls, but a big penalty for the stupidity. You're not getting out of zip ties and tape though, not even a magician could, and I doubt you're trained for that. Anyway," he raised a hand showing the white plastic shopping bag, "I have your next experience right here."

Alfred's eyes fluttered open. "What? Where am I? Oh hell, I'm still here."

"That's right, big boy." Jim walked behind Alfred. "Now I'm curious, have you ever asphyxiated anyone before?"

"A few times."

"Was it a fast death or ugly?"

"Depends on when you do it. If they're asleep, painless

and easy." Alfred's eyes wandered to the plastic bag. "If they know it's coming, ugly and miserable. It only lasts for a minute or two though. Then they pass out."

"Supposing you never got the treatment. You're about to learn all about it firsthand."

"Not the worst thing in the..." Alfred was cut off by the bag now enveloping his vision. He laid still as the crinkles met his ears.

"Not going to move, eh? Don't want me to have fun? Fine by me." Jim tightened the grip of the bag around his neck. "You will have to breath eventually and will involuntarily start jerking. I can play the waiting game."

Seconds eventually turned to a minute, and Alfred started moving.

"Feeling the lungs burning? You know, if I got to choose the way I die, this would be right at the bottom. That feeling of helplessness, inability to breathe, and no way to end it other than passing out is pure horror to me. How's it feeling?"

Alfred declined to answer in favor of his movements becoming more erratic and pronounced now as time wore on. His body jerked as much as his constraints would allow. His arms and legs yanked against the bindings. He tried to roll to no avail as Jim kept the bag wrapped firmly around his face and neck.

"Alright." Jim released the hold and pulled the bag off.

Alfred gasped for breath and panted.

"Anything like what you imagined? Was the lung burning more of a sensation, or more of a desperate ache?"

"I'm going to kill you when I get out of these."

"Which step was anger on the five steps? Let's see..." Jim paused and snapped his fingers, "It was denial, anger, bargaining, depression and acceptance, right? You were in denial earlier probably mentally. Now it's anger." He raised the bag over Alfred's head again and descended. "And pretty soon you'll start begging for your life." He watched the man under his arms jerk and twist in agony. "How many people did this exact same thing for you? You're the expert after all. He lifted the veil after a minute.

"Fucking none." Alfred huffed and puffed. "I'm not a rank amateur. Mine were quick and painless. Poison tends to look like illness anyway. They think they're sick, not being murdered. You say you're not a sadist, but damn if you don't feel like one right now."

Jim tossed the bag down beside him. "Is that right? Answer me something. Have you slept lately?"

"What?"

"You couldn't have slept for long if you did. You drove clear across the country in a night and managed to track my ass down at the motel. Nice work on that by the way, but you couldn't have slept much if at all."

"No, I didn't."

"Good to know for later today. You and me are going to spend all day together. Tell me, do you like music?"

"No."

"Good. You may have noticed the stereo system over in the corner. He walked over to it and turned it on. "See, one of the neighbors is on vacation, and the other keeps to himself. So no one will be interrupting us; and even if they did, so what? I'll be the one going upstairs and, as you learned earlier, you won't be." He twisted one of the knobs and loud electronic music with pronounced bass started blaring in the room.

Jim moved back to the stairs and ascended. He yelled over the music. "Have fun. I'll be back in a bit. Don't go sleeping on me now." He shut the door and immediately moved back to the front room to see the next-door neighbor exiting his house and stomping over. He opened the door preemptively.

"Turn that blasted music down, you young buck," the older gentleman demanded.

"Sure thing, old timer. Sorry about that. Sorry about that." He quickly shut the door on the muttering man and made his way back to the basement. He switched off the music. "Did you like that?"

"Yeah," Alfred's dry voice said. "I liked the beat in it."

"Good. I love to hear that." Jim picked up the wireless headset perched above the system and came over. He placed them on Alfred's head. "Good thing I kept the tape down here." He said, reaching over and ripping off pieces before affixing the headset to Alfred's head. "It doesn't matter if we damage your hearing, so I'm going to give you more of that sweet music," he said, finishing his work. He patted Alfred's bald head and got back up. He switched the output to the headset and cranked it up again. He held up a thumb and tilted his head with a smirk. "Enjoying?

Alfred made no effort to respond and only cringed as Jim turned the volume up higher. He rolled around in agony as Jim turned the dial all the way up.

"Have fun with that, asshole." He stopped when the cell phone in his pocket chirped. He sat on the stairs and answered it, raising it to his ear. "Yeah? Doing anything fun yet?"

Cynthia's voice could be heard over the line. "If you call class fun. I just got an interesting text from the cranky old guy next door. Apparently my boyfriend is causing a ruckus."

"I smoothed it over with him already. I had to get a bit creative with my entertainment."

"Well, I'll be back in a bit. Don't piss off the neighbors anymore, yeah?"

"Of course. Just listening to a bit of music right now." Jim leaned back and watched Alfred's writhing form. "Relaxing."

"Should you really be relaxing right now? You better know what you're doing."

"Have a little faith. We got this far, didn't we? All work and no play makes Jim a dull boy."

"You are anything but dull if I've learned anything," Cynthia said. "Just no more surprises, okay? Is there anything I should know?"

"I'll be heading out tonight to go shopping, but that's about all. You know how it is. We always need something."

"Right. I'm getting in the car now, so I'll talk to you in a bit. Have fun relaxing or whatever it is you're doing."

"Oh, I will." Jim smiled. "I will." He hung up and kept his gaze on the suffering man in the middle of the concrete basement. "Where should I bury his ass tonight? Oh, I know. I could go camping - well, say I'm going camping anyway. I would still need a tent and all the typical supplies just in case anyone came sniffing around. I'd just need a nice remote area. Not near the border though. The last thing I need is border patrol coming by in the middle of my digging. It sure would be nice to have an extra pair of hands though. Not that Cyn will go with me. Wait, today's Friday. She could go if I convinced her. I'd just have her help me dig a bit, and then she could relax. No, she'd never go for it. I don't want her to be near a dead body. Shit. Who could I turn to? Am I really going to dig a six feet deep grave by my damned self? Looks like it."

Alfred's voice was louder than before. "Fine, I'll do whatever you want - just take these damned things off." He rolled back and forth, shaking his head, attempting to dislodge the headset. "I can't take this shitty music anymore."

"He'll be fine for another few hours until I figure this out." Jim watched his would-be killer roll into the wall and try and bang his head on it repeatedly. "Crap, he'll try to kill himself if I leave him. Then we'll have blood everywhere down here. Fuck! Fine, I'll take it off." He stepped over and ripped off the tape and lifted the speaker. "Happy now?"

"I thought I was cruel," Alfred said. "That is just unusual and depraved. What do you want from me? To give up the contract? It's not like it's impossible to do, you know."

"You sure moved from anger to bargaining quickly. There's only one problem. How could I trust a man hired to kill me and mine?"

"I was only after you, not after whoever you're protecting. I know nobody else. The point is, if I tell the higher ups it's not worth it, they'll listen to me."

"You expect me to believe an enforcer like you can sway the higher ups from a contract? How stupid do you think I am?" Jim frowned.

Alfred shook his head. "I wouldn't try to convince them of the contract, just that you're untouchable. With the heat surrounding you, the media coverage and publicity, it'd be bad for business. I can make this work."

"A free lancer is going to convince a boss to give up money because it's too hard? That'd be a big hit to your rep."

"Better than dying and being buried in the desert. That's what you were going to do, isn't it? Besides, I have enough money to retire on. I don't need this anymore. I'm getting too old for this shit business."

"Why should I trust you of all people. You were hired to kill me - you just admitted as much. It doesn't seem wise to just cut you loose."

"Bring me a burner phone, and I'll prove it to you. I'll call the shot caller who contracted me out to this job. He'll spread word that no one takes the job, but I can't guarantee other families won't try. It's the best I can do. I will say this - you won't have a problem with anyone else's men. I am the best."

"Says the man hog tied on a basement floor," Jim said. "Tell you what - I'll go get you a burner and see if you can deliver. We'll go from there. How about that?"

"Fair enough."

"Good." He pulled out his phone and dialed Cynthia's number.

"What? The only reason I'm answering is I'm at a stop light."

"Can you stop and pick me up a burner phone?"

Cynthia paused before answering. "What's a burner phone? You mean one of those cheap things that don't require a plan and you toss away?"

"Yes. I have an idea, and I need one. It'll be cleaner if you do and would really help me out."

He could hear Cynthia sigh over the line "Fine. I'm right by a place that sells them anyway. You're going to explain what it's for when I get home. You know that."

"Of course, sweetie. Drive safe." He hung up and looked over at Alfred. "You'll get your chance. Now don't blow it, and you may yet go home alive. You cross me, and you already know what'll happen. Bad music will be the least of your worries."

"You'll kill me. I get it. A tip from your elder, don't over-play the murder angle. People get desensitized to it and get desperate. Desperate people do unpredictable things. Unpredictable things can get you killed."

"I'm just going to ignore the irony in what you just said

and answer with this." He moved closer and grabbed the tape. He pulled it out and placed one end on the wall and the other across Alfred's body until it made contact with the wall on the other side. He repeated the process as he spoke. "I can't have you getting cute and trying anything else on me while I head upstairs. You understand."

"Smart." Alfred's dry voice answered. "Not efficient in the least, but smart. Not like I can use my hands or feet anyway.

Jim finished the fifteenth application and took a few steps back to admire his work. "How's that?"

"I'm stuck. What do you want me to say?"

Jim reached down and yanked at the makeshift bonds. "Yeah, seems you're right."

"Don't trust my word?"

"Would you trust the word of a man sent to kill you?" Jim stood up straight. "Now don't go anywhere. I'll be back soon enough. I recommend you think of what you'll say to your boss."

"I'll be waiting with bated breath."

Jim made for the stairs and climbed them before closing the door behind him. He went to the front room and peeked out the window to see Cynthia's car pulling into the driveway. "Perfect timing." He swung the door open and welcomed her inside.

"What was so important you had me stop on the way home?" Cynthia placed the shopping bag on the kitchen counter.

"Our hitman wants to call his boss to call off the hit."

Cynthia's eyes widened. "You thought this was a good idea? He's just going to tell them to send more. You know that, right?"

"He's macho for sure, but I don't think he's suicidal."

"You don't know that for sure."

Jim rolled his eyes. "So you'd rather I just put him down? That's quite the change for you isn't it?"

Cynthia averted her eyes. "Well, I just thought you were going to."

"You bitched at me before about my plan of doing just that; but now that I give an alternative, you complain about that too? Good Lord, I can't win either way. Look, the only reason I'm even entertaining this is a logistics problem."

"What does that mean?" She planted her hands on her hips. "Logistics? With what?"

"With hiding his body after the fact. You think I can just kill him in the basement and leave it there? No. I have to take his ass into the desert at night and bury it. Now I don't know if you've ever tried to dig a grave before, but I doubt it since I haven't. They're harder to make than the movies make it out to be. If I did it by myself, it'd probably take every bit of five to six hours. That's assuming I can have the time uninterrupted."

"Just do what you did before."

"Before, I just left the body where it laid. Either making it look like a suicide or bolting off after making sure no DNA was left. It's a different animal doing this."

"Damn." Cynthia bit her pink lipstick clad lip. "We can't just call anyone to help with this either. It has to be us. You want me to go with you and help? Is that it?"

"I don't want you anywhere near this."

"A little late for that, isn't it?" Cynthia asked. "I'm already involved. At this point I'm going to prison, even if I'm not the one digging the hole. The best I can do is make sure it goes off without a hitch. Right? If that means I pick up a shovel and do some labor, then so be it. I have tomorrow off from class, so it works out. Mostly."

"Mostly?"

"I do have a paper due Monday, but I can get that done on Saturday and Sunday. If we were to commit to this, we'd have to have an alibi for anybody coming by."

"Difficult to explain digging a hole in the desert, wouldn't you say?" Jim asked. "We can't just say we're going to sleep in it. Nobody would be brain dead enough to believe that."

"Hot air rises, right?"

"Don't even entertain the idea."

"We could say we're digging a latrine."

"A six feet deep latrine that's perfectly shaped like a guy, in the middle of the night?"

Cynthia's eyes narrowed. "How about you give an idea instead of shooting all of mine down, Mr. Negative?"

"Find an already dug hole?"

"Just drive through the desert until we find a perfectly sized hole? Jesus, I thought my ideas were dumb."

"The cartel's south of the border do this shit all the time. It's feasible."

"So, piss off another bunch of nasty people? Bad idea."

"The only other idea I have is we both dig it together and keep the body in the trunk until we're done. We could even wait until we're there to end him. The body wouldn't smell that way either. If anyone asks why we're digging, we go with the latrine option. If they call us on it, we're totally new campers. It would require us to get a tent though, along with all the other crap people get doing that."

"This is getting more expensive all the time."

"It's to avoid death. I think it's worth the expense. We just need to find a place not too near the border and away from roads. Prying eyes would be the end of us. You know any camping spots around here?"

"Without people going to them and with cover? Possibly the lake an hour away. Buchanan I think it's called. It's got plenty of tree cover. It's got some campers, but at this time of the year it should be pretty empty. It might technically be in Texas, but it doesn't matter. Camping in a different state just adds credibility if anyone asks. It's not desert, but does soil matter if we bring shovels?"

"Not a bit." He leaned forward and planted a kiss on her forehead. "Thanks for the brilliant idea. Too bad about the phone though." He picked up the device still encased in plastic. "I'll find a use for this later."

"If we're going to have all this ready for tonight, we'll need to get shopping now. At least we have a reason to be shopping for shovels - camping and all. Shouldn't look too suspicious. At least I know there's quite a few campgrounds near the place. It shouldn't be too difficult to find one uninhabited. The question is, where is the guy? In the basement?"

"Tied up, and I can guarantee he isn't going anywhere until we want him to," Jim said, sitting down on a nearby stool. "He still thinks he's going to get a shot to call off the hit."

Cynthia leaned back onto the bar. "He'll blow a gasket when he finds out his fate is to be buried in a park tonight then."

"Does it matter? He's not long for this world."

"You still have a mask I can borrow for a second?" Cynthia asked.

"Yeah." Jim pointed to his backpack in the corner near the door. "Why?"

Cynthia approached and dug around in it for a moment. "Just going to double check your work. No offense, but if I'm going to be party to a homicide, I want to be sure we checked all our t's and dotted our i's. Get me?"

"Sure, sure." Jim stood up and led the pair toward the basement door. "Follow my lead and don't say anything, regardless of what he says."

"Got it."

Jim pulled open the door and descended first. He motioned Cynthia to come down with him.

"Well?" Alfred asked, "Do you have a phone for me?"

"Not quite yet, buddy."

"Who is that?" Alfred's eyes followed Cynthia's mask clad form skip down the stairs. "Your girlfriend or something? She want to watch round two? Is she into that kind of stuff? Is that where you learned your sadistic tendencies? Kinky."

She approached him and leaned forward, inspecting the tape binding. She grabbed hold and pulled. She stood up and moved to the other side, testing it as well. Nodding, she moved to Jim's side.

"You get the seal of approval, kid? She must be your boss, eh? Didn't take you for the pussy whipped type. You seemed like a real man after all."

"Say whatever you like if it makes you feel better."

"Your boyfriend must be incompetent for you to have to double check his work, missy. How about you untie me and get with a real man? I can make you feel funny in ways you never dreamed." He wiggled his eyebrows.

"Disgusting prick," Cynthia said at Jim's side. She wrapped an arm around Jim's side and leaned in close. "You're a slave to your contractor. That doesn't sound like a real man to me."

"Spunky." Alfred licked his lips. "I like that. I'll have you soon enough."

"You wish." Cynthia turned and smacked her butt. "Kiss my ass." She looked up at Jim. "Have him ready, and we'll see if he holds up his end of the deal tonight." She left without further word, leaving the two men alone.

"I like her," Alfred said. "She's wasted on you."

"You are correct in that at least. However, you did earn yourself this." He picked up the nearby roll of tape and placed it over his mouth.

17

Cynthia answered the ringing phone from the passenger's seat. She stared ahead at the increasingly rural landscape as she spoke. "Not really a good time, Charlie."

"Why's that? You're never doing anything on a Friday night. Is that an engine I hear? Oh, I see. You two are going on a date. I see how it is."

"No, not at all." Cynthia looked over at Jim's grinning face. "We're just taking a little trip is all."

"A trip where?"

"Is that any of your business?"

"You're trying to hide this, and it just makes me all the more interested. I know you, and you don't hide trivial things. What are you two doing on this trip?"

"We're camping. Happy now?"

"Ooh, I'll come along."

"No, you won't."

Charlie chuckled. "Oh, so it is a date, and you don't want little old me intruding. I see how it is."

"You are so annoying."

"Fine, I get it. You want a house sitter for your little honeymoon?"

"You just want a place to crash. Admit it."

"Guilty as charged. Seriously though, I'll watch the place for you." Charlie cleared his throat. "I don't know if you heard, but the neighborhood is a bit more dangerous nowadays. Murders have been happening, and my bet is theft will follow soon after. I've got nothing to do this weekend, so why not?"

"Fine, if it makes you feel better. Go ahead. You know where my spare key is, right?"

"Sure do. Thanks for this. You two have fun out there. This has been a long time coming. I'm glad you two finally got to it already."

"Whatever, bye." Cynthia hung up with a huff.

"What did he want?"

"Wanted to know what we were doing tonight. Then wanted to come along." She looked around her seat toward the back. "I didn't allow that, given our cargo. It would be troublesome to say the least. He did offer to watch the house while we were gone though. Personally, I think he just wants a place to smoke since no parties are happening, but I can't deny having someone there would give some peace of mind."

Jim stopped the car for a moment before waving a car on. "Keep your eyes peeled for a suitable place. Nice idea with the rag by the way. He won't be causing noise that way and it may save us the trouble later."

"What do you mean?"

Jim hit the gas. "I mean taping that rag doused in that solution to his face will keep him out. Why do you think I did it? It could kill him too. He's not getting oxygen in that setup. Or at least very much of it. He'll be dead weight now, which will suck to carry, but it's better than him kicking and fighting us every inch of the way. Don't think too much about it. It was my idea to actually implement it."

"Christ, I didn't even think about that."

"He was sent to kill me. Don't feel too bad about it. Besides, like I said, it was me that did it. It's on my hands. Sign says there's a camp site ahead. Check to your right and see if there're many cars there."

"Right," she said, turning her head. She saw a parking lot along with a board with assorted messages clipped to it. "There're no cars there. I think it's our place. We're not even technically in the park proper, but that's why there's no one there I bet."

"Works for me." Jim slowed the car down and pulled off the highway onto the small dirt road leading to the asphalt parking lot. He backed into the deepest spot. "The only question now is how we're going to move the body from here to wherever we dig. The road's right there."

"It's getting dark." Cynthia unbuckled her safety belt. "Unless someone shines a light over here later, no one will see." She jabbed a thumb over her shoulder. "Besides, there are trees right back there. If we can move him ten feet, we'll be in the clear. We should scout out the place first and make sure there are no campers, to be safe anyway."

"Good idea." Jim followed suit and hopped out. "Let's unload our gear and get the tent set up. We'll worry about that other thing later."

The pair got out and circled around the vehicle, opening the back door, and picking up what they could. Jim grabbed the rolled-up tent, while Cynthia grabbed the cooler and assorted bags. They slammed the door shut and took a stroll into the woods.

"This might actually end up being fun," Cynthia said. She glanced over at Jim's amused face. "What? I've never been camping before."

"It'll be a once in a lifetime thing, that's for sure." Jim sneezed. "Excuse me. Let's just try and keep our bearings straight here. We don't want to get lost."

"True, and I doubt many will be following us this late. If they're not here already and setup, they won't try to do it after dark. Let's just find an open meadow and setup."

"There's one off to the right." Jim pointed across his body to a clearing. "Not many twigs to clean up before I set this thing up either. No hills - it's perfect." He kicked a few stray pieces of wood away and tossed the package down. "We'll see if this is as easy to setup as the clerk claimed."

"I'll help. Lord knows you're not a handyman." She carefully sat down the bags and ambled over.

The pair barely got the tent setup before night fell. They stood side by side looking at their accomplishment.

Jim reached down and plucked the handle of the lantern poking out of one of the bags, pulled it out, and switched it on, illuminating the nearby area. "I think we did a surprisingly good job all things considered. It should be big enough, and even if it rains now we'll be good."

"At least it's not cold yet," Cynthia said. "Means we won't need a fire. We still need to get the sleeping bags out." She reached into her pants pocket and retrieved a handheld flashlight. "And you said these were a waste of money."

"I thought we'd get here earlier," he said, pulling out his own and turning it on. He followed her back toward the car.

"Always better to be prepared. Isn't that the scout's motto?"

"No clue. Probably. I wasn't a scout."

The pair made their way back to the vehicle and retrieved the rolled up sleeping bags from the back and lugged them back to the campsite.

"I'll get these ready inside. You had better make preparations for our main job tonight. It'll be totally dark soon, and that's our window."

"Prep? All we're doing is carrying his ass to the drop site."

"Then find the damned drop site. We can't do it here for God's sake. Bad enough I'm roughing it out here. I will not rough it out here while next to that. Make sure it's at least a distance away. We're not that far off the road."

"Sure," Jim said. "You still have your phone, right?"

"Of course, why?"

"Just in case I get lost."

"I will have your gps location, don't worry. I'll guide your dumbass back. If it weren't for me, you'd be useless out here."

"Probably." Jim smiled. "Alright, I'm heading out then."

Jim pushed ahead further into the woods. "I don't even know what kind of spot I should be looking for," he muttered to himself. "I'll just head in a straight line. It should be easy enough to not get lost that way. It'd be nice to have some tree cover on all sides as well for prying eyes." He weaved around a tree in his way and waved his flashlight around, watching his surroundings for a few minutes. The sound of owls, crickets, and assorted other wildlife echoed around him. "It's kind of creepy out here this late." He pushed forward through some thick foliage and found a small clearing. Trees surrounded it along with bushes on every side. "This is as good as it gets I think."

He pulled out his phone and called Cynthia back at the

tent. "I think I found a suitable spot. It's not too far away but within reach." He whirled around in the middle of said clearing. "Trees are all around, plenty of cover, and ample space to dig. "You want to come check it out?"

"I trust you to pick out a spot," Cynthia said. "While you've been doing that, I've been gathering rocks and twigs. I know we don't need a campfire, but it would be fun."

"Fun. Yeah, that's why we're out here. Still, a firepit would be safer. I'll be heading back now, as soon as I can remember which direction it was."

He heard her sigh over the line. "Hold still and stop spinning."

He did so.

"It's to your left and straight ahead."

He followed the directions and started walking. "What would I do without you?"

"Get lost in the forest and go missing apparently. Get back here and we can start this fire." She hung up without any further words.

He followed suit and pocketed the phone, dodging low hanging branches all the while. "She's treating this like an actual camping trip. Bless her heart. At least it'll look legitimate if anyone comes by, right?"

His trip back to camp was uneventful aside from a mosquito biting him in the neck followed by a slap.

"Took you long enough." Cynthia looked up from the circle of rocks she had just created. "How's it look?"

"Like a fire pit I guess. I'm not sure. We may want to get another layer or two, just to be safe. I don't think one is enough."

"Oh man, it took long enough to find all these, but hey, at least now you're here to help."

"The things I do for you."

A few hours later.

"I'd say it turned out pretty well." Cynthia peered out of the tent at the roaring fire outside.

"Sure." Jim pulled out his phone and looked at the time. "It's midnight. Just about time to get started on the real reason for us coming here, wouldn't you say?"

"I knew you'd bring it up sooner or later. Yeah, you're right. Who knows how long it'll take. At least we've already got the shovels here."

"Well, I thought we should dig the pit inside the circle for added security anyway, and it'd make this easier." Jim climbed out and grabbed one of the nearby shovels. He yanked it out of the ground causing a bit of dirt to fly out. "Thinking ahead pays off."

She climbed out and zipped up the tent behind her. "A feeling unfamiliar to you I'm sure." She grabbed the remaining one and hefted it over her petite shoulder. "Let's get this over with then."

The pair made their way back to the clearing and planted their shovels nearby before heading back to the tent in silence. On their way to the car, Cynthia spoke up.

"Don't suppose you've thought of a way to deal with him if he's just asleep?"

"I'd rather not make a mess," Jim said, stepping over a larger log. "We could just strangle him. No fuss, no muss, and it's over inside of five minutes. Every other way that comes to mind involves a lot of blood or noise. I don't think we'll have to worry about it though. He's had no air for hours now other than through that drenched rag. His respiratory system couldn't possibly still be working."

"Says the man with no medical degree. Still, I hope you're right." Cynthia broke the tree line and saw their car. "Come on, muscles, don't make me wait all night."

"There are worse nicknames to be given." He stepped over the last twig and into the clearing. He hurried over and stuck the key in the driver's side door. He leaned forward. "Ready?"

"As I'll ever be."

He popped the trunk and closed the door, hurried over, and threw it up. "Head or legs?"

"Uh, legs."

Jim reached inside and put his arms below Alfred's shoulders. He waited until Cynthia got her hands below his legs. "On three we lift. If he falls - whatever. It'll just make it easier to get a hold. One, two, three." The pair lifted and dumped him onto the pavement below with a wet smack of flesh.

"No time to waste." Jim bent and snaked his arms under Alfred's arms. He dragged him back, leaving Cynthia at the car. "Close the trunk and I'll get him out of sight. Help me afterward." He disappeared out of sight.

Cynthia slammed the trunk shut and jogged after him. She caught up and managed to grab hold of his ankles and lifted the body off the ground. "Couldn't wait two seconds?"

"Did you want to keep us exposed any longer than needed?"

"Good point. God, he's heavy," Cynthia said.

"He's got a lot of muscle on him. Tell me if I'm about to back into anything, would you?"

"You're fine. Our campsite's just ahead, so make sure to angle around the fire."

Jim turned his head and navigated around the circle of fire leading the trio deeper into the woods toward their designated site.

"I feel like a character in one of those movies," Cynthia said, straining.

"Talking about that vigilante who was actually a lawyer you love? Yeah, probably not a good thing to want to emulate."

"Yet here I am, thanks to you. I do wonder if it'll have a happy ending like the movie."

"You mean whether you'll pass the bar exam? Also, I've never asked, did you want to become a prosecutor, or a defender?"

"I can tell how much you've listened when I talked before about my future. I've only said it dozens of times now. I yearn to be a defense attorney. God knows if you ever get caught, you'll need one."

"Aren't you supposed to not represent people you know? Conflict of interest and emotions overriding common sense or something?"

Cynthia gave him a dour look. "Who's the one studying legal ethics? Me or you?"

"Right. I'll try not to give you a job later in life, yeah?"

"Boy, wouldn't that be nice. Not like you have a history of that or anything." Her voice was laden in sarcasm. "Kind of like this dumbass we're hauling to dig a grave for."

"Yeah, I screwed up. Will I never hear the ending of it?"

"No."

"At least you're honest." He checked behind him. "Almost there. Don't worry - the heavy labor is only beginning."

"Comforting to hear." She stepped through the final bush and dropped Alfred.

Jim followed suit and picked up one of the shovels. "Let's get started then." He pointed down at the ground. "You start over here, and I'll start over there."

"Is that six feet apart?

"He's five foot eight, for one, and two - no. We're going to start on one side and work our way over. If we have to fold his legs under his body, then so be it. We don't care about his comfort level, right? All that matters is the depth of the hole." He jammed the metal down into the soil and placed his foot on it, pushing it deeper before hefting it out and dumping the contents to the side.

She did the same, not quite as deep, but poured hers on the other side. "This is going to take a while. It's only a few inches deep."

"After a whole one dig, yeah. I bet it'll take two or three hours of this with help, so get settled in for the long haul."

"At least I can look forward to some good old fashioned roasted marshmallows after this."

Jim dumped another load of dirt to the side. "You brought those?"

"If I'm going to do this, I wanted to have something to look forward to afterward. You think I wanted to sit in the tent and play cards like we were doing the last two hours after digging the fire pit? No, I've always wanted to try them. I've heard they were good."

"I love your priority system. Just think of it this way - getting the dirt back in will be twice as easy. At least then gravity will be on our side."

"I'm sure my back will thank it for that by the end of this. You had better be fetching everything for me the next few days if I'm to work on my damned paper tomorrow."

"I'll be a regular errand boy for you, miss."

"You'd better."

"Let's just focus on this for now before I dig myself into a deeper hole."

"Ha! Ha!" Cynthia's dry voice said.

———

An hour and a half later.

"See?" Jim wiped sweat off his forehead and stood up straight. He climbed out of the hole after helping Cynthia out. "Not so bad."

Cynthia looked down at the hole they'd created. "Are we sure that's six feet deep?"

"Why do you think I bought this tape measure?" Jim pulled one out of his other pants pocket and pulled it out to full length. "See? Six feet." He stuck the end into the hole and it was indeed a perfect six foot hole. He pulled it out and released it, causing the tape to snap back into the device. "The length of the hole however," he moved around Cynthia and repeated the process, "is only five feet and six inches. That will work, given his height. He might be crumpled, but who gives a shit?" He tossed the shovel aside a few feet. "Now let's get him inside."

Cynthia tossed hers nearby and slowly made her way over. "I'm beat already, but yeah, okay."

Together they slid him over to the makeshift grave and kicked him inside.

"You'd better be right about this being easier," Cynthia said grabbing her tool again. She shoveled a load into the hole.

Jim started on the other side after grabbing his again. "See? Much easier."

"It doesn't feel much easier."

"You don't have to kick into the soil now, do you? It's easier." He shoveled a load of dirt onto Alfred's unmoving body. "You can barely see him already under all that dirt."

"I never thought I'd hear that line in my life outside of movies or novels. Now I've heard everything."

"I'm just a string of firsts for you, aren't I?" Jim waggled his eyebrows. "I'll make it up to you. I already promised."

"Not the first I was thinking of."

"What was that?"

Cynthia turned away. "Nothing. You're hearing things. You must be sleep deprived and exhausted. It really is going faster now though. Wait, what was that?"

"What was what? I didn't hear anything," Jim said, continuing the work. The sound of moving earth met their ears.

"No, not that." She pointed down into the pit. "He's moving I think."

"It doesn't matter."

"It doesn't?"

Jim shook his head. "No, it doesn't. He's dying anyway. Would you prefer I jump down there and strangle him in front of you?"

"As opposed to burying him alive? I don't know."

"Just keep shoveling. He probably doesn't even realize where he is or what's going on. Consider it a mercy. He's in a drug fueled haze. Just let him fall back asleep."

She continued dumping more soil onto his legs as they kicked forward. "I don't like this."

"It'll be over soon enough. You're not the one that is

covering his head anyway. I'll be the one suffocating him like this."

"Because that keeps my hands clean. I'm still shoveling over here. I'm an accomplice to homicide no matter how you look at it."

"Just," Jim paused, "keep your mind on the task at hand. Don't think about him. Focus on your marshmallows or whatever you brought. We'll be roasting them over a fire before you know it. If he was out of this hole, he'd be out killing. Think of this as a public service if you must."

"At least we can't see him anymore. He's completely under now. It must be a foot or more of dirt at this point." Cynthia crinkled her nose. "That doesn't make me feel better though."

"Me neither honestly."

The pair fell into silence for a few minutes, piling dirt onto the figure below.

"You think Charlie is having a better time than us?" Jim asked.

"Obviously. No doubt he's stoned, laying on the couch watching television while we're out here breaking our backs for this. We'll get back tomorrow to find him passed out."

Jim tossed another pile down into the hole. "May have to take him up on his offer this time. We're going to be sore as hell."

"Never buried a hitman alive before. You think so?"

"I know so. unless little miss college student does back breaking manual labor every day I don't know about. My side's already killing me, but I'm good."

"You would tell me if it's reopened? You'd better. Don't try and be a tough guy."

Jim lowered a hand to the wound before continuing his

work. "We'll check back at the tent, but it doesn't feel like anything's ripped."

"Good, because we didn't bring a ton of first aid supplies. You'd have to make due with bandages and no disinfectant. We were in so much of a hurry we forgot it." Cynthia spiked her shovel into the ground, pressed her hands into the small of her back, and stretched. She looked down at their work. "What do you know. You were right for once. This'll be a hell of a lot faster."

"The 'for once' part was unnecessary. It seems we're over halfway done now. Keep at it and we'll be eating marshmallows before you know it and driving home tomorrow."

The pair fell into silence as time passed by. The dirt above ground slowly but surely fell into the pit from whence it had come. Thirty minutes later Jim slung the shovel over his shoulder.

"You want to do the honors?" he asked.

Cynthia dumped the last load of soil onto the earth. "Are we done now?"

"Looks like it." Jim evened out the soil and moved away from the newfound grave. He kicked a bunch of brush over it as she looked on.

"Having fun?"

"Trying to make it look less suspicious. Don't want some hiker getting curious, do we?"

"Guess not." Cynthia moved to the other side and followed suit.

"How does that look?" Jim angled his flashlight down toward the fresh dig site.

"Like a small uneven pile of dirt with leaves and twigs on top. Does it looks suspicious? I'd say no. Who the hell looks at the ground and thinks it looks weird?"

"Good point." He moved over and nodded toward the tent. "Let's head back and relax. We earned it."

"I call first dibs on the roasted marshmallows." She bent down and picked up a suitably large stick. "This one's mine. Find your own."

"That's fair. You did help me out after all."

"Damned skippy. Now gather some more wood. The fire's probably nearly burned out already."

"Bossy tonight, aren't we?"

"I earned it."

"True that."

18

"I hate you for this." Cynthia grimaced as the car jolted after hitting a speed bump. "I hurt all over and hold you personally responsible. My back, my legs, arms, every part of me is sore. They don't put that part in the media."

"Not as glamorous as they make it out to be." Jim flinched as he turned the wheel. "We're almost home. Don't worry. You'll have me to order around and fetch you everything as you work on your paper."

"Oh yeah, joy of joys, working on my paper. Don't make me too excited now. I am going to make you tend to my every beck and whim."

Jim pulled into the driveway alongside Charlie's jeep. "Wouldn't have it any other way, darling." He headed over to the door and unlocked it. Swinging it open, he stepped inside.

He immediately reached behind him, pulled out his firearm, and kept it at the ready. He heard Cynthia come in behind him and shut the door. "Quiet."

The entire foyer was wrecked. Assorted things littered

the floor, plant pots were overturned, a hole the size of a fist was in the wall, along with other signs of a struggle.

"Charlie?" Jim called out. "Are you there, bud?" His voice lowered. "Get your weapon out now, and do not ask questions," he told Cynthia behind him.

She undid the safety and followed behind Jim. "I don't like this."

Jim crept around the corner, keeping his weapon at the ready, and saw Charlie laying on the floor face down. He pointed at Charlie's unmoving form and moved past it, checking the remaining bit of the ground floor. Once satisfied no one was there, he made for the stairs. "He alright?" he asked before ascending.

"Oh my God. He's breathing, but beat to hell."

"Stay down here. I'll make sure we're alone." Jim reached the top of the stairs and swung left and right. No one met him as he cleared each room one by one. He made his way downstairs and moved toward the basement door. He threw it open and saw only one thing out of place. A letter hung from the ceiling affixed to a string that was taped to the ceiling. He angled his weapon down below the stairs and circled around until he was sure no one was waiting for him. He cautiously made his way over to the envelope and snatched it before bringing it back upstairs with him.

"I have to call an ambulance. He needs more than I can provide." She pulled out her phone and looked up at Jim. "He could have a concussion or God knows what else."

"Go ahead. I just don't know what we're going to tell them beyond what we know. He was housesitting, and we came back to him like this."

"Agreed." She dialed the three numbers and brought it up to her ear. "Yes, I need an ambulance. 1792 Oak Avenue. Yes. I came back from a trip to find my house sitter here. I think someone broke in and beat him up. He's still breathing, but he's not waking up. Okay. Yes, I can stay on the line."

Jim positioned the envelope in front of Cynthia. He held one finger up to his mouth along with a shushing sound.

"Yes, I understand." She hung up. "They needed the line. They're sending over police and an ambulance. What is that?"

"I don't know yet. I haven't opened it. It was strung up above just waiting for us. I assume it's from whoever did this. By the by, should we stay here for the authorities? I mean, look at us." He gestured down at their dirt covered clothes.

"They'll ask where we were no doubt." Cynthia bit her cherry pink lips. "It'd look bad on us if we just left. Tell you what. I'll stay here and wash up while I wait on them. You leave and see what you can dig up on whatever that," she gestured to the envelope, "is. I'll call you when the coast is clear and you can come back. If they take forever, I'll just go to you under the pretense that I need quiet for studying."

"Got it." Jim pocketed the envelope and went to the door. "Be careful, and don't say too much."

"As if I need you to tell me." Cynthia rolled her eyes. "Now get going before they get here. We should have a few minutes still, and I need to change clothes and wash my face." She dashed up the stairs.

Jim jogged outside and hopped back into his car before backing out onto the street once again. He put it into drive and managed to turn off the street before he heard the faint noise of sirens in the distance. "Just in the nick of time," he muttered to himself. "If only it'd been the same for Charlie. Those sons of bitches, whoever did it." He drove a few more streets over and stopped in a nearby store's parking lot. He pulled out the envelope and ripped it open.

"Let's see here. You are as tenacious as they come. We are pleased you've taken our words to heart. Know this - we had no plans on hurting anyone when we paid you a little visit. Your friend, however, was not so calm. We had to subdue him. You should know we have no plans on seeking retribution on him, mainly since he is an associate of yours. Just remind him that he needs to hold his tongue and not draw his firearm so quickly." Jim looked up. "Charlie drew on whoever it was. I have an inkling who it is based on this, but let's see what they want."

He kept reading. "This is not why we left this letter, however. While we are ecstatic that you dealt with the would-be assassin the degenerates sent after you, your work is not yet done. You dealt with the symptom, not the root disease. They will send more killers after you when they find where you buried their first option. This is do or die for them. They fear for their lives. So should you. There is nothing more dangerous than a desperate fool who knows true justice is headed their way. You, my brother, are just that. While you were dealing with the lackey of the insects, we did some more digging into your problem. We found the shot caller of the local child trafficking ring. Those you've went after before were not the top of the food chain, merely the middlemen and the bottom rungs. You've pissed off some powerful people. At the bottom of this letter, we've included a private url on the deep web. Only you and I have the link. Don't worry, nobody else can see it. It will show you everything you need to know about who we're dealing with."

Jim wiped a bead of sweat off his forehead as he pulled out the other lone sheet of paper and started reading. "What you have done so far is merely the beginning. Ahead of you lies the hardest trials yet. Fear not, we have judged you worthy to complete this test. Check in your girlfriend's back-yard, under the balcony in the garden for a boon in your newest tribulation. That along with that address is all we can do to aid you in this. Good luck, brother. Succeed, and you will have our respect and finally be free of those who seek vengeance upon you. You have our word."

"Like your word means a damned thing to me. For all I know you'll blackmail me with what you know down the line if I don't play fetch," Jim muttered in distaste. He tucked the messages back into the envelope and tossed them into the passenger's seat. "Good thing we brought the laptop on our little camping excursion. It still has a charge I hope." He stretched and reached into the back seat to retrieve the device. Hefting it onto his lap, he opened it and turned it on. "Hopefully this place has free wi-fi," he said under his breath. He deftly moved the cursor over to the ethernet connectivity hub and connected. "Bonus points for connecting to the deep web via a public hotspot too. I think that's more secure, so the internet says anyway." He opened the deep web browser and started the arduous task of typing in the address manually from the letter, having to stop and open the note every few letters. "This shit's for the birds. It would have been so much easier if he'd sent an email. Hardly secure that way though I guess," he angrily muttered.

"There." He finished typing in the random assortment of letters and pressed enter. The page went straight white for more than a few moments. Jim tapped his finger on the side of the laptop and rolled his eyes. "Goddamn infrastructure of the deep web. Always slower than normal. Oh," the screen went black, and the page loaded. A picture of a man in a suit and dark sunglasses appeared front and center on the screen. Assorted paragraphs of text appeared on the side. "So he's the big man behind the child trafficking, huh? That is, if their intel gathering is correct. How much do I trust vigilantes and their info, especially ones who beat up Charlie? That's the question. Still, they did good with the assassin. I have to take that into account. I can't help but feel they're manipulating me though. Let's see here. His name is Oswald Planter. Swanky name that. He's CEO of a local franchise. Who knew some big wig grew up around here and spread his business around the country? I thought we were all yokels out here. Grocery chain, eh? That would give him a decent way of moving the kids. All he'd need are a few corrupt drivers and loaders, and he'd be in business. He'd have access to warehouses to house them before he sold them off. Jesus, what am I in the middle of? This is like waging war on a goddamned warlord of sorts."

"Be that as it may, I should go see how Charlie's holding up before I get too far down this rabbit hole." He turned the ignition back on and pulled out of the parking lot.

At the hospital...

"I'm sorry, sir, there's no one here by that name." The receptionist frowned and stared at the computer screen in front of her. "Are you sure that's the name?"

Jim ran a hand down the front of his face with an exhale. "Yes, he's my best friend. I got a call saying he was in this hospital after getting beat up pretty badly."

"I'm sorry, sir, but they must have been mistaken. There is no Charles Baskin checked in."

"This makes no sense."

"I'm sorry, but I must ask you to step out of line. Others are waiting."

Jim glanced behind him at the ever-growing line. "Right. Thanks for your time." He sidestepped and got out of line.

"Next," he heard the lady say behind him.

He sighed and made his way outside into the parking lot. He went back to his car and hopped inside. He pulled out his phone and noticed Cynthia had called while he was inside. He dialed her back. "Cyn?"

"Did you get my message?"

"About Charlie? Yeah, I was just calling about that."

"Is he hurt bad?"

"That's just it. He's not here."

A pregnant pause permeated the line. "What are you talking about?"

"He's not here. I just tried to visit him, and the receptionist said no one with his name had checked in today or anytime in the past week. He did get picked up by the ambulance, right?"

"So far as I know. By the time I got out of the bathroom, the place already had cops inside. They asked me a bunch of questions, but Charlie was gone. I assumed he had been transported to the hospital. What the hell's going on?"

"Not sure. Are they still over there?"

"Yeah, but I left for the night. I'm not staying the night at a crime scene with CSI all over the place. Not with this paper due."

"I've got news, but I don't want to say it over the phone. Where are you staying for the night?"

"Is your place still a no-go zone?" Cynthia asked.

"I hadn't checked. Let's swing by and see. If nothing else, one of us can leave our car there and head out. I have something to show you, but it can't be at one of our houses."

"Sounds sketchy, but yeah, alright then. I'll see you there."

"See you soon." Jim hung up and started the engine. "Sketch doesn't even begin to describe it," he muttered to himself and pulled out onto the busy street. "Come to think of it, do I even have a working door at my place after that jackass kicked it in? I guess I can replace it if need be. How hard can installing a door be?" He tossed the phone into the passenger seat and moved back onto the street heading for his home. He zoned out as he drove watching the cityscape pass him by.

"Not like I trust these guys, but they're the only lead I have on whoever's gunning for me. I don't have much choice in this, do I?" he asked himself.

19

———————

"What was so important we can't look at it here?" Cynthia stepped out of her car. "Nice open house by the way." She gestured toward the open doorway without a door. "Cops must have taken the door for evidence or some such, eh? Guess we're not staying here tonight."

"Not unless we want to replace the door in the dark," Jim said with an exhale. "Not to mention I don't have the experience to even know how to do it. I doubt you do either." Jim came over, leaned against her vehicle, and crossed his arms. "We need to head to someplace with wifi so I can show you our newest development. I have your laptop in the back. Let me get it really quick, and I'll hop in yours." He jogged over to his own car and retrieved the device. He slammed the door shut and tucked the electronic under his arm as he swung open her passenger side door. "Alright." He shut the door beside him and plopped it on his lap. "Let's get out of here."

"Right." Cynthia backed up, her head on a swivel, looking behind them as she spoke. "Are you planning on giving me a hint as to what you're being so cryptic about? Or are you trying to keep it a surprise? Also, did you notice if my document is still on there?"

"I saved it, yes. I figured you wanted it backed up." Jim smiled with a wry grin. "Thank me later. The note from before essentially gave a url along with a note." He pointed ahead. "That place should have wifi."

"You'd know this how?" she asked with a roll of her eyes while slowing down. "Stop here for coffee often?"

"Actually, yes. Now stop interrupting if you please. I've got some news. You remember the envelope from before?"

Cynthia's jovial smile disappeared. "Yes, and regarding that, I haven't had any luck finding Charlie either. You're sure they said they hadn't seen him at the hospital?"

"Yes. I annoyed the nurse about four times asking and spelling out his name. He hasn't been there. Now so far as this envelope business - get your laptop and we'll see together, since I haven't had a chance to look at it yet either. It gave me an address about who my supposed final target is before they leave me alone. Personally, I don't believe them. Not when they won't show their faces to me."

"Wouldn't expect them to." Cynthia opened the laptop sitting on her lap and pushed the power button. "Give it a minute." She looked out the window to her side. "Will this ever be done, you think?"

"I'm sure it will. You worried?"

"Damn right I am."

"Right."

Cynthia looked back at the screen when the bootup music played. She typed the password in and pressed the enter button. "Give me that." She held her hand out and grabbed the paper when it was given. "I don't recognize this kind of address."

"It's not on the regular internet is why. It's a deep net address. Did I uninstall that browser already?"

"I don't recognize the installer here. Is this your handiwork? Thanks for installing random programs on my work laptop without asking."

"Had to be done. You know how it is."

"Right. So I just install this, wait for it to work itself out and connect to the network, and then type this in?"

Jim grunted. "About the large and small of it. Easy enough to figure it out, huh?"

"Not difficult." She squinted her eyes and typed out the address slowly in the darkened cabin. "Turn the light on, yeah? This is going to give me a headache otherwise."

Jim reached up and switched on the cabin light. "Better?"

"Much better."

She finished typing the address and pressed enter. "Now we wait for the moment of truth. Did they say who this target was?" Her eyes ran down the printed note. "Of course not. Just that they're behind the damned child cases around here. Cryptic as always. As for this boon they mentioned, we better hope they hid it well. The cops are combing my place over."

"We'll see. We'll worry about that part for later. Right now my priorities are where Charlie is and about this kingpin."

"He was in no condition to get up and walk out." She saw the screen change to the one Jim saw earlier detailing their supposed target. "This is the guy?"

"According to that group, yeah." Jim said, leaning over and looking at the screen. "You ever heard of him?"

"Everybody's heard of Oswald Planter in passing. It's not

like I researched the guy before. He owns a chain of grocery stores across the country. Why?"

"Think about it," Jim said, elbowing her in the side gently. "He has a supply chain of trucks to transport kids, warehouses to house them, and all it would take is a few corrupt workers to make it work."

"You believe them?"

"I don't take them at their word, no." Jim shook his head. "I do see how it would work though. I'd have to do some investigating."

"Even if he is, I don't believe they'd stop hounding even if you do this." Cynthia's eyes danced down the lines of text of the screen as she spoke. "This all stinks of them trying to recruit you if you ask me."

"I'm not joining these people. They're useful, but I'm not joining them."

"At least you still have some sense," Cynthia said, placing the laptop on the dash between them. "How do you propose investigating a bigwig like this? You can't just walk up to the guy or stalk him. He's bound to hire private security, especially if he traffics children as you suspect. I don't see a way for you to confirm any of their intelligence without exposing yourself."

"They don't know their first assassin is dead yet," Jim said. "It follows that they think I'm going to die soon to the best of their knowledge. While he will have a bodyguard and perhaps even more than a few men, I have an idea."

"I'm not going to like this, am I?" Cynthia asked with a whining voice "What numbskull plan are you concocting this time?"

Jim reached over and rested a hand on her shoulder, showing a reassuring smile. "Do you trust me?"

"Yeah. Now answer the question. The seduction play's not going to work."

"Excuse the hell out of me for trying to be comforting, but fine." Jim cleared his throat and continued. "It gives his daily routine on that page," he said pointing at the screen. "I can watch from a distance. I'd just look like traffic from his security's point of view."

"Until they notice that car's been following them for a prolonged period. They're trained to notice such things I'm pretty sure."

"What do you suggest?" Jim asked.

"It said in there where he keeps the kids if you actually read the whole thing. You skimmed it, didn't you?"

"I was in a hurry."

"It says where he keeps the kids. I can't believe I'm about to say this as a law student, but I think a little breaking and entering is called for here." Cynthia winced. "I never said that officially."

"Right. You want me to add cat burglar to my resumé? If the kids are there, there's going to be security, alarms, guards, etc."

"Not if there really are kids there."

"I don't follow."

"Of course. Think about it." Cynthia tapped the side of her head with her index finger. "The dude isn't going to want a loud ass alarm system if he's illegally storing kids there. At most there might be a guard or two. Maybe they're honest, maybe they're not. Your worst obstacle would be the locked doors they inevitably have there."

"I can't pick locks. What would you have me do? Break them down, causing everybody to know I was there?"

"Obviously not. See, there is this thing called the internet."

"You're not saying what I think you are?"

"It's time to learn how to lock pick from videos on the internet."

"I'd have to practice on something before I'd want to go there. You realize that. Assuming I can regularly unlock the practice door, I'd do it. You have a place in mind?"

Cynthia nodded. "Policeman told me I'd be fine to come back and sleep in my own house."

"Weird how when it's my house, they kick me out; but when it's you, it's different."

"No one was dead in my house. Besides, who knows police procedures besides the police themselves? I don't pretend to. The point is, we can go back to my place tonight and practice. You can go tomorrow night, and hopefully this whole business will be settled. You'll either have your proof he is trafficking kids, or he's not. One or the other."

"If he is?" Jim asked. "What then?"

"You'll do what you want I assume. I doubt he'll be at the warehouse himself, but at least you'll have proof. Think of this as your superhero moment." Her voice turned dramatic. "You swoop into the warehouse in the dead of night, sneaking past guards, and setting kids free. You drop them off at their houses, and when you're at last done you plot to give the big baddie his just desserts."

"You are so full of shit." Jim couldn't conceal the grin appearing on his face.

"You were the one who always worshiped those comic superheroes as a kid."

"Granted," Jim said. "Now let's do some recon on this place I'm breaking into before we go too far here." He reached up to the laptop and set about researching the warehouse location he was given. "It looks like it's not too far away."

"It's in a quiet part of town - it's almost all industrial there. You evade security, and it looks like you're in." Cynthia leaned over, studying the picture he'd pulled up. She pointed to the screen. "It has a checkpoint leading in, so the front door's out."

"It has a fence around the perimeter. What do you suggest?"

"You can't climb that. For all we know it's an electric fence," Cynthia said. "What about that?" She pointed to the edge of the picture. "See that road behind?"

"Yeah, it looks like the official employee entrance or exit."

"It only has one guard box area thingy," Cynthia said. "That's your best chance."

"This is quickly becoming a full-fledged job. You think I can sneak past a security guard there?"

"It's better than trying your luck against three at the front gate. It'd be a lot easier if you had a distraction. Now who do we know that could do that?"

"You don't mean?"

"Oh right. I could do that. Thanks for suggesting it."

"What possible reason could you have to want in when they ask?" Jim asked. "They will ask. You know that."

"I'll just make something up. I was wanting a statement from them for a paper I'm doing for college."

"You're a law student."

"They don't know that. For all they know I'm some liberal arts student worried about cruelty to animals. I'll hound the guard about their meat products being inhumane. Don't worry, they won't be focusing on you slipping inside. They'll be too busy dealing with me."

"Seems it's settled then. I just need to study the places layout. I don't want to get lost once I'm inside the place or while getting out. I'll bring a pocket camera just to make extraction easier."

"How would that work?"

"I don't want to try and get them out by myself while sneaking out. I'll get in, find them, get out, and call it in. Before I leave, I'll take a picture and send that with my report to the police. They can't ignore that then. If I spray paint the container, they can't miss it. We'll have to buy a can of that before we go."

"Let's get back to your place then. We'll see how many police are still at my house, and we'll get ready. You can study there too. Also, get a cup of coffee because it sounds like you'll need all the energy you can get for tonight."

"What I wouldn't give for you to say that under other circumstances," Jim said with a waggle of his eyebrows and a lascivious grin.

"Sometimes I wonder if boys ever grow up."

Later that night...

"I feel like I'm planning a robbery hiding in this damned bush," Cynthia said in a hushed whisper.

"Don't worry. You're not planning a robbery." Jim placed a hand on her shoulder. He smiled. "You're planning a breaking and entering."

Her voice was soaked in sarcasm. "That's a lot better."

"When it's to save children, it is." He gently poked the tip of her nose as he spoke.

"Of course." She exhaled. She looked at the guard checkpoint about fifty feet in front of them. She looked over her shoulder at the car they drove to get here. "I'll go back to the car and gather some of my notebooks and such. When I get back, will you be ready?"

"Need some props to really sell it? Yeah, I'll be ready by then." Jim pulled on a black ski mask and his leather gloves.

"What am I doing with my life?" Cynthia asked herself as she got out of the bush and walked back to the car.

"More like what am I doing to your life?" Jim watched her leave. His eyes turned back to the checkpoint, mentally running simulations of what was about to happen. "The best option, ironically, is moving right in front of her. He won't be looking down in front of the counter when she's bitching at him. The camera mounted on top of the building wouldn't see me from there either. I'll have to zip left and avoid the camera on the right side of the building I'm going in."

"Right where the door is, that's where you're going in." Cynthia returned to the bush carrying a large red three ring binder. "Just be careful inside. There's no telling how many are in there or where they are. The good news is if the kids are in there, there likely aren't any guards; or if there are, they're corrupt and in on it. Still, don't shoot unless you have to. It'll make getting out ten times harder."

"I'm not looking to alert the whole place. You just do your part, and I'll manage somehow," Jim whispered back.

"Are you ready?"

"Whenever you are."

Cynthia backed out of the cover and made her way back to the car. She opened the door and reached inside. She carried the binder in her arms and bumped the door shut with her hip. She marched over to the guard station.

A man's voice met Jim's ears. "Yes, miss? How can I help you?"

Jim crept through the foliage and broke through to the

other side. He veered to his right, staying out of the guard's line of sight until he got perpendicular to the outpost. His crouched form approached from the side.

Cynthia took a step back. "What do you mean? I was told over the phone that I'd be allowed to get some answers."

Jim took the opportunity to pass by under the window as the two bickered.

"I wasn't informed of any visitors tonight, miss. I'm sorry," the man's voice said. "I'm going to have to ask you to leave now."

Jim passed the checkpoint and made for the nearest cover near the building. A large delivery truck was parked next to the tall chain link fence.

Cynthia glanced over to where Jim disappeared behind the vehicle and looked back to the guard. "Fine. I don't know what I'm going to tell my professor. He'll give me an F for this you know." She sighed and put on her best puppy dog face. "I'll just leave and fail this semester then." She turned away from the building, her shoulders slumped, and walked back to her car.

Jim watched her get in and drive away. "She should get to my extraction point in a few minutes. It'll leave more than enough time for me to get in and out," he said under his breath.

He peeked around the back corner of the large truck. "No patrols out here. The cameras are all I need to worry about it looks like." He looked over at the nearby guard station. The back door he could see remained shut. "The quicker I go, the quicker I'm out." He looked away from the building toward his main objective. "Camera's there." He looked up at the surveillance camera mounted to his right. He looked to the left at numerous other delivery trucks parked. "There's my route." He looked over his shoulder, seeing no movement from the guard outpost.

"It's now or never." Jim ducked out of cover to his left and rushed over to the next truck. He dashed out of the newfound cover all the way to the main building, staying away from the stationary camera mounted on the side of the building. He put his back to the side of the building and looked to his right, spotting a door leading inside. "Now to just open this, and I'm golden." He trudged over and got to a knee. "Let's hope this works." He got out his lockpick and got to work.

Seconds turned to minutes until he heard a click. He looked over his shoulder and saw nobody. He put the lockpick back in his pocket and grabbed the unregistered gun out of the back of his belt line. He stood up, got ready, reached forward with his left hand, and pulled the door open. He slipped inside once he saw the inside was vacant and shut the door behind him.

He made for a nearby stack of crates and placed his back to it. He heard a faint voice from somewhere in the building, getting louder as the seconds passed. "Yeah, I'm just going to go get some coffee. You want me to get you anything?" a female voice asked. "Alright. Two black coffees it is. I'll be a little while. I can't believe they still haven't given this building a coffee machine."

The sounds of footsteps got closer. Jim bit his lower lip, seeing a shadow get closer to his hiding place. He sidestepped away to the opposite side of the crates as she approached. He peeked around the corner as his intruder stepped ever closer and turned the corner just before the woman circled around the corner and swiftly opened the door he'd just entered.

He heard the door close behind him. He remembered

back to the document he was given, recalling the numbers he didn't understand. Looking at the crate beside him, it clicked. The numbers indicated which crate the children were supposedly inside of. "Judging from these numbers increasing, the one I'm looking for is a little further ahead." Jim barely spoke to himself above a whisper.

His feet moved fast, but not enough to draw attention as he progressed further into the warehouse of sorts. He kept track of the numbers on the side of every box he passed and mentally had a better guess where his target was with every number.

Eventually he stopped when he'd found the number he was looking for. He peeked around the nearby corner and saw what could only have been the man he'd heard talking earlier walking his way. "Fuck," Jim said under his breath. He positioned himself around the corner from the man and readied his right fist.

Once his quarry got into view on his right, he blind-sided the man with a punch to the side of the skull, causing him to fall to his left. The man crumpled to the ground, his head smacking against the concrete below with a wet sound.

Jim pounced on the man's body only to find him knocked out. "Don't know if it was from the punch or your head bouncing off the floor, but I'm not arguing," Jim said to himself. Without further pause, he got back to the steel shipping container. "Shit, how do you open these again?"

He twisted the two metal pieces above the right side handles until they were above them. "I think that's right." He gripped the two metal handles and rotated them the only way they would move, outward until a loud metal noise erupted from the crate. Once that noise was gone, it was replaced with muffled talking inside. "Son of a bitch," he said to himself as he yanked the now unlocked door out toward him with a high pitched noise.

He could barely see in the dark shipping container but could make out the sound of numerous squeaks and shushed whispers. "Are you kids alright?" he instinctively asked. "I'm not here to hurt you. I'm here to get you out of this and back home." He squinted, barely making out the silhouettes chained to fixtures on the walls of the container.

One brave young boy near him dared speak up. "Who are you? How are you going to get us out, mister? We're chained in here, and I'm betting you don't have the key."

"Call me Masked Justice. I don't need a key. I'm not doing the heavy lifting myself. I'm getting out of here and calling this in. The police will get you out and back to your families. "I just need to do one thing before calling to be sure they answer." He dug into his back pants pocket and retrieved the handheld camera. "Say cheese."

"What does that mean?" The boy asked as a flash of light erupted from the handheld device in Jim's hands. "That hurt my eyes, mister."

"You'll thank me when a policeman is getting you all out of here. Without this picture they might think this is a prank. I won't let that happen. Now I'm going to have to close this back up, but within an hour you all will be free. I promise on my mother's life."

"Please don't leave us." A different voice begged. The little girl struggled against the bindings around her wrist.

Another small boy beside the girl shook his head. "Don't leave us alone in the dark again, sir. It's scary in here. I want to go home to mom now. I don't want that scary guard to come in here again. Just get us out now."

Jim could hear the desperation in the children's voices.

His voice grew soft. "I'm sorry. Look, I already knocked out the scary guard. He won't be coming in here again."

"You promise?" the little boy asked.

"I promise. They won't hurt you anymore. All I ask is for you to be brave, and you'll be home before you know it." He backed up as he spoke. He grabbed the two swinging metal doors.

"Please no!" The voices became muffled as he slammed the doors shut. He didn't bother relocking the container. He could hear quiet yelling from inside as he got the spray paint out and shook it. He painted a red 'x' on the side of the corrugated metal container and turned to the guard he knocked out earlier. "You son of a bitch," he whispered under his breath before turning toward the door he entered and jogged back.

He heard the door open and quickly ducked around the nearest stack of boxes. He circled around as the footsteps got louder. He managed to push the still closing door open and sprinted as fast as he could manage back toward the guard station. He crouched and got below the guard's sight line. He got off the property and got back to the car they rode in.

He slammed the door shut with a sigh. "They were in there alright. Now take us to the nearest payphone."

"Do those still exist?"

"I've seen one by the post office, so take us there. I can't call on my own phone."

"Got it," Cynthia said, starting the car. "How did it go in there?" she asked, pulling out of the parking lot. "It better have gone well, because that guard has been eying me up and down while you were in there. He probably thought I was up to something."

"You were."

"That's not the point."

"There was only one guy in there while I was there," Jim said, buckling his safety belt.

She gave him a sideways look. "You managed to open a steel crate while there was a guard inside? What? Was he deaf?"

"Not really. I knocked him out."

"Knocked him out? This isn't a tv show. How did you manage that?"

"I hid behind a corner, waited for him to come around, and punched him."

"Jesus, you might have killed the guy. Did you at least catch him as he fell?"

"Considering I was scared shitless, and the kids afterward said he was evil, no, I didn't. He'll be fine. It was just a punch."

"You and I both hope so. Because if he is dead, I don't know." Cynthia said, pulling up to the post office. "Now go make your call. I'll stay in here. There's a camera up there," she said, pointing up to the right. "Keep your back to it if you know what's good for you."

"Got it, be right back." Jim threw the door open. He kept his back turned to the camera she pointed out and ducked into the pay phone booth. He dialed the same number he'd memorized all those years ago when he started his hobby.

"Yes, this is the police, state your emergency." A monotone male voice answered.

Jim spoke in a slightly deeper voice. "There is a shipping container full of children at the Small Grizzly warehouse located on 1679 Helos Street. I believe they are being trafficked. You need to send people there now." Without waiting for a response, he hung up and returned to the car with Cynthia.

"That was fast."

Jim closed the door. "I wasn't trying to recite an epic, just telling them what I know without giving away any personal information. Now let's go home for the night. I need to send them this picture I found to cement it. They'll have to move after they see this." He whipped out the handheld electronic camera and pulled up the photo he recently took. "See this? It's inhumane. These are the kind of people we're dealing with."

Cynthia leaned over and took a look at the picture with children chained by their necks to the wall. She could see a bucket between every few children. "Christ. That's what you found?"

"Yeah. It broke my heart too. They were begging me to get them out right then. There was no way I could manage that though, you know. So, I promised them I'd call it in and get the police to free them."

"They just left them in that dark room, for how long?" She started the engine and resumed the trek home.

"No telling. It could have been for days, weeks, or even months. They look pretty skinny to me," Jim said, looking down at the miniature screen. "I'll put this on my laptop, use a vpn, and send it from a public network to the police. It's why I'm in a hurry. I want those kids out of that hellhole."

"I get it," Cynthia said. "Those poor kids. They don't deserve that. I don't think I'd have had the heart to leave after seeing that," she said, turning the wheel.

"It hurt me doing it, but I knew I couldn't pick that many locks, get them all to follow me out without anyone noticing, or fitting them all in here. No offense."

"None taken. You're probably right, but it doesn't change their situation."

"No. It doesn't." Jim's voice turned somber. "We're getting

them out as soon as I get home, I'm sending the police this picture. They can't ignore that, right?"

"It's invalid evidence if it goes to court, but at least by the time that would happen, the kids would be home safe."

"That's what's important in my book," Jim said. "Now get us home. I have a job to finish."

"I can't wait to get some sleep tonight," she said. "School's been rough lately."

"I haven't helped with that I'm sure."

"No, you haven't."

"You could at least lie to make me feel better."

"With you?" She looked over when she came to a stop at a stop sign. "Never."

"Stone cold."

"That's what they teach you in law school."

20

"There," Jim said with a press of the enter key. "They now have the photo of the kids, That along with the anonymous tip I gave earlier should get their asses over there tonight."

"By tomorrow morning it'll be on the news, and everyone will know." Cynthia yawned. "You're sure you took all the necessary precautions? The last thing you need is police coming and asking why you had such pictures."

"I used a vpn, created a new email on the deep web, and used a public wifi. It's as much as I can do."

"Not much else to do on that front then. I look forward to the news report tomorrow morning. It should cast public doubt on Oswald. He'll be scrambling with such bad press. Someone's going down for a hot minute, but I doubt he'll be the one."

"Even if he was the mastermind?"

She sent a sarcastic glare over toward him. "You think a millionaire will admit fault? No, he's going to blame his subordinates and play the victim." She tried to imitate a male's voice. "Well, I had no ideas such atrocities were being committed on my property. I will hire more security, fire those responsible, and hope they get the maximum penalty the law deems appropriate." Her voice returned to normal. "I can see it now.

"He'd have to worry about them squealing though."

"Squeal what?" Cynthia asked. "You think the big boss man ever talked to them and let them know he was in on it? Odds are, if the guards are in on it, they're talking to a middleman between the owner and the traffickers. They won't know shit."

"This was a band-aid fix then?"

"If you must look at this from a negative light, yes, I guess it was. Just remember you saved all those kids from a horrific place. They won't know your name, but they'll always remember you for the rest of their lives. That has to mean something."

"I'll tell you what I'll remember the rest of my life." Jim sat the laptop down beside him on the couch. "I recall the smell. It was outright rancid. There were buckets every few kids filled with waste. I'll never forget their desperation when they were begging me to get them out right then. When I told them I'd have them out inside of an hour, their faces contorted into pure fear. They pleaded, begged, and grabbed for me as if I was the last life jacket on a sinking ship. That's what I'll remember."

"Christ." Cynthia leaned her head over to Jim's shoulder and rested it. "Don't focus on that. Think about how those kids will be back in school thinking of ways to sneak out of classes like you used to. Imagine that decades down the line they'll be telling their kids about the time a man saved them from a dark hell."

"You're right. Of course you are," Jim said. "Now what should we do for Oswald Planter? He's in on it. He has to be.

There's no way someone could use his warehouse without his go ahead. I won't rest until he's either behind bars or taken care of."

"You realize this little crusade is never ending?" She angled her face to look up at him. "You're never going to catch them all. You'd get yourself killed a hundred times over before you even made a dent. There will always be one more job. You know that."

"Maybe, but when has that line of thinking ever stopped me before? To me that just means that someone has to start working on it."

"You really are an idiot. The hero complex is a dangerous thing, and you're developing it right before my eyes. I don't think you realize how scared I am of it." She broke eye contact and nuzzled into his neck. Her next words were muffled yet audible. "I don't want to wake up one day and either see you on television or get that phone call from your parents once your luck runs out. You can't chase bad guys your whole life. You're not Superhero dude over here. You're a simple human with dreams bigger than your body can cash."

"Thanks for the vote of confidence," Jim said, a sarcastic bite in his voice. His left arm raised up and fell over Cynthia's shoulder, pulling her close. "For right now, I'm happy. That has to count for something." He rested his chin on the top of her head, a faint smile gracing his features.

"Oh, crap." Cynthia pulled away from the embrace. "We never did look to see what they left. Remember? They promised a supposed boon when they beat the shit out of Charlie."

"Who left? Oh right, in the note they said they left us something." She pulled Jim up to a standing position and led them outside into her backyard. "It said under the balcony in the garden, right?" She hopped down onto the grass covered backyard. She looked over at a small patch of dirt. "There's the garden." She looked up and pointed. "There. See that?"

Jim looked above to see the bottom of the balcony on her second floor. He could see something white against the black backdrop only because of the full moon above. "It looks like an envelope," he said, squinting into the relative darkness. He reached up and jumped, grabbing for the white object to no avail.

He squatted and looked back at her. "Get on my shoulders."

"We're not teenagers anymore," Cynthia said.

"Put your embarrassment aside. I can't grab it. Get on my shoulders and grab the thing."

"Alright, but you better not enjoy it." Cynthia carefully stepped over Jim's form and sat down on his shoulder.

He grabbed the side of her legs wrapped around his head to keep her steady and slowly got back to his feet, making sure to keep her steady all the while. "I do not mind this."

"I bet you don't, pervert." Cynthia reached above her and grasped the envelope. She untied it from the short length of wire. "Stop rubbing your cheeks on my thighs and get me down already."

"Can't a guy have a little fun every now and then? Oh fine then." He lowered himself to one knee and let her get back onto the ground.

She extricated herself from him and grabbed his arm with her free hand, leading him inside. "Let's get inside and read this. It's a little late now, but you never know if it could be useful." She led the pair inside and over to the dining table where her laptop was sitting. She tore open the envelope and read in silence for a moment before handing it over without a word.

"What's up?" Jim asked, taking the paper. "Let's see here. Your friend is fine. We are sorry for the mess we all caused. Regarding the boon we promised, you will find it at the bottom of this message." He read it aloud.

"It's a web address it looks like," Cynthia said from beside him. "I'm not sure how a web address is supposed to help you take down the guy, but we'll see."

"We shall see. Let me see your laptop for a minute," Jim said, holding his hand out at his side without looking.

"What's the magic word?" Cynthia asked.

"Please?"

"Correct. See? Manners cost nothing, and yet you rarely use them with your best friend. Was that so hard?"

"Pedantic as always I see." Jim opened the deep web browser and started typing in the seemingly random string of numbers and letters. "Let's see here. I'm almost done."

"There's nothing more annoying than having to type all those random inputs. They couldn't just leave a thumb drive with the url," Cynthia pouted. "That'd be too easy."

"That's their style." Jim pressed the enter button. "Now let's see what they left me."

The page loaded showing a play button at the bottom, a timeline, and a volume indicator along with a black screen above them.

"It's a video." Cynthia got closer to Jim's side and leaned forward.

Jim clicked play. The black screen disappeared, being replaced by a video feed of the warehouse from above, taken by drone. White text appeared on the screen. He paused and read the text. "You may think us nothing but ruthless killers, but this should help you save the children being held in the shipping container. Pay attention to this before you go to maximize any rescue attempt."

"Oops," Jim said.

"No kidding."

The video feed from above cut to a security camera footage from inside the warehouse. "That's inside the place. I remember because," he pointed toward the top of the screen, "that's the box they were being held in."

The same distorted voice from their meetings spoke over the video feed. "Inside there are two guards stationed. One is an honest guard who does nothing but his job. The other is the one running interference and keeping the children quiet. The male guard is just trying to make ends meet. He is dutiful and does his best at the job. If one of the two patrols, odds are it's him. The other guard, that's the scum of the pair." The voice paused. "She occasionally gets coffee for the two of them and appears to have a nice working relationship. What her partner does not know is when he leaves for the night or for any appreciable length of time, she keeps the kids in line."

The boring static video of the empty warehouse fast forwarded. The male guard left via a nearby door. The female guard watched him leave and moved toward the door he exited. She cracked it open and peered through before turning back toward the shipping container Jim motioned toward earlier. She opened the door with deft movements and moved inside.

"Oh my Lord," Cynthia said, covering her mouth. "Is that the guard you knocked out?"

Jim didn't answer verbally, choosing instead to watch the video.

She came back out of the box and pointed at one of the

occupants before saying something. She slammed the doors shut and relocked them.

"No," Jim said. "I overheard the woman going to get coffee. I figured the one staying behind was the dirty one. It makes sense. It'd give him time to check on the kids."

"You were wrong. You knocked out the wrong guy, and the woman is still on the loose," Cynthia said at his side. "Did I get that right?"

"Why don't you just rub it in my face? I preferred it when I was rubbing my face against your thi-"

Cynthia's face lit up in a fierce blush. She smacked him in the shoulder hard. "Stop deflecting already. Be serious for a minute. This is big."

Jim didn't respond for a minute before answering. "Yeah. It is." His voice lacked the usual confidence. "I still got the kids out though. That's what matters to me. The corrupt will get their due eventually. If it comes to saving the kids or violence, I choose the kids."

"You certainly did that. Now let's head to bed and see what happens. We need to stay rested."

"True that."

The next morning...

Cynthia pushed the door open to Jim's room and stalked over to him, making as little noise as possible. A devious grin was plastered on her face all the while. She placed both hands on his shoulders and inhaled deeply. She shook him as she yelled. "Time to get up, sleepyhead!"

"Christ alive." Jim rolled to the side away from her and fell out of the bed with a loud thump. A moan escaped his lips. "Some things never change I see."

"It's been a hot minute since I've done that." Cynthia tried to hide her laugh but failed. Her muffled laughs erupted behind her hand. "It never gets old; but seriously, get up."

Jim clawed his way to a kneeling position and stood up, completely shirtless, revealing his toned muscled physique. He ran a hand through his hair and scratched his bare chest with the other. "I'm up already. What was so important to wake me up like this?"

She did her best to hide her blush from the still half-asleep man and averted her eyes at the show he was inadvertently putting on. "I heard on the morning news that coming up was a story about a certain little warehouse. I figured we'd both want to see what they have to say."

"I see." Jim rubbed his eyes and focused on her once he was done. "You want to leave the room, or you want to watch me change clothes? It makes no difference to me. Just stand right there and watch. You'll enjoy it."

"You're still a teenager mentally." Cynthia turned around and stepped into the hallway. "Hurry up, it'll be on soon," she said with a slam of the white wooden door.

Jim got to work putting on what few clothes he had and followed after her into the main living room area. "I'm here." He plopped down on the sofa facing the television next to Cynthia. "Did I make it?"

"Quiet." She shushed him as the news show came back from commercials.

The television showed a man and woman sitting in front of a large desk. "Welcome back, everyone," said the male newscaster. "We have breaking news that a large shipping container full of children was found at a nearby warehouse owned by Oswald Planter. Investigators suspect they were to be sold to the highest bidder. Sources say one child at the hospital credited a 'Masked Justice' with their rescue from the inhumane circumstances."

"Masked Justice?" Cynthia asked. "That was the best you could come up with? You sound like a Saturday morning cartoon vigilante."

"It was spur of the moment, alright? I didn't have a lot of time for my PR spiel."

The woman to his left spoke up. "That's not all. One of the guards was found knocked to the ground when police got there. An ambulance was called while the man remained lucid enough to answer questions. Unfortunately, when he arrived at the hospital he was unconscious." Her tone turned dour. "Shortly after, he was dead. Medical experts suspect a subdural hematoma from apparent head trauma."

"Excuse me?" Jim said, voice raised. "I just punched the guy once. That's all, and now you're telling me he's dead?" He raised a hand to his face with a moan. "This can't be happening."

"Oh my God." Cynthia's hands both covered her nose and mouth. Her muffled voice came through. "Look at what we've done. An innocent man is dead. It's all because of us."

"Our own Tricia is at the scene."

The camera cut to the inside of the warehouse with two women standing. The one with a microphone raised it to her mouth as she spoke. "Thank you. We have a witness to what happened last night. Miss Cassie Washington, please tell us what you saw."

"Well, Tricia, I went out to get us our evening coffees as I normally do. Burt was acting the same as he always does, but when I got back inside he was already on the ground. Someone had gotten inside and opened the container. I saw all the kids inside." She pointed off screen. "I immediately ran to the office and called the police, and here we are." She covered her mouth, tears threatening to fall as her voice faltered. "I just can't believe Burt was party to something like this."

"The bitch is even trying to play the hero in all this," Jim said, a scowl on his face. "She's the one who was keeping the kids under lock and key."

"Thank you, Miss Washington. Back to you in the studio."

Jim reached for the remote and turned the television off.

"It was smart." Cynthia's voice was frail and far away sounding. "She saw the guy's body lying there, so she called the police, knowing it was going to be found either way. She got ahead of it."

Jim turned to her after hearing her brittle voice. "Are you alright?"

"I just..." She stood up and walked around to the back of the couch, "I can't do this right now." She marched back to her room and slammed the door shut, leaving Jim all by his lonesome in the living room.

His head sagged forward, his body slumping into the couch. "What am I doing?" He leaned forward, cradling his head in his hands. "This isn't why I started doing this - to have an innocent man end up dead by my hand." He fought back tears as he spoke through his hands.

He looked up from his self-inflicted pity party with renewed hatred in his eyes. "Oswald's the reason for all this. To avenge the innocent, he has got to go down." His eyes softened. "Is that for justice," he looked down at his clenched right fist, "or for my own conscience? Who knows or cares anymore. I'm finishing this thing soon come hell or high water."

21

"Why are you on my laptop?" Cynthia asked as she walked into the main room. The fading light from outside the nearby windows hit her form. Her eyes were red and puffy, indicating crying had been done earlier.

"I do still work during the day you know," Jim said, typing as he spoke.

"Just working? Nothing else?"

Jim spared her a momentary glance before looking back at the monitor. "Mostly."

"What does that mean? You're not done after this morning?"

"The kingpin is still at large. If I don't complete this, they'll come after us again. You know that as well as I do."

"Damn the consequences?" Cynthia asked.

"I'm broke up about that, but it doesn't change that we're still under the literal gun here. I don't want to die. I don't want you to die. It's that simple as I see it."

"Fine," she said with an exasperated sigh. "I'll help with this one last thing, but I'm done after this. You understand me? Done with all this. I also want you to go back to your place when we're done with this."

"You're..." Jim trailed off, his face contorting to a face of sadness, "kicking me out?"

"You heard me," she said, a sullen tone to her voice.

"You can't mean that." Jim slid the laptop to the side. "I didn't mean to kill that guy. You know me. It was one punch."

"It doesn't change what happened. An innocent man is dead because of us. I can't be party to this anymore after this job. I just can't. I could lose my license to practice law after I graduate. My future is at stake while you're still doing this crusade of yours. Answer me this." She crossed her arms, a stern look on her face. "Are you planning on stopping this whole thing?"

Jim remained silent and looked away.

"That's what I thought. Now that that's out of the way, what's your plan for this?"

"I can get out now if you want." Jim pushed the chair out from the dining table and stood up. "I'd rather you not feel worse than you already do." He turned around and started walking when he felt her hand grasping his and holding him still.

"Just listen to me for once, you dumbass. I said I'll help this one last time, and I meant it. I'm involved now too whether I like it or not. So let's fix this."

"Alright." He turned to face her and moved back to the table. He placed both hands on the table and leaned forward. "See that?"

She moved beside him and looked at the monitor, "I see Planter's house. At least I assume that's his house. It's posh enough to be his."

"Correct," Jim said. "We got the kids out. Now to take out the mastermind."

"I assume you have a plan. That place looks defended. I see a guard just from here." She gestured toward the screen showing a visibly armed man patrolling left to right on the screen in the darkened front yard. "It looks like a fortress. I don't see a way you can get in and out without being seen."

"It's one guard. I've been watching this feed for the last hour while working on the side. He keeps one guard on duty at all times."

"You just keep this feed up at all times? Also, how did you even find this? Why is there a stream of the front of his house?"

"One question at a time. Yes, a quick search, and there's some disgruntled customer upset with Oswald after the news today. She's been protesting outside his house all day on a livestream. It doubles as surveillance for me."

"You're going to attempt to sneak in there with a pissed off Karen watching the front all night? This is a dumb plan."

Jim shook his head, "I never said the front. Logic says if there's a front entrance, there's a back entrance. Look, I've done a background check on the guy." He pulled up a different window showing the website he used before.

"You can't just run a background check on some guy on a whim."

"Says who? You underestimate the internet." He showed the results he'd gathered earlier. "See? He's divorced, living separate from his wife and kid."

"So, he had a gold digger wife. What's that got to do with this?"

"It means," Jim tapped the side of his head, "that he's in there alone. I have a genius plan to get in and out quietly. I even have a back-up plan in case that one isn't relevant. Plan one is to get in the house and cut the gas line. It'll look like an accident."

"Couldn't that blowback on other nearby houses? I'm not a scientist, but it seems like if it exploded, it'd travel back through the city pipes. I don't like this idea."

"If he has his own tank out back, it'd be fine. However, in case he doesn't, I have a second idea. I get in, take care of him while he's asleep, and get out quietly. No chance of innocents getting caught in the crossfire."

"Okay, that'd be fine. Do you have a plan on getting inside?"

"Sneak in like I did the warehouse. That lockpicking video should serve us well. It's fresh in my mind."

"If he has an alarm system?"

"You have an answer for everything." Jim bit his lower lip.

"He lives close to the police station. You'd have approximately five minutes. It'd be cutting it close. Neither of us know how to disarm a system. You'd either have to bail or rush."

"That's a risk we'll have to take. I'll make a judgement call. There's just one thing I want you to promise me." Jim turned to her and grabbed her hands. "If you hear sirens, I want you to get out of there and leave me. I'm prepared for that."

"Yeah."

"That's it?"

"Yes."

"I expected at least a 'I can't just leave you' or something. Jesus, alright fine." Jim released her hands. "Make sure you carry a mask just in case. You won't be going inside, but I don't want you anywhere near this. We'll take my car to be safe."

"It's far too late to keep me away from this you know," her flat voice said.

"Yeah. Anyway, we'll park around the back, I'll hop the small fence once the guard passes by, lockpick the door, and do what I'm going there for."

"Murder. Don't try and church it up. You're planning a murder here."

Jim paused, seeing her staring at him. "Let's get this started."

Later that night out back of Oswald Planter's house…

"Remember, keep that mask on hand. Don't put it on until you have to. It'll be suspicious otherwise."

"I'll try to keep that in mind. Now go murder the man. Christ, look at my life. This is what it's come to. It's all because of you."

Jim donned his own black mask and put on his leather gloves. He made sure his knife was where it was supposed to be along with his unregistered firearm tucked into his belt line. "I know it doesn't mean much coming from me," he locked eyes with Cynthia in the driver's seat, "but I am sorry. Not just for getting you involved with all this, but for the way I am. But I cannot change how I am. I'll be back in a few minutes." He saw the guard turn the corner and disappear from view.

She did not respond to him and watched him exit the car.

He jogged up to the waist high fence and hopped over it. He spotted assorted bushes lining the backside of the house along with a swing fence hanging from chains a few feet to the side of the back door. He sneaked across the backyard until finally nearing the house. He heard crunching grass to his right and immediately got into the nearest bush. He laid flat on his stomach as crunching grass got closer.

"I could have sworn I heard something," a male voice said nearby.

Jim saw a circle of light on the ground a few feet away dart further off.

"Nobody's out here besides me. Fine then." The noise of grass being crushed faded away until Jim could no longer see any beams of light from his hiding spot. He crawled out of the bush trying to make as little noise as possible, being only marginally successful. He held his breath as he heard the sound of the guard's footsteps stop again, only to release the breath when he heard them start again. He immediately rushed to the back door and got to work.

The door opened with a quiet click under his ministra- tions. He opened the door and ducked inside, closing it behind him as quietly as he could muster. "No alarm," he whispered to himself. "That's one worry out of the way. Now to double check that no one else is in here. I don't want a repeat of last time. No more innocent blood will be on my hands." He creeped through the near pitch-black interior of the house.

He cleared the ground floor of the house slowly, checking room by room, seeing no other occupants. He felt his way around until he found the stairs leading upstairs. "Paydirt," he said under his breath.

He climbed the stairs, one step at a time. He took his time carefully testing each step, making sure he wouldn't stumble at the top. Reaching the top, he pulled out his knife and gun in each hand. His right hand gripped the firearm tightly. His left hand kept the knife in his grip as he crouched and moved forward.

He stopped in his tracks as he heard muffled cries to his

left. He used his left hand to feel around in the near complete darkness until it bumped into something resembling wood. The noises stopped and were replaced by a voice.

"Please no, sir. Not again. Please not again tonight."

No way, Jim thought. He felt around until he felt the doorknob. He sheathed his weapons and set about lock-picking this door in the dark. It took longer than the backdoor, but eventually a click signaled the door was unlocked. He opened the door, seeing a dimly lit room with what looked like a teenage girl sitting on the bed, looking at him.

"Well, at least if I die tonight, it'd be better than this living hell. Mister, are you going to kill me? You're certainly dressed like a killer," she said.

"What? Good God, no." He stepped inside and closed the door behind him. "Who are you? The intel I had said he didn't have a daughter."

"That psychopath?" She asked in a shrill, but shushed tone. "Fuck no, man. I was bought by him. He's kept me locked up in here for months. He feeds me twice a day, but look around." She gestured to the relatively barren room, barring the television across the room and assorted dressers lining the walls.

"How old are you?"

"Fourteen. Why do you care?"

"Because I'm going to get you out of here and back to your parents. What's your name?"

"Wait, seriously? It's Ashley." She leaned forward, eyes widening. "You're not lying, right?"

"Seriously. Now I have a little business to finish with your kidnapper, and I'll be back to get you out."

"When you said finish business, what does that mean?"

Jim paused a minute and looked over to her. "He won't bother you ever again. Let's put it that way."

"You're going to kill him? Good fucking riddance."

"Quite. Now just stay quiet in here, Ashley, and I'll be right back. Do you know where his room is by chance?"

"Of course I do. The sick asshole doesn't take me in here. He drags me to his bed first." She hopped off the bed. "I'm going to accompany you and watch. Don't worry I'll be quiet."

"You shouldn't see it. Trust me when I say it'll leave a mark on your psyche."

"My psyche is beyond fucked. Seeing that dickhead bleed will help more than anything after all he's done to me. This isn't a discussion. I'm coming along."

"Just stay behind me and stay quiet then. Don't do anything crazy, and we'll be good. You got it?"

"I understand." She walked over to him. "Let's go then. What was your name again?"

Jim sighed. "Call me Masked Justice."

"Oh my God. You're him? The guy who rescued a bunch of kids from that warehouse?" She circled around him. "Now you're here to get me out too."

"Yes. Now please," he raised a finger to his lips in a shushing motion, "let me deal with your captor."

"Yes sir."

"Good." He gestured her over and grabbed the doorknob leading out into the corridor. "Here we go. Last chance to not have to witness this."

"Not a chance."

"On your head be it." He twisted the knob and gently pulled the door open. He got out into the hallway with his newest companion. He felt a hand on his shoulder. He looked over it to see Ashley pointing further down the hallway to the right. He nodded and continued towards it.

The pair skulked down the hallway. The underweight girl behind him tapped him on the shoulder as they got closer, grabbing his attention as she pointed at the now nearby double doors on their right.

"Right in there," she said, scarcely above a whisper.

"Got it." Jim turned around to face her. "As soon as this is done, we're making a break for the outside. I've got a car waiting, so no loitering around."

"I want out of this shithole - no worries there."

"Right." Jim prepared the knife and gun in his hands.

She grabbed the doorknob, twisted it, and pushed it open for him.

He nodded without a word of thanks and sneaked into the dark room. All he could make out in the room was the vague outline of the bed and an almost inaudible breathing coming from on top of it. He moved beside the bed, and readied his knife. He confirmed where Oswald was in the bed by quite literally feeling the top of the bed. Once he'd hit the giant lump, he knew he'd found his target.

Unfortunately his game of touchy feely awakened the executive from his slumber.

"Hm?" Oswald muttered, rolling to his side, facing Jim. He stopped moving once he felt Jim's arm. "Who the hell?"

Jim didn't bother answering, choosing instead to thrust the knife forward as fast as he could into Oswald's neck - rather, what he assumed was his neck in the near pitch black bedroom. A squelch along with a scream of unadulterated pain erupted from Oswald's mouth. He adjusted his position so he now sat on Oswald's torso. He threw his right hand forward again and again. Blood sprayed all over Jim's black hoodie.

Howls of anguished pain were muffled by Jim's left hand as he pressed his left palm against Oswald's mouth as the stabbings continued. His victim got slower as he thrashed around below him. Sensing his opportunity, he withdrew his right hand one more time and jabbed forward into the executive's throat and twisted the blade before yanking it free.

His latest target brought one hand to his throat and his other to his punctured abdomen, trying in vain to staunch the bleeding. "Let go you piece of shit. Just die already and do everybody a favor." A feral look of bloodlust was painted on Jim's features. He dragged the blade to the side, effectively slitting Oswald's throat.

The body below him gurgled for a minute or more until it stopped moving. He climbed off the bed. "It's done," he said loud enough to be heard by Ashley, who was posted in the doorway staring at the spectacle.

"Fucking hell. You really killed him," he could hear her say.

"Yeah." Jim slid past her and got back into the hallway. He looked down at his now blood drenched hoodie. "Shit. I can't go outside like this or someone will call the cops on me."

"Just take something of his then. It's not like he needs it anymore."

"Fuck it. I'll just go like this. I don't want to spend any more time here, and I doubt you do either. Now let's get out of here and get you back home." He gestured for her to follow him down the hallway and back down the stairs. "We're going out the back door. We'll have to hop a fence, and the car is right there. Can you manage that?"

"I don't know. He didn't feed me all that much. I'm

already tired. He never wanted me to be able to fight back you see."

"That monster," Jim growled. "Fine. I can work with that. I'll get you over that fence. Do you mind if I help you over then?"

"I don't give a damn so long as I get out of this place."

"Good. Then follow my lead." He looked back at her as they reached the back door. His hand rested on the knob. "Just stay quiet and follow my lead." He leaned to his left and peeked out the curtains overlooking the backyard. He saw the patrolling guard disappearing from sight to his right. "It's almost time. We're going to have to be fast to get out before he comes back here, so no wasting time."

"No arguments from me."

"Let's go." Jim opened the back door and led the pair outside. He looked over his shoulder every few seconds, confirming Ashley was still behind him. "Can you climb a fence?" he asked in a quiet voice.

"I can try," she said, stepping up to the waist high chain link fence. She lifted one leg up and rested it on top of the fence and struggled for a minute before Jim stepped in.

"Here." Jim guided her leg down to the grass below and cupped his hands together. "I'll give you a boost."

She placed her foot in his grasp and felt him lift her up far enough so she could climb over the obstruction.

Jim got the firearm back out and prepared to climb over himself when he heard a male voice interrupt him.

"Holy shit! You stay right there."

Jim closed his eyes and turned around, weapon still in his grasp. "Look, man. Do you know who you work for?"

"Damned right I do. Mr. Planter pays very well. Now don't try anything."

Jim stepped to the side, showing the guard Ashley's skinny visage behind the fence. "What's your name?"

"Jeff. What does that matter?" The guard answered.

"Jeff, do you know what your boss gets up to behind closed doors? This young girl was locked in a room up there and abused for years. You don't want to be party to that, right? Just let us go. You can call the police afterwards, but just let us go. You don't want to align yourselves with people like him."

"He hired me to deal with situations like this. I can't just let this go." Jeff's hands disappeared behind him.

"Bad move, Jeff." Jim raised his weapon toward him. "Your hands move again and you're dead. Is it worth it?"

Jeff froze at the threat. "It's a phone, not a gun. Will you let me move my arms?"

"No."

"Well, shit."

"You don't try anything cute, and we all go home tonight. You do something else stupid, and only we do. I'm getting this girl out, full stop. There's no arguing this. I beg you, don't try me. I don't want to put you down."

"There's cameras out here, man." Jeff pleaded. "If I don't do my job, they'll be after me. They'll kill me."

"Sucks to be you then."

Jim watched Jeff's hands move from behind him. He could make out a large item as it blurred in movement. "Damn it!" He instinctively squeezed the trigger twice in quick succession, putting Jeff down on the grass."

Without waiting, he turned around and hopped the fence. He grabbed Ashley's hand and guided her back to the nearby waiting parked car. "He threw open the back door and helped Ashely inside before hopping in himself. "Get us out of here," he said to Cynthia in the front seat.

"Who the hell is this?" Cynthia turned around while starting the motor.

"I'll tell you later," Jim said. "Just get us out."

"Fine then." Cynthia put the car in drive and pulled onto the small road behind Oswald's multistory house.

"Cute girl. Is she your girlfriend?" Ashley asked.

"Shit, you don't have your mask on."

"I didn't want someone to see me and call the police. A person sitting in a car alone with a mask on is pretty shady," Cynthia said. "I didn't expect you to return with anybody."

"It wasn't on my agenda, but when I found her locked in a room, underfed like this, I couldn't just leave her."

"Don't worry. Talk about me like I'm not even here. It's cool," Ashley said.

"Sorry," Jim said. "Just do me a favor, and don't tell anybody about her, would you?"

"For you? The guy who got me out of that hell? Consider it a done deal. I don't know who you are, lady, but I thank you two for freeing me from that pervert."

Cynthia looked up into the rear-view mirror. "Since you already know my face, my name's Cynthia." Her attention returned to the road. "Did you get what you wanted done?"

"Oswald's dead," Jim said, "if that's what you're asking."

"Good. Then you remember what I said earlier?"

"That you're done, and you want me out of your house. Yeah, I remember. Speaking of which," he turned to Ashley, "where do your parents live?"

A sour look washed over Ashley's features. "I'm not going back there. Those sacks of shit sold me to that psychopath."

"Wait," Cynthia said from the front. "What now? They sold you into slavery?"

"Basically." Ashley looked out the window to her right as

she spoke. "Dad had a problem with gambling. Mom wasn't too much better with her getting sloshed off wine every damned day. I still don't know if she even noticed or cared that I was sold off."

"Christ," Jim said. "I'm sorry."

"I'm used to it. I've had more than enough time to think about them over the years. I am not going back to live with them again though. I'd rather go homeless on the streets and take my chances."

"I'm not going to let you go homeless," Jim said. He looked up front. "Take us back to your place. I'll pack up and figure this out."

Ashley looked up front and back to Jim beside her. "You two live together?"

"We did due to extenuating circumstances. I'll explain later."

"So are you two boyfriend and girlfriend?"

"Not anymore," Cynthia said, steel in her voice. "I'm done with him."

"Good."

"What?"

"Nothing." Ashley looked away, a devious grin on her face.

Back at Jim's place...

"Do you mind if I ask you a question?" Ashley asked as they pulled into the driveway.

Jim parked the car and removed the keys before turning to her. "You've already seen both my and Cyn's face. Go for it."

"Why were you two living together?"

Jim opened his door. "Come on in, and I'll explain." He

led the pair to the front door. "See this?" He gestured to the new door.

"A door?"

"Yeah. This used to be an open doorway after the incident not too long ago." He led her inside the house and closed the door behind them. "See, I used to catfish predators online. I got this guy to come over. I wanted to gather evidence and turn it all in to the police. Well, he came back, busted the door down, and tried to kill me. I put him down and this place was a crime scene. I'm just lucky the police left a message saying it was finally clear to come back." He knocked on the new door. "I just appreciate that someone replaced my damned door."

"Wait, let me get this straight." Ashley took a seat on the nearby couch lining the wall. "You killed a child predator after he tried to kill you, and that's why you lived with her?"

"Yeah," Jim said, walking into the kitchen. "When was the last time you ate? I mean this in the nicest way possible, but you look hungry."

"I think it was," she took a minute to answer, "two days ago?"

"Well, I don't exactly have a lot in the house. Do you mind eating cereal before we go to sleep and figure everything out? You need to eat something."

"I'm not going to complain with whatever you have," Ashley said. "You know what they say, hunger is the best spice."

"True." He prepared the simple meal and brought it to her. He handed it over and sat on the other end of the sofa. "It goes without saying, but treat this as your home while you're here." He pointed back to where he came from. "The bathroom and shower are through there all the way in the back."

"A shower. That will be heavenly."

"Don't tell me…" Jim trailed off.

"I wasn't allowed to take showers. The sick fuck gave me sponge baths after chaining me to the bed."

"I'm sorry." Jim looked away from her toward the powered off television.

"For what?" she asked between swallows of the breakfast food.

Jim looked at her for a moment. "I don't know," he shrugged. "For not getting you out sooner I guess."

"You like putting the weight of the world on your shoulders, don't you? Then again," she started with an impish grin, "what can I expect from a wannabe superhero who calls himself Masked Justice?"

A brilliant flush radiated from Jim's cheeks. He kept looking away from her, trying to hide it. "That name was a spur of the moment thing. I didn't know what to tell those kids when they asked for my name."

"It's fitting though," Ashley said. "To me you are a superhero, even if you are just a man."

"That's nice of you to say, but trust me when I say I'm not a hero. I'm just a man who doesn't know when to quit."

Ashley finished her bowl and placed it on the coffee table in front of them. "Any person who puts their lives on the line to help out the weak and helpless is a hero. It doesn't matter if it's a lawyer, policeman, or yes, even a vigilante. They can be heroes too."

"Whatever you say. I'm no hero. You heard about the kids in the shipping container I assume since you heard my name before."

"Television was the one luxury that kept me from going totally crazy. I even imagined Masked Justice coming to my rescue. Imagine my shock when a masked man enters the room and sets me free."

Jim's voice turned somber. "You know the guard who ended up dead?"

"The crooked guard?"

"The news thinks he was crooked. He was not. One guard was honest, one was corrupt. I found out after the fact that he was the honest one." His voice started shaking. "I didn't mean to. All I did was punch him. He fell, hit his head, and ended up dying. I just wanted to free the kids, and I accidentally killed an innocent man just doing his job. That's why Cynthia kicked my ass out, and I don't blame her."

"You had no way of knowing he was innocent. He was guarding a bunch of kids in a box."

"I had my suspicions, but no concrete proof. I was so sure the one getting coffee for the two of them was innocent. It was a front, a ruse - trying to keep herself looking legitimate."

"Wait, she?" Ashley asked. "You mean the woman who told the story to the news?"

"That's the one. She was the one who kept those kids locked up and kept them quiet. I was so sure." He shook his head. "I thought why would the innocent guy stay back near the kids?"

"You got them out in the end though."

"Yeah. I did."

"That's what matters," Ashley said. "Think of it this way. You're fighting a war. Every war has casualties. While you don't want to disregard them, you focus on the next move instead of dwelling on your past mistakes. You're only human."

"Look at me." Jim showed a small smile. "Getting

cheered up by the same girl who's been through worse hell than I ever went through. Anyway, that's why Cynthia left me. She couldn't stand being an accomplice to a guy who killed an innocent." He looked down at the floor at his feet. "I don't blame her honestly. I don't deserve her. I've known that since I was a kid."

"Let's focus less on depressing things," Ashley said. "Where am I sleeping tonight?"

"You can sleep in my spare bedroom upstairs for the night, unless you need a tv to sleep. In which case you'd need to sleep here. I don't have one in that room."

"I've grown accustomed to sleeping with the tv on."

"Then I guess you're sleeping here." He pushed himself up to a standing position. "I'll get out of your way and let you rest." He walked past her toward the stairs when he felt her hand grab his nearby wrist, stopping him.

"Hm?" He looked back at her. "What's wrong?"

"I know I've said it before, but I have to say it once again. Thank you so much for tonight. You've no idea what it means to me."

Jim smiled at her. "You just get some rest. We'll figure out what we're doing in the morning. We both need the rest." He gently removed his hand from her grasp, flicked the nearby light switch, cloaking the front room in darkness and turned to walk up the stairs. "I'll be right back with a pillow and some covers. Get comfortable."

She watched him climb the stairs before reaching for the television remote and turning it on and lowering the volume. She laid down and got comfortable, feeling secure for the first time in years. She closed her eyes with a warm smile on her face.

22

J im closed the front door behind him, eliciting a groan from the nearby couch. "Sorry about that." A large white plastic bag hung from his right hand as he walked past.

Ashley grunted, swinging her legs to the side. She blinked her brown eyes repeatedly, staring down at her bare feet. "Where did you go?"

"My laptop is still being held as evidence, and since I still need to work, I needed another one." He placed the large white bag on the kitchen table. "This baby sure isn't top of the line, but for working it'll do in a pinch. Besides, it's all I can afford right now."

"Of course you have a job," she said before yawning. "What do you do for your day job?"

"Ever heard of data entry? It's boring, monotonous, and doesn't pay extremely well. The plus side is, the more time you have, the more work you can do. It fits my needs perfectly well."

"Yeah, work all day and save children at night."

"That's the dream right there," Jim said. He walked

back to the door frame between the kitchen and the main room and leaned to his side against the wall. "I got you some clothes, but don't get your hopes up. They're probably oversized. We can order you clothes that fit later. I imagined you wanted a change of clothes sooner rather than later."

"Yeah. That fat fuck only let me change clothes once a week or sometimes less. Thanks again."

"Don't worry about it. Now we do need to talk about the future."

"Alright." She looked at him with wary eyes. "What does that mean?"

"It means, you said you don't want to go back to your parents, yes?"

Her eyes narrowed and her voice gained an edge. "I'm not going back to the same people who sold me off to pay a little debt."

"I get that," Jim said. "How do you feel about the foster system? For the record, I'm not trying to get rid of you. I'm just trying to think of what would be best for you."

"I'd rather not."

"Alright then. Well, I don't mind you staying here, but I can't imagine you'd want to stay with a guy after your ordeal to put it lightly."

Ashley looked at him, "I don't mind. Not if it's you."

"I appreciate the sentiment, but I'm not exactly father of the year material here. I'll do my best if that's what you really want though."

"You don't need to be father of the year. All I ask is you give me a roof over my head, food, and teach me what you can."

"That I can manage. Then we'd just need to come up with a story for when my parents come over. I can't exactly tell them I got you out of the crime scene where Oswald Planter and his guard were found dead, now can I?"

"You could say you adopted me I guess."

"No, that process takes a while I think, and I've never mentioned it to them. They'd never buy that." He brought his right hand up under his chin and thought it over. "How about I tell them you're a friend's kid who moved away. He didn't want you to switch schools this late in the year, and I'm your pseudo godfather? Does that sound alright?"

"Better than I can come up with. What's the name you're going to use?"

"Say you're the kid of Izzy."

"Who's Izzy?"

"It's the name of a guy I used to know from high school. We were buddies. He moved away recently so the stories match up. No one will ever know the difference. Speaking of high school, we'll have to get you enrolled back in school if we want to sell this story."

A whining noise escaped Ashley. "School? Really?"

"Your whole story for staying here is so you can stay in school. It kind of falls apart if they stop by one afternoon and here you are. Besides, I would like you to get an education - for your own future if nothing else."

She crossed her arms. "Fine. I don't want you getting in trouble. I'll go to school."

"Good," Jim said. "Then we just need your documents, which I'm guessing you don't have right now." Jim thought for a second. "How would we go about getting those?"

Ashley's eyes lit up for a second. "I got it. Do you have a phone here?"

"Why?"

"I'm going to talk to my parents and convince them to give me my documents. Do you have a PO box?"

"Yeah, fine." He dug out a phone from a nearby bag sitting on the floor. "It's a burner, so it should be alright. I look forward to seeing how you're going to manage this." He grabbed a nearby pen and paper and jotted down the PO box information and handed it over.

She took the phone and paper from his grasp and dialed the number. "Yeah, this is Ashley. Yeah, that Ashley. You remember me I assume? The daughter you sold to pay for your debts. The same one you took life insurance out for. I know the police haven't declared me dead yet - that's not the point. Look, listen. I don't want much. I only want my birth certificate, my social security card, and any other piece of ID. You deliver that to where I designate, and I go away. I never call the police and tell them you fuckers sold your own daughter out for a quick payday and your insurance fraud never comes to light. Do you understand me?"

She waited as the sound of a faint male voice entered her ear. "Yeah, birth certificate, social security number, and every other document you have of me. Why? I want to create my own life. It's none of your damned business. You lost that right when you sold me. Do we have a deal?"

Jim waited, his eyebrows raised in amusement at the blackmailing going on right in front of him. He couldn't hide his smile as she rattled off the PO box information.

"Now get that there by tomorrow, and we're good. You fail, and your whole world falls apart. Just like when you sold me to that pervert. Except instead of being abused by one old man, you'll be abused by bubba in the big house. I hear they don't take child abusers kindly in there, and selling your own flesh and blood would earn you a shank I bet. Yeah, you'd better." She hung up and tossed him the phone back. "Do with that whatever you normally do. The documents will be delivered by tomorrow."

"I didn't expect that strategy when I handed you the phone if I'm honest."

Ashley smirked. "You didn't expect me to be nice to them? No, never. They're the reason all of that happened to me."

"Whatever works." Jim kept the phone in his hand. "With those documents, we should be able to enroll you in school and get settled in on that front."

"What about the other?"

"You're referring to Masked Justice?"

"Who else?"

"Ordinarily I wouldn't want you getting involved, but you already know who I am so that's out the window. I now know what kind of negotiator you are, so I won't even argue. All I ask is you follow my lead, don't improvise, and do what I say. Does that sound fair?"

"For now."

"You realize you won't be going inside with me on my jobs, right? At least not until I train you a bit. I don't want you getting hurt or caught."

Ashley nodded. "I just want to help the up-and-coming famous vigilante save more children. Is that so wrong?"

"Just promise me that your first focus will be your schoolwork and fine, I'll allow it."

"I promise."

That night...

Jim sat in the recliner across from the sofa where Ashley sat watching television. He finished typing and placed the laptop down by his feet to the side. "Is it already ten? Crap, I guess I overdid it with work today. It's about time I finished the business I left unfinished before."

"What does that mean?" Ashley asked, her eyes still glued to the screen.

"Remember the guard from the warehouse I told you about?"

"The corrupt one that got away?"

"She's not getting away - not under my watch. She kept those and God knows how many other kids petrified and huddled in metal boxes. She's likely been doing it for years. I'm not letting her go."

"What do I get to do to help?"

"Before we leave, I'm going to show you how to utilize this in the field." He gestured to the laptop. "This thing will be what keeps my ass alive and out of prison. Do you think you can handle being my overwatch?"

"Overwatch?" She watched him pick up the laptop and bring it over to the couch. He sat beside her and turned it back on.

"The one who watches my surroundings while I'm inside, so I don't walk into a trap."

"How can I do that on a laptop? Wouldn't I need access to a camera feed or something to make that work?"

"That would be ideal, but unless you know how to digitally infiltrate and pull that off, then no. I meant like keeping a picture of the blueprint up and guiding me through the place so I don't get lost or run into a dead end. It's a big responsibility though. If you're not up to it, I understand."

"I can manage that."

"Good," Jim smiled. "Then I should show you how to get a blueprint of whatever building you want. It's actually relatively simple if you know where to look. This will be your job from now on, so pay attention."

She leaned her head over further to get a good look at the monitor on his lap.

He noticed her look of concentration and continued his lesson as the night continued on.

Once he was done some ten minutes later he closed the laptop, double checked it's charge, and closed it. "I think you're about ready. Any questions?"

"I get it. It's a simple search from the website you have bookmarked. I may have to do a little improvising depending on the building, but it seemed simple enough. Reading floor plans will take a bit of practice though. I understand the basics to guide you through her house though. Speaking of which, how did you find her house?"

"She was on the news. They said her name, remember?" Jim asked. "Her name was Cassie Washington." He switched browsers to the background check service he used before. "I simply ran a background check." He went through the motions without actually searching, showing the process. "Inevitably there will be duplicates in a big city. That's when you have to do some real virtual leg work. I research where they work by following social media or, if you're lucky, it'll say right in the report. Anyway, I looked her up. It said she worked in the same warehouse, so I knew I had the right woman. This," he pointed at the screen, "is her address." He handed the laptop over. "Here, it's your turn. See if you can find a floor plan layout with that information. Don't worry, we're in no rush tonight. The required crypto is already funded, so don't worry about the cost. It's peanuts."

He watched her run the background check the way he taught her and navigate the webpages with great alacrity. "Geez, you're better with a computer than I am. I'm impressed."

"Here." She ended her search with an address appearing on the screen. "Is that it?"

"That's the same address I came up with, so I'd say you

got it. Now can you read the floor layout? Use this local site to find the floor plans. Oh yes, this is important. Make sure you're on a vpn when you do this." He showed the virtual private network and how to activate it. "The last thing we need is local authorities getting curious as to why we as a private household need information on a place where shortly someone dead will be found. Never, and I mean never, forget this. In fact, it'd be better if we did this from a public network, like our lazy neighbor's." He switched to the public connection and activated the vpn before handing it back to her. "Now find us the floor plans if you would, and prove to me you're ready."

She navigated away from the service and searched the archives. The search took a few silence filled minutes She pulled up the requested plans before turning to him. "Done. If I'm reading this floor plan right, it's a single floor. It seems simple enough to guide you." She trailed her finger a few inches from the screen as she spoke. "I can tell how her whole house is laid out." She turned to him. "Would this really help Masked Justice?"

"It would certainly help me. I don't want to get lost in there. Whether Masked Justice will live up to your expectations is another thing entirely," Jim said. "I'm just a man."

"A man that's saved almost a dozen children from terrible fates. If this will help you, it'll do for now."

"For now?"

Ashley waved his concern aside. "Don't worry about that. Just know I'll follow orders and help out."

"You know how to start a car engine, yes?"

"I can learn."

"Good, because I'll need the engine still running when I get out. Just try your best to stay out of sight."

23

"Is this how you've done every other job?" Ashley asked from the passenger seat. "You just pull up in a car, get out, and get it done all while in a hair net?"

"You'd prefer I walk there instead?" Jim asked, pulling the mask over his head. "I avoid the traffic cameras by and large. Also this," he pointed to his entrapped hair, "keeps my DNA out of the crime scenes."

"I guess I just thought you'd have like a justice-mobile or something."

Jim paused and looked at her. "Do I look like a billionaire playboy? You've read too many comics or watched too many Saturday morning cartoons about superheroes, haven't you?"

"Maybe."

"You definitely have." He made sure his two weapons were secured as he talked. "Now this will be relatively simple compared to my last few jobs." He brought a finger to his ear. "Testing."

She mirrored his actions. "I can hear you."

"Then we're good. Keep the line open while I'm in there.

Now keep that map up, and be ready. When I'm ready to leave I'll need you to guide me out."

"Then go take out the bitch," Ashley said. "If she was the one keeping those kids in there like you say, I want her in pain."

"She'll get what's coming to her," Jim unsheathed the knife, letting the moonlight bounce off the steel before sheathing it and resting his left hand on the door. "Let's do this." He opened the door and slipped outside onto the street side. His head swiveled left and right, seeing no lights on in the houses he passed by.

He hopped the fence on his left and dashed through the dark open backyard. He slowed down and approached the back door. He reached for it and grabbed it, trying to twist. No such luck as it refused to budge. "Of course," he said under his breath. He got to a knee and set about unlocking the lock with his limited experience. It took him a few minutes with only a little pestering from Ashely in his ear all the while.

"I guess you weren't bullshitting." Ashley's voice came into his ear. "Where did you learn to do that?"

"I'll tell you later," he said quietly. He quickly pulled the door open and closed it behind him. "Now where is her bedroom at from the back door?"

"It's to your right, through a long hallway. It should be either the last door on your left or right, depending on which bedroom she liked the most. Be careful in there. There was something wrong with that woman if you ask me. There was something in her eyes."

"I'll keep that in mind," Jim said, taking cautious steps in the indicated direction.

Ashley kept talking in his ear. "I'd like to think I recognize mental illness when I see it. I had to see Oswald's psychopathic ass every few nights. I used to people watch on television talk shows to try and remain sane."

"Not to be an ass here as this is interesting, but do you think this could wait until the drive home?" He sneaked through the house, staying as quiet as he could while whispering.

"Oh, right."

Jim followed the directions until he came to the two doors. "Left or right, that's the question." He heard noises to his right, making that decision easy. Instead of snores, he instead heard lewd noises. He heard shuffling bed sheets and sounds of passion. "You're joking."

"About what?" Ashley asked, when she heard a rather loud female moan. "No way. Well, she's busy, so get in there. It'll be easier."

"With a guy in there? How is that easier? He's balls deep in her. He isn't going to allow me to stab her and go on my way," he spoke as quietly as he was able a few feet away from the door.

"She's busy. He's naked. They're vulnerable. You have a weapon. Do the math, man," Ashley said. "You'll be fine. Just hurry up before he finishes. Then it'll get harder - excuse the pun."

"Fuck it. Fine." Jim gripped the knife in his hand and reached for the door. He was stopped as the female moans continued inside, but the male noises turned from pleasure filled to fear. He froze in confusion, then opened the door far enough to peek inside.

His eyes went wide at what he saw inside. Instead of the scene of carnal passion his imagination had been painting in his head, he saw a different scene entirely. His target was sitting on her male guest's groin facing away from the door as he imagined, only in her right hand he saw a blade. Her hand disappeared in front of her.

"Quiet now lover," he could hear her coo to the groaning man below her. "If you make much more noise, I'm going to have to cut deeper quicker. You don't want that now, do you?" Her voice was one of a teasing wife. "Then I'd have to clean up all this blood even sooner. Just be a good boy and suffer in silence if you want to live a little longer."

"I'd rather die quickly than endure any more of this you psycho bitch!" Jim could see Cassie's knife hand being grabbed by her victim's own hand.

"You little shit," Cassie growled.

He watched the two struggle for supremacy as both grunted in exertion until he saw her right hand fall out of sight along with a cry.

"You just couldn't be a good boy, could you?" she asked, venom in her voice. "All you had to do was lay there and let me have my fun. You couldn't even manage that."

His only response was a wheezing gurgle and the sound of steel penetrating flesh. She wrenched the knife up above her head, red staining the blade even in the dim light.

"Christ alive," Jim whispered to himself.

"Did she just do what I think she did? She killed him? He must have been a two-pump chump, or she's just a legitimate psycho bitch like I said before."

Jim waited for her to dig the metal implement into her victim. He heard the telltale sound of steel intruding into flesh before he pushed the door open, not squeaking as it did so. He held the melee weapon in his right hand in a death grip.

In his careful approach he heard the horrified screams of Cassie's victim. He managed to approach unheard due to the racket the pair were making on the bed. He readied his right arm and angled the knife's approach so that it embedded itself into his target's throat.

Before he could drag the blade across he felt a sharp pain in his side. His left hand gripped the appendage attached to the blade dug into his side. His eyes moved back to Cassie who had her head turned to face him as best she could manage, steel still jammed into her neck.

Her voice was garbled but still understandable. "Who the fuck are you?"

"The man putting a stop to you. Your days of trafficking kids for abusers are done. This," he looked down at the still man below her, "is just another reason I'm putting you down." He kept her hand still but could feel her trying to twist it. "Come on now," he exerted the remaining energy into sliding his blade to the side. He was rewarded with her eyes going wide and her free hand jumping to the cut in her neck. She let go of the knife firmly embedded in Jim's side in a vain attempt at staunching the bleeding. She fell down on top of her would be lover.

Jim kept a hand on the knife jammed in his abdomen and looked down at the guy. "Dude? You alright? It's over now. She dead or dying. I'm not sure which, but she's done." He reached down with a wince with his left hand. He shook the man's shoulder and noticed his chest wasn't moving along with the veritable pool of blood he was standing over. "Can't tell if it was hers or his. Fuck." He looked down at the wound that was bleeding already. "Shit. I'm already bleeding, I'll have to improvise here."

"Improvise how?" Ashley asked. "Your DNA is already there."

"Bring me the gas can from my trunk."

"You keep a can of gas in your car?" The sound of a car

door opening and closing accentuated her question. "Wouldn't that like explode if someone hit you?"

"You watch way too many movies. No, now hurry up." He saw a folded towel on the nearby hope box at the foot of the bed. He grabbed it, stuffing it into his newfound wound haphazardly. "That should do for now. You almost in here?"

"I got the gasoline. Just give me a minute." Her voice was no longer only in his ear, he could hear her natural voice.

"Bring it in here quick."

"Do I want to know what we're doing?"

"We have to burn this place, at least where my blood could be, so that includes the bed and the carpet. We'll call the fire department after we're sure the evidence of my being here is gone." He turned around as the door swung open to reveal Ashley carrying said container.

"The floor and the bed you said?"

Jim held the cloth to his new wound and got out of the way, back at the door. "Yeah. Be careful not to get any on you."

"Duh." Ashley poured the fuel on the designated spots and again for good measure. She doused the entire carpeted floor and emptied the rest on the now two dead bodies laying in the bed. "Christ. She did a number on him, didn't she?" She looked down at the young man's mutilated naked chest, evidence of stab wounds, dragged nails, and ripping greeting her eyes. I told you something was off about her. I just didn't expect her to be quite this psycho."

"She trafficked children. Never underestimate their depravity," Jim grunted. His free hand dug into his hoodie's pocket and produced a match box. He handed it to the returning girl and took the can. "Here, do the honors."

She extracted a match and struck it against the box.

"Getting rid of the evidence is all well and good, but what about your injury?"

"I have a guy who can fix this." Jim grit his teeth.

Ashley tossed the lit flame into the room and the pair exited the room in haste. They went back the way they came and exited through the back door. They got back into the car when faint hints of smoke were coming from the house.

Jim sat down in the driver's seat. "Good. You kept it running." He put the car in drive and got them away from the soon to be inferno.

"She got you good." Ashley leaned closer to look at the injury.

Jim kept his right hand plastered to his right side, his left turning the wheel as needed. "Yeah. I got careless. I should have immobilized her knife hand before I stuck her in the throat."

"Still, that's one less person transporting kids out there," Ashley said. "Are you sure you're good to drive? You're bleeding pretty good there."

"It looks worse than it is. Besides the doctor I mentioned isn't that far away from here."

"Hey," Ashley looked out the window at the all too familiar motel they were passing by. "Wasn't that the place they found a dead guy not too long ago?"

"What?" Jim looked over and saw where she was glancing. "Oh, right. That guy lured small boys into his room."

"You were behind that?"

"Yeah. He was a real piece of work. He worked at a local arcade. That's where he found his prey."

"How'd you even know about the guy? An arcade doesn't seem like the kind of place you'd frequent."

Jim turned the wheel. "I used to go there all the time as a kid. As for how I knew to check him out, I'll tell you when we get home." He slowed the car down to a stop and got out. "Come on in. He's still open, and it could be a little while. Just don't ask any questions about his business is all I ask. It's his one rule. You know how back-alley doctors are."

"Not really, but I'll trust you on this one." Ashley got out of the passenger seat and followed Jim to the door in the back alley.

Jim pounded on the door and waited.

The door flung open to reveal Edmund. "Look who it is again." He looked left and right. "No Ray here with you this time? Also, who's the girl? Your little sister? Come on in."

"Not quite."

"I would ask what the problem is, but I can see the knife still stuck in your side. Smart that, not removing it. You'd have been bleeding like a stuck pig if you had." He pointed to a chair in the middle of the room surrounded by a rolling metal tray and a stool. "Sit there and take your shirt off. I assume you have money."

"I always carry enough to pay you when I go out like this. Don't worry." He extracted his wallet before sitting down and taking off the hoodie and t-shirt. He took out a number of one hundred dollar bills and slapped them down on Edmund's palm. "There. Is that enough?"

"For this? I suppose it's enough. If you'd pulled that out, it'd be three hundred more for the amount of work. Though I see you didn't listen to my advice about quitting this shit."

"I am known for being hardheaded."

"Apparently. It's good for business for me so I won't push farther." He sat on the stool with a grunt. "Let's get this started." He removed the impromptu field dressing with an unpleasant expression. "What even is this?" He held the cloth at arms length, a disgusted face all the while. "Is this a towel?"

"I think so," Jim said, leaning his back on the chair. "I was in a hurry."

"I see. Is there a reason I smell the faint aroma of smoke?"

"I was pretty sure this was a no questions kind of place," Jim said, a wry grin plastered on his face. "Or was I wrong?"

"Just making conversation." He put on a pair of gloves with a snap.

"Then try and pick a less incriminating topic," Ashley said, standing at the side.

"Sure, girl." He looked to Jim. "Now this is going to hurt like fuck and bleed, but it has to be done. The blade has to come out." He looked at Ashley. "Girl, I'd look away if I were you. Especially if you're squeamish."

"I'll be fine."

"Sure you will." Edmund grabbed the handle of the knife and winced. "Here we go." He pulled the blade out of Jim's flesh, dropped it on the metal tray, and immediately moved to staunch the moderate bleeding. "It's not as bad as I first thought," Edmund said, applying pressure with the gauze. He kept pushing with his left hand while his right grabbed a nearby bottle. He threw the used gauze in the nearby trash bin and unscrewed the bottle's top. "Prepare yourself. This is going to hurt, but it has to be disinfected." He poured the disinfectant over the now open wound as Jim writhed in the chair. "Is anyone else getting déjà vu?"

As this was all going on, the door they entered opened again to reveal Raymond entering. "I'm back. Oh, I didn't think you'd have a customer so late." He walked over and leaned to look at Jim's face. "Well, look who it is again. Are you still playing at superhero? I'm guessing so, judging by this injury." He saw Ashley standing to the side? "Who's this girl?"

"Did you hear about the kids locked in the shipping container?" Jim asked as Edmund now got out a needle. "The guy in charge of that had her imprisoned in his house."

"As his little fuck toy," Ashley said, a snarl now covering her face. "Literally."

Edmund raised his eyebrows. "I heard he was found dead in his bedroom. News was he was stabbed to death in his own bed." He jabbed the threaded needle and started stitching. "He kidnapped you?"

"Fuck no. My parents sold me to him for money."

"This guy got you out?" He gestured to Jim with a thumb. "I find that hard to believe." He finished the stitching and placed a pad over the injury. He taped the dressing to the site and leaned back.

"He did." She locked gazes with him until Edmund turned away.

"It seems you've surprised me yet again. What is it they call you now? Masked Justice was it? That's what some of the kids referred to their rescuer as."

"You stay up to date with current events I see," Jim said.

"Also heard one of the guards died during that little rescue attempt," Edmund said, his tone neutral as he applied another wrapping on top of the previous.

Jim looked away. "That was an accident. I just tried to knock him out. He was between me and the kids."

"So you hit him in the head. He falls to the floor and cracks his head? Did I get that right?" Edmund sighed. "Shit don't work like that in real life, son."

"I realize that now."

"You should have just used that stuff I made for you."

"It was already used up."

"The kid got the children free, didn't he?" Raymond

slapped Jim's shoulder with a smile. "I count that as a net gain."

Edmund made sure the dressing was secure. "True."

"What's the prognosis, doc?" Jim asked, now struggling to reclothe himself.

Raymond jumped into action and helped Jim put his clothes back on. "I'm no doctor, but I can tell that'll hurt like hell for a few weeks."

"Quite," Edmund said, voice dry. "If you insist on keeping this lifestyle, those stiches will probably tear, and you'll be right back at the beginning. If for no other reason than that, take a short break. In a few weeks, you'll be medically cleared to keep doing this hard and fast lifestyle you've cultivated."

"I'll keep that in mind." Jim got his black hoodie back on. "Oh, and I expect everyone present to keep quiet."

"I don't want to be known as Masked Justice's doctor. No offense, but that would be bad publicity. I'd be arrested and thrown in prison. I'll keep your secret so long as you keep my side business quiet."

"As for me, it'd be better if I'm just known as that homeless guy. I don't want attention. I'd be better help to you in the future if nobody knows me anyway."

"Just saying. No offense, but I'd rather none of you know. It's a little late for that though."

"I'm not looking to pass judgement here, son." Edmund removed the gloves and tossed them in a nearby trash can. "Just know I'm not looking to heal senseless serial killers, which you are not. You keep it that way, and we'll be fine."

"I hear that." Jim's face contorted in pain as he tried to get up only to fall back in the chair.

"Like I said, you'll be out of commission for a while.

You'll need your new charge there to help you back to your car. Hold on while I get you one last thing for the road."

"Don't worry, girl. I'll help get him there too," Raymond said.

"Uh, thanks, old man."

"Remind me to get him a present when we get home," Jim said.

"You don't have to do that."

"No, but I want to," Jim said. "Look forward to it old timer, for all your help."

Edmund was across the room, unlocking one of the cabinets and reached inside to retrieve a pill bottle. He walked back and handed Jim the bottle. Take these antibiotics everyday as directed on the bottle until every pill is gone." He looked to Ashley. "You make sure he takes them all."

"I will."

"Oh yes, and one more thing." Edmund reached down under the rolling metal tray and grabbed a box. "You'll need these. That dressing needs changed at least once a day. Use the rest of these until you can get some for yourself. There's not a lot of pads left in there, but you should have a few days to get some. You'll have to either do it yourself or find someone willing to change it. Just remember to do so. You don't want it to get infected."

"I'll manage. Don't worry, doc." Jim managed to stand up.

Ashley moved to stand beside him. "Put your arm around my shoulder."

Raymond mirrored her movements and got to his other side. "Don't argue now, tough guy. Let's get you to your car and back home.

Jim sighed and did as instructed. "I don't have broken legs you know, but fine. If it'll make you two feel better."

Jim allowed himself to be guided back to the door. "I'll see you around, Doc!" he said over his shoulder as Raymond pushed the door open.

"No offense, but I'd rather you not come back too often now, you hear?"

"Got it."

Ashley closed the door behind them with her foot. "Were those two friends of yours?"

"You could say that." Jim climbed in the driver's seat with her help before closing his door. He looked to his side at the teenage girl in the passenger seat. "The old man saved my ass, and the doctor patched me up when I was just beginning."

"You're not worried about them knowing?"

Jim started the engine and pulled out onto the road, heading home. "Unless I plan on not ever getting injured, I need a private doctor. He doesn't want publicity any more than I do. As for Ray, he's already incriminated himself by helping me - same as you actually."

Ashley looked over at Jim. "Incriminated myself? What did I do?"

"You're party to arson and possibly murder, depending on legal shenanigans I think. You brought in the gasoline used to set the place on fire. You're an accessory now. I think that's the technical term," Jim said.

"That woman was part of Planter's business you said?"

"She kept those poor kids in a shipping container reeking of crap and piss." Jim's voice gained an edge. "She sealed her fate when she tortured children for a little money."

"How did you figure that out?"

"I have my sources," Jim said, turning the wheel. "Sources whose intel has been good so far. That, and judging by what we both saw, she was fucked in the head. That much is obvious."

"Sources? What? Do you have someone in the local newspaper?"

"Reading is a dying media. Think more technological in nature." Jim pulled onto his street finally. "I'll elaborate more inside." His eyes saw an all too familiar vehicle parked in his driveway. "I'll be damned."

"What? Whose jeep is that?"

"It looks like Charlie's. He disappeared under mysterious circumstances before is why I'm confused." He pulled in beside Charlie's car and turned the engine off.

"Who's Charlie?" Ashley asked.

"I'll explain after this. Just know he's a friend of mine that went missing."

"So mysterious," she said, climbing out of the now still vehicle.

24

———

Jim pushed the door open gingerly, favoring his injured side. "Charlie? Are you in here? I saw your car outside?"

Ashley closed the door behind them and kept a wary eye on her surroundings.

"Jim, old buddy, you've seen better days judging by how you're walking." Charlie came down the stairs. "Did Cassie give you some trouble? Yeah, she's always been a psychopath, but I knew you'd come out on top."

"Alright. One," Jim held out a lone index finger, "I have lots of questions."

"I'm here to answer them, old friend, so shoot." Charlie sat down on the bottom step, keeping his distance from the pair.

Jim fell onto the couch and continued. "Where the hell did you end up after the day we found you at Cynthia's laying on the floor? We were beyond confused."

"After I delivered the letters I couldn't let myself be questioned by the police, old friend. I beat myself up because I didn't want you all to put it together that I was with your allies. We were quite surprised that the infamous Masked Justice would call the police, but it makes sense now. You were trying to lay low, and what citizen wouldn't call the police? It was a miscalculation."

"What? Were you carrying bud or something?"

Charlie erupted in boisterous laughter. "Sorry." He quieted down and kept talking. "No, though I do enjoy a little smoke every now and then. I have a confession to make, buddy. I'm not the thrill seeking psychonaut I've painted myself as. The truth is I have always been more interested in your hobby. I've kept watch on how you've progressed for my group. I was here to deliver the two letters you received. I must say, we expected you to read both before leaping into action, but you're a man of action. You only needed one."

"Your group? You don't mean the PHR?"

"The very same." Charlie clapped. "Bravo on being so quick, Jim old boy. Did you never wonder why I was always so interested in your livestreams or why I was always out and about? I was scouting you while doing my job for the PHR. Being a hippy stoner always high was the perfect cover."

"For how long?"

"Ever since we graduated high school and was scouted by them. I then became a scout, and I knew you were perfect for us."

"Scouting me?" Jim asked. "Was our friendship a sham then?"

"Not at all," Charlie said, a warm smile on his face. "You know the only reason Cynthia didn't get roughed up that one night was because I was the one on duty. Yeah, that was me that tied her up. Orders were to rough her up, but I couldn't bring myself to do that."

"How generous of you," Jim said, voice not conveying gratitude. "So let me get this straight. You, under the guise of house sitting for her, delivered the two notes, beat yourself up, and got out when I left and she got a shower?"

"That's about the large and small of it," Charlie said. "I was just there to deliver intel and instill a sense of fear in you. We figured it'd motivate you, and it did just that. You took care of matters just as I knew you would."

"Which brings us to the present," Jim said. "Why are you here now?"

Charlie looked over at Ashley. "Who is this girl?"

Ashley broke her silence on the couch. "The girl who just helped him on his last job."

"I got her out of Planter's house. He had her locked up and had been having his way with her."

"Not anymore." Her voice was laden with venom. "Never again."

"I had heard he was dead. I didn't know he had a girl. Is she living here?"

"Yeah," Ashley said. "Why?"

"I won't tell the group about this then. I know you're not going to do anything, but there are more fervent members who may not be as understanding of this situation you've found yourselves in."

"You never did tell me why you're here," Jim said.

"I'm here to extend an invitation."

"What? To join your little republic? Why would I?"

"Logistical support for one," Charlie said. "The street level vigilante schtick is cute and all, but we can give you technology and devices that would make it much easier for you. You'd gain an infrastructure of support and supplies."

"If I said no?"

"You don't want to do that. Look, I don't want to elaborate on why, but trust me when I say don't do that."

"This isn't an invitation, is it? This is more like a threat. Join us or else we tell the police what you were up to is more like it," Jim said, a scowl finding its way onto his face.

"That's one way to look at it. Another is, gain many boons or make another enemy."

"So he's either with you or against you? That's not much of a friendly thing to say," Ashley said.

"We're entwined now, Jim old boy," Charlie said. "You know how we operate, and we know things you've done. It's in everybody's best interest if we join forces and take down more molesters, yeah? Imagine what you could do with almost limitless intel at your fingertips. We have men and women in almost every major US city. Policemen, judges, government officials - you name it, we have it. We're not just a group of lunatics like the media portrays us. We're simply sick of child touchers getting away with it, same as you."

"Join or we out you, is that the short version?"

"If you must boil it down to such extremes."

"It sounds like you're not leaving me much choice here. I obviously can't fight back in my condition." Jim's right hand fell to his recent stab wound.

"Glad to have you aboard then, my friend."

"Before you get ahead of yourself, just know I'm nobody's errand boy. I do my own jobs."

"That's fine. We're not stringent on deciding what our members do. You can do your own jobs. We only ask two things. One, never betray our values - meaning, don't touch kids. That along with rule two, try to minimize civilian casualties. I'd be your handler in case the higher ups need to contact you. Basically, you'd do what you normally do until a job comes along. Fair enough?"

"Something's telling me you're hiding something. What happens if a big target appears near here? You're going to task me in taking care of it?"

"Possibly. But would you really mind though? If we had confirmed they're a pedo, I didn't think you'd be squeamish."

"So he does the work, while you sit around?"

Charlie gave a bemused look toward Ashley. "I've put my field work in already, little lady. It's called seniority."

"Still, it's join or go to prison," Jim said. "Fine. It's not like I have a choice in this apparently."

"Wise choice, my friend. I'll pass along your compliance to the higher ups. They will be pleased." He took out a sheet of notepad paper and taped it to the nearby guard rail. "Monitor this email address every day. If we have a job for you, it'll appear there. Any questions?"

"Questions? Not really. Just realize my doctor says I can't go in the next couple of weeks. Stab wounds tend to incapacitate me. You know how it is."

"I will keep that in mind. Do let me know when you've recovered. If any jobs come for you, I'll sub them for any that can be delayed a few weeks due to your injury. Fair enough?"

"It's as good as I'm going to get," Jim said.

"Good, then I will take my leave. You have a good night, you two." He got up from the bottom stair and moved to the door. "Take it easy, buddy," he said before exiting the house, leaving the man and teenager on the couch.

"I can't believe he was a part of that group all this time." Jim leaned his head back and stared at the ceiling. "Looking back, I should have put it together."

"He was kind of an ass," Ashley said. "Friends don't blackmail friends."

"I certainly found out a lot of things about Charlie tonight. That's for sure. Now let's get ready for bed. I've had a hell of a day."

25

"You remember the story we agreed on?" Jim asked Ashley.

"I'm staying here so I don't have to switch schools since my parents moved away."

"Good. We'll get you enrolled in school as soon as possible too. Which is for the best anyway." The sound of an engine outside interrupted Jim. "They're here." He got up with a wince and walked over to the door. "Here we go." He opened the door. "Hey Mom, hey Dad." He greeted his parents getting out of the car.

"Son, it's been too long," Dennis said. "Oh, who's this?" he asked as the pair entered the house.

"That's Izzy's kid. He moved away but didn't want her to have to switch schools so late in the year. I'm watching her while she finishes the year out."

"It's nice to meet you," Jill said, looking at Ashley. "It must be difficult for a poor dear like you to live with your father's friend." Jill drew Ashley into a warm hug. "Forgive my son if he does something wrong. He's never been too good with girls."

"Thanks, mom. I think I can handle it."

Dennis let out a hearty laugh. "Don't smother the poor girl, honey."

Jill released her hold on a visibly relieved Ashley. "I was just worried about the girl is all," she pouted. "Our son is a lot of things, but babysitter was never one of them." She looked back at Ashley. "He is remembering to feed the two of you, yes? He's been known to get so enveloped in work he forgets to."

"He's been doing a good job so far." Ashley's normally confident voice was now mousy and shy.

"Good to hear." Dennis led his wife to sit down on the couch while Jim sat in the lone recliner, leaving the last spot on the couch for Ashley. "Have you been following the news, son?"

"Not really."

"Apparently Oswald Planter, along with an employee of his, were found dead recently. To add on to that, a crate of kids were found in Planter's warehouse. The kids were going on about some guy named Masked Justice who freed them."

"Masked Justice? What a lame name," Jim said.

"My thoughts exactly," his father said. "A lot of guys on the force are split on him. Some say he's a force for good. Others think he's a no-good vigilante who thinks he's above the law."

"What do you think, Dad?" Jim asked.

"You know I've never been fond of vigilantes. No one is above the law. He may be saving kids, but he should leave it to the proper authorities. He'll get more people killed than he'll save, if you ask me."

"Don't get so worked up, dear." Jill placed a gentle hand on Dennis's shoulder. "Think of your blood pressure." She looked over at Jim. "You know better than to get him so worked up."

"Sorry, Mom," Jim said.

"The fact that there're any men or women with a badge who don't mind this crazy running around playing superhero sets me off," Dennis continued, unabated. "He's not trained, and he doesn't follow proper procedures. He killed that guard in the warehouse. Did you know that?"

"Was it a dirty guard?" Ashley asked. "Someone had to be keeping the kids in there."

"Even if it was, the man is not judge, jury, and executioner. Mind you, we don't know if the guy was innocent or guilty. It seems Masked Justice doesn't care either since he killed the other guard last night and torched her house - I'd bet to get rid of any evidence."

"You think," Jill said. "You said yourself your friends told you that there's no evidence of that."

"I'm just following logic," Dennis said. "She worked at the same warehouse. This so called Masked Justice just couldn't leave any guards alive. He's dangerous is what he is."

"Alright already," Jim said, trying to calm down his father.

"How are your classes going?" Jill asked, turning to look at Ashley.

"As good as can be expected. I just wish they gave less homework."

Jim smirked. "Good luck with that." A beep from the laptop beside the recliner grabbed his attention. "Give me one second. That's work related." He leaned to his left, feeling his right side light on fire in pain. He picked up the laptop and plopped it onto his legs. He saw a message in the email Charlie left.

His parents continued talking with Ashley as he silently read the message he received. "Greetings, Masked Justice. We are pleased you have decided to join us on our righteous crusade. Know that you are part of a brotherhood of sorts now. We look after our own. You still have to be careful, but there are members in law enforcement near you that can aid you. As for why we sent this message, we have heard of your recent injury and have a job for you that can wait a few weeks to be done. We have tasked you with eliminating this target. The details can be found on the address found at the bottom of this message. Do not click it. Type it in on a public wifi along with vpns. You know how operational security works. Rest well, brother."

He closed the laptop and looked up.

"Everything alright with work?" Dennis asked.

Jim smiled. "Yeah, Dad. Everything's just fine."

"So tell me how you managed to piss off Cynthia," his father asked. "You know she's perfect for you."

"Come on, guys," Jim said.

"She's such a dear," Jill said. "You need to say you're sorry and apologize. Maybe she'll take you back."

"I doubt that, Mom..."

THANK YOU FOR READING!

The adventure continues in Masked Justice. If you want to help support this work, please consider leaving an honest review on Amazon. Have a great day!

ABOUT THE AUTHOR

Alex J Fischer has been writing for close to a decade and has won five National Novel Writing Month challenges in a row.

Alex grew up in a small town in Ohio and still resides there. Hobbies include writing, video games, and watching crime shows.

ALSO BY ALEX J. FISCHER

The Morris Crime Family:

Welcome to the Family

The Silver Lining

Any Means Necessary

The Fourth Bullet

A New Generation

The Order of Vengeance:

The Order of Vengeance: Motorcycle Club

Vengeance Above All